Traumata

TRAUMATA

...bereaved, broken and suspected of murder.
Can her father save her from a life sentence?

Douglas Renwick

By the same author

Prologue

North-East Afghanistan, June 2017

In Khuh Tabar, a remote Pashtun community high up in the foothills of the Hindu Kush where the snow-capped peaks of the Himalayas touch the sky, a baby cries. He has blue eyes, like his mother. She pleads for his life while his father, the son of the headman, lies crumpled nearby; he's still warm.

There are bundles of clothes on the ground – women's clothes: firaqs, partugs, head-scarves, shawls and rags. Ragdolls, rag and bone, flesh and bone. Some shudder in agony, some cry out in anguish, some crawl in hope of reaching safety. Other bundles just lie there, quietly without moving, failing to hide the crimson creeping out from beneath them, staining the hallowed earth of their beloved paradise.

Two years later, the once-mother – the widow – returns to England, bereaved and broken, haunted by the memories and still deafened by the screams. The smell of cordite still lingers in her nostrils. Her baby's cry still reverberates around the echo chamber of her skull.

Kind hearts welcome her to the professional care of Beechwood Hall, a psychiatric hospital near London, to begin her recovery. Four months into her treatment, she discovers the identity of the murderer; her polite name for him is Mr Nasty. He's alive and well and just happens to live less than twenty miles away.

Chapter 1

How can one be happy and sad at the same time? That's how Michael felt when he got Melanie's email. Happy he was needed – and happy his grown-up daughter believed she could come to him for help. But sad she was in trouble and had no-one else to turn to – and terrified he might fail her.

She had no brothers or sisters to give some same-generation sympathy. No mum to offer sensible female advice and a cuddle. And no partner to share life's journey. No Mr Right – yet – despite a string of hopefuls.

He was proud she'd followed in his footsteps and became a doctor, but then she joined the Army. At first, he was pleased; he imagined she would meet some nice young medically qualified officer and settle down. But it did not go according to plan, at least not to his plan. She was posted to Afghanistan, of all places, where it had all gone dreadfully wrong.

From: Melanie Green
Subject: I need you
To: Dr Michael Green
07/09/19
>

Hi Dad – Remember Mr Nasty, the slime-ball who led the raid? He's dead. Good news, because I no longer feel angry. But the police have been round asking questions. They didn't tell me how it happened, but I hope it was bad. Obviously, I didn't have anything to do with it – as much as I would've liked to have finished him off.

Damn right he remembered Mr Nasty, and what he'd done. He'd heard all about him when she first came home to be treated for post-traumatic stress disorder. His instinct was to believe her, but at the time she was having memory problems – and trouble distinguishing between real events and dreaming.

Whatever had happened out there, the death of the man was good news as it would reduce her anxiety level. Bad news, though, about the police questioning her; that could have the opposite effect.

But it's complicated. A friend had been advising me on the anger issue. His name's Rand. I met him on a

Facebook forum some weeks ago, a bereavement support group. He persuaded me to talk about things, and I found this very helpful. After he replied to my post, we just exchanged emails. We got on, but now I can't get hold of him. So I'm feeling a bit alone. Any chance of you popping over for a few days? I could book the guest suite for you, like last time.

Lots of love,

Melly xxxx

P.S. Attached are my email exchanges with Rand – background reading for you. Some of it you know, some you don't. I just can't go over it all again.

He was pleased she'd found a new friend who'd been helping her, yet disappointed he'd stopped replying to her emails. It was just the sort of thing which could set her back a few weeks. Would he, her dad, drop everything and fly to the UK to see her? Of course he would.

"Daniela? Could you come in, please?" No sooner had he released the intercom button than his PA-cum-receptionist bounced in with a big smile, eager as ever to please her British boss. His appointment as one of the five GPs who served the resort of La Manga in southern Spain was not well paid, but it came with free membership of the golf club and a modern and well-equipped surgery with air conditioning. However, the greatest perk was his staff: Daniela, a bright-eyed 25-year-old local girl who was only too willing to manage his diary and run errands for him, bring him endless cups of strong coffee and generally mother him, as well as being his gate-keeper and front-of-house manager.

"I need to fly to London – to visit my daughter as soon as possible. Just a one-way flight, as I'm not sure when I'll be back. And car hire at Gatwick, open-ended if that's possible."

"Certainly, Dr Green. Would you like to fly first class?"

"No. Just EasyJet, but next to a window near the front would be nice, with lots of leg-room if possible." Folding his six-foot frame into an aircraft seat was becoming more difficult for him, as he approached his sixty-third year. At least he had no trouble sliding into one next to the window, not like some of his patients who were built more for comfort than speed. He had to be careful what he said to them.

"Sure, eet's done!" and with a swirl of her skirt, she trotted away.

He reckoned he'd need legal advice, as his knowledge of the law was limited to what he'd gleaned from being a Grisham fan; UK procedures would be different. He wondered if his old mate from uni days might be able to help, or at least put him in touch with someone who can.

"And Daniela!"

She raced back, still smiling.

"Could you look up a number for me, please? A firm of solicitors, Matthew, Finch and Trowbridge. In London. In fact, could you give them a ring and ask if David Goodman is still there? If so, I'd like to see him. Perhaps I could take him out to lunch, maybe the day after I land. See what you can do."

"Sure, with pleasure."

Zoom. She was gone. He knew she'd do an excellent job of running things in his absence. She would share his patients among his fellow GPs in the resort, as they always did when one of them was away. And with the holiday season coming to an end, the pressures would ease.

Now, he thought, I wonder what Melly's file is all about. He had to admit he always found it intriguing to hear about her new friends – especially the male ones. One day, he hoped, Mr Almost-Right would come along. Surely not Rand, not if he's abandoned her. He flicked through the first few pages on his screen.

From: Rand@djb9x2103i9.com
Subject:
To: Melanie55@gmail.com
15/08/19
>
Just do it.

Rand

>

>

From: Melanie Green

Subject:

To: Rand

15/08/19

>

Do what? Who are you, by the way? Is that all you've got to say?

Melanie Green

>

>

From: Rand@djb9x2103i9.com

Subject:

To: Melanie55@gmail.com

20/08/19

>

Kill him. If he is still alive and justice has not run its course. If you can be sure of your facts I suggest you avenge him. The anger will then go.

>

>

From: Melanie Green

Subject:

To: Rand

20/08/19

>

He is still alive, and so far he's escaped justice. I can't bear it – but I couldn't kill him. I couldn't kill anyone.

I only joined the army as a doctor because I wanted to help soldiers survive the horrors of war; to save those young lives. Is Rand your first name or last? Is it really Rand, or did you make it up?

Melanie

>

>

From: Rand@djb9x2103i9.com
Subject:
To: Melanie55@gmail.com
21/08/19

>

Think of it as divine retribution. An eye for an eye. Or a justifiable homicide. Should you allow this person to live? Perhaps it is your duty to take him out. I assume you have explored and exhausted any possibility of bringing him to justice yourself.

Rand (contraction of Randolph)

>

>

From: Melanie Green
Subject:
To: Rand
21/08/19

>

Dear Contraction of Randolph,

Thank you for your email advising me to kill my partner's murderer. I think this is an excellent idea, and the thought of it made me smile. Probably for the first time in many months.

However, despite my army training, I don't think I'm capable of doing it for two reasons. Mentally, I couldn't bring myself to do such a thing; practically, I can't think of a way to do it and get away with it. But any suggestions of how to 'execute' the deed would be very gratefully received, so I can imagine them in my dreams: the nastier the means, the better.

I want to watch him die slowly, in pain, terrified. But I don't suppose you know anything about bumping people off. It's easy for you to just say 'kill him'. He escaped justice – so far – because he is an evil, lying scumbag, and I'm such an unreliable witness that nobody would ever believe me. I suppose I could report him. I'll give it some thought.

    Yours sincerely,
    Miss Melanie Green

Not Mr Almost-Right. Not nearly. As for his daughter, he remembered she was always inclined to make a joke of everything – but this was no joking matter. He'd have a word with her about it. Then he read Rand's reply. Perhaps he was a sensible sort of fellow, after all.

From: Rand@djb9x2103i9.com
Subject:
To: Melanie55@gmail.com
23/08/19

>

The thought of killing anybody should not make you smile. It is a grave matter which does not lend itself to flippancy. I may be able to give you some ideas, but not until I know the circumstances which justify the target being eliminated. You may be mentally unstable, and I would not wish to abet an unjustifiable felony perpetrated by a madwoman.

Just Rand will do fine

>

>

From: Melanie Green
Subject:
To: Rand
23/08/19

>

Hi, Just Rand!

Killing someone is only a grave matter if you actually do it. Get it? No? Thought not. You think I may be mentally unstable? Seriously, you could be right. But I'm making progress. To be frank, you're giving me hope. Perhaps I could kill the bastard if you helped me plan it. I've got a suggestion. You tell me about you and then I'll tell you about me. Agreed?

Melanie

>

>

From: Rand@djb9x2103i9.com
Subject:
To: Melanie55@gmail.com

24/08/19

>

No. Ladies first

>

>

From: Melanie Green

Subject:

To: Rand

24/08/19

>

Just Rand – do you realise how annoying you are? I send you an email in the morning, then I have to wait until the following morning for you to reply. That's bad enough, but when that reply comprises only three flaming words, it ain't half irritating.

So, you want to hear about me. Brought up in South East England, went to a Catholic convent which put me off any kind of religion, then decided to do medicine. My father's a doctor, and Mum was a physio, so it's in the blood.

Cash was tight at Med School, so I joined the Royal Army Medical Corps and got paid. I became a doctor, did my basic army training and got posted to Afghanistan. My parents were kind of pleased, but I think my father worried.

Talk about being busy! We worked eighteen-hour days in six-hour shifts. Satisfying when they pulled through; otherwise, it was not so good. Some joked about dying when they knew they were on their way; difficult not to know when your guts are slithering around you on the stretcher. Soldier humour, I suppose.

Sometimes I'd go out in the helicopter to pick up a casualty. Not in one of those big double-rotor jobs with a full-blown MERT (medical emergency recovery team), but in whatever was available.

Often I'd go with Foxy, or Lance Corporal Foxton to give him his full name. He was a medical orderly and much more experienced than I was in battlefield first aid. I was a captain by then, and in theory his boss. But we were great friends and got on really well.

He had to stop. It was too long to go through the whole thing there and then, so he printed off a copy to read on the plane, and with a paper version he would be able to make notes in the margin if necessary. He pressed the button on the intercom. "Next patient, please."

By lunchtime, Daniela had come up with a taxi booking from Michael's villa to the airport picking him up at three, an e-ticket from Murcia-Corvera to Gatwick taking off at 5.15 pm, and an appointment for lunch the following day at noon with Sir David Goodman in London.

"Thank you, Daniela, that's so kind. My daughter's in a bit of trouble."

"Oh no! Ees there anything I can do to help?"

"Not that I can think of, but it's a kind offer. Thank you. If anyone calls, it's probably better if you don't say I've gone to England."

He had only two patients that afternoon. He was never abrupt with his clientele, but on that occasion, he kept small-talk to a minimum. When he'd seen them, he replied to his daughter's email with his ETA and went home to pack his hold bag and briefcase.

He included his own file on the shooting. Not that it contained much, just his letter to the MoD reporting the crime, plus the reply he got back saying they would look into it. It was from a Major Birch, a staff officer in the PR department. Michael hoped her email exchange with Rand might contain a first-hand account of the incident which would encourage them to take the matter further.

Chapter 2

Shortly after take-off, he settled down with Melanie's file on his knees and continued reading.

Anyway, one day – as they say in the sort of books I read – Foxy and I went out on an early morning casevac and unexpectedly came under some sporadic small arms fire. We were flying high so it wasn't effective., but when the odd bullet hit the Makrolon plates under the cockpit, we would feel the thump. Slightly alarming but it soon passed, and we landed safely at the pick-up point in the courtyard of a tumbledown farm in the middle of nowhere.

Our flash briefing said there was one casualty but sod's law being what it is there were two, both alive but stretcher cases. As Foxy and I loaded up the first one, I noticed liquid dripping from the heli onto the sandy ground. I bent down and smelled it. AVTUR – aviation fuel, in other words, paraffin. I told Rupert, one of the two pilots, who said we must leave straight away, and not to load up the second casualty, as weight must be minimised.

We reckoned the second guy was in a bad way and had to get back to the field hospital straight away. When I was doing the once-over, he regained consciousness. He smiled when he saw my Brit uniform. He was young, I guess in his mid-twenties. I told him he'd be OK. He moved his good hand and pointed to his jacket pocket. Inside was an envelope with a US address. It wasn't stuck down, so I took out the handwritten letter.

It started 'Dear Mom and Dad... If you receive this'... The usual thing; for me, they always jerk a tear. I stuck it back in the envelope, and with a broad smile I returned it to the pocket, assuring him he would be fine and in a few days he would be able to write another one with better news. Having told him that, I was damned if I was going to leave him in that God-forsaken place, so Foxy and I loaded him into the aircraft, and we off-loaded my box of medical tricks to save more weight.

Foxy, bless him, offered to stay and be picked up later. So typical. I wasn't going to let him, so I jumped down and ordered him onto the heli. He refused, and I threatened to court-martial him for disobeying a direct order from a superior officer. Not that I ever felt superior to him. Anyway, he climbed into the damn thing, and Rupert wound it up for take-off.

This is where it gets difficult. I knew they'd send another heli to pick me up, and my box of medical kit. We weren't in a hot zone enemy-wise, so I wasn't too fussed. Also, it had been a long flight, and I felt queasy, so it was a relief to have my feet on solid ground and be breathing fresh air.

I watched the helicopter as it ascended under full power. After a few seconds, I could see the aircraft above the dust cloud. I waved to Rupert and Sergeant Jones, the second pilot. They waved back. I watched it get smaller and smaller as it ascended into the vivid blue sky. I noticed a faint trail of white smoke chasing it.

It's strange what you remember on such occasions. When the bright orange bubble disappeared, I noticed the rotors were still going around, and I wondered if the thing had survived the hit. Then, ever so slowly, the craft – or what was left of it – started to tumble, rotors still turning. Then one broke off. I suppose you would have said something like 'Holy Cow!'. But I started with shit and worked my way up to something much worse, shouting at the top of my voice.

I'd seen lots of deaths by then, but close up; seeing the wreckage falling to the ground was somehow worse, imagining it crashing in some far off rocky ravine never to be seen again. It was like seeing a road accident from afar. You cannot comfort the dying. Five of them: Rupert the pilot, Sergeant Jones his mate, the two casualties and Foxy.

It soon dawned on me I'd ordered him to his death. It should have been me on that aircraft. I should have died, and Foxy should have lived. I wondered how many others would die because Foxy wouldn't be around to save them.

I thought about my two patients, their good fortune to be found and casevacked, only to be blown to bits in the heli. I regretted stuffing that letter back in the guy's pocket, as I realised it would never get delivered. I tried to remember the address, vowing to write to his parents as soon as I got back to base, to tell them I was with him shortly before he died and about his letter urging them to be brave.

In a way, I died too. Our ops centre would have assumed I was on that aircraft, and I realised there would be no rescue helicopter coming to pick me up. I hadn't a clue where I was, and as for tabbing it back to base camp. Across that terrain? No way.

I was stuck. I remember wondering what they would put in my records: KIA, MIA, or PKIA? I don't suppose you know what those letters stand for. Well, work it out, sunshine.

I worried about Mum and Dad. They were wonderful parents. I was an only child, and they doted on me. I imagined Dad opening the front door and seeing the families officer standing there in full service-dress and Sam Browne (a leather belt and cross-strap). I knew they'd be heart-broken.

Dad especially was looking forward to being a grandparent. The last thing I would ever have wanted was to let him down in that respect. I think he was disappointed I was a girl. I tried to be more like a son, probably another reason I joined the Army. I wanted him to be proud of me. I'm going to have to stop. I can hardly focus on the keyboard.

Mel

He was shocked by the final paragraph. Proud of her? No father could have been more proud of his daughter. Disappointed? What rubbish. He had to admit he did look forward to her finding the right person and settling down, and having a family. But it was her life. The last thing in the world he had ever wanted was to apply any sort of pressure.

She was wrong about one thing. He never opened the front door to see the families officer standing there. He and Dawn were returning home from a trip to the supermarket. As they rounded the corner into their road, he saw the car, a black Ford, parked outside the house. He knew straight away what it was doing there, and his stomach turned to liquid. The man was standing by the front door and looking at his watch. Melly was right about a couple of things. The officer was in full service-dress wearing a Sam Browne – and he and Dawn were heartbroken.

Michael was intrigued to see that the next email was from Rand telling Melanie more about himself. Perhaps he's not such a mystery-man after all. But the bio raised more questions than it answered.

From: Rand@djb9x2103i9.com
Subject:
To: Melanie55@gmail.com
25/08/19

>

Full name: Randolph O'Brian
Place of birth: Pierre, South Dakota, USA
Date of birth: 03/03/1990
Parents: Joseph O'Brian, Martha O'Brian
Specialisms: Special Forces Operations (Airborne)
Courses attended: Unstructured clandestine operations (UCO), hand-to-hand combat, close-quarter fire-arms usage, close observation and reconnaissance.

UCO is a technical term covering abductions, annihilations and assassinations. And those are just the 'a's. I am currently stationed in Greater London in deep cover awaiting assignment. Thank you for telling me about you. Most people experience bereavement from time to time, but at your age, you've had more than your fair share. I will try to help. Tell me more.

>

>

From: Melanie Green
Subject:
To: Rand
25/08/19

>

Hi, Just Rand – thank you for your bio. Do you really expect me to believe it? But I'll go along with it, just to keep you in a good mood. South Dakota? Does that mean you're a red-neck? I've just googled 'Jokes about South Dakota'. My favourite is, 'What does a South Dakota girl do if she's not in bed by 10 pm? She goes home'.

I guess you've done some interesting training, or are you making it all up? You're not a Walter Mitty by any chance? In Greater London, are we? Well, I'm surprised we haven't bumped into each other, because I, too, am in Greater London.

Perhaps we ought to meet up. Save all this typing. But there again, would I feel safe with a trained assassin, probably a ruthless psychopath, doling out death to anyone who got in his way? Or do you do it for money, or for the CIA or whatever government agency you might work for? I don't know about these things.

Thanks, by the way, for your renewed offer to help. That's kind of you; a CIA-trained assassin can't have much time on his hands – perhaps just blood, m'lud. And did my acute sense of awareness, heightened by repeated trauma, detect a slight note of sympathy in your email? Of course, I could be quite wrong; assassins don't do sympathy, do they? But if I'm right, thanks for that also.

Always welcome, a sympathetic shoulder to cry on. Not many of those about these days. My father did come here to see me when I finally returned to UK, but then he went back to Spain.

Michael was glad Melly hadn't fallen for all that nonsense about the man being a trained assassin. Surely that would be the end of their brief over-the-internet encounter. But he had many more pages to go.

He was touched Melly mentioned him. His visit to Beechwood Hall had been many months ago. It had been a difficult time for both of them. And he had had the awful task of breaking the news to Melly of her mother's death.

He'd spent four days there, in the guest suite, but at every opportunity, he and Mel would meet and go for a walk if it was fine, or a drive if not. They would talk endlessly, for much of the time about Dawn, Melanie's mother, and of the great times the three of them had when Mel was a girl. He was pleased there was nothing wrong with her long-term memory, but when he'd pressed her for details of more recent events she'd struggled.

That was when she'd talked of the massacre, a raid on the village led by a British Army officer. She reckoned he'd shot and killed at least one unarmed male civilian. But her account had been so sketchy it could hardly be regarded as reliable evidence. Perhaps her emails to Rand would give more details.

Right. I'd better get on and tell you the next episode. There I am, alone, miles from anywhere, standing in a dusty courtyard surrounded by ruined farm buildings. It's mid-morning, and the sun is beating down on me from a clear blue sky. A few minutes ago, my transport took off without me, only to be whacked by a missile (Stinger? Redeye? SA-7? God knows), killing all on board.

I felt I'd had a lucky escape until I realised that everyone back at the ranch would assume I was on board. I'll be listed PKIA – presumed killed in action if you didn't get it. And after suitable pretences of regret, I'll become just another war statistic. No one would be coming to find me.

I should point out that I was not equipped for being dumped behind enemy lines in hostile terrain, and I didn't have a clue where I was. I had no means of communication, no map, no water, no food; just a plastic box with rudimentary medical supplies. And I had no weapon of any kind. The two casualties had semis, but SOPs say you're to recover the casualties' firearms, so the baddies don't get their hands on them.

But on that day, would you believe it, began the best and most rewarding period of my life. The first thing I did, once I'd pulled myself together, was to take stock of my surroundings. I was in no hurry. I had nothing to do for a change. And probably for the first time in six months, I appreciated the pure natural beauty of the country.

I had a wander around the abandoned farm buildings. Not in them, because of the IED risk. I'd seen a few results of those to make me very cautious. I did notice that there was a well in the courtyard, and there were goat or sheep droppings on the ground, fresh ones. So it was unlikely that any tripwires had been set up outside.

The silence was wonderful. I'd been to other beautiful places in the region, but usually by helicopter for a rapid pick-up-and-go, so the sound of its turbine would be roaring in my ears all the while.

Having survived for six months on probably no more than five hours per night – or rather per 24 hours – I was short of the zeds. But I'd been too busy to notice. Now, here on my own with nothing to do, no patients to patch up, it all caught up with me. Perhaps I should have panicked or started walking south until I hit the Arabian Sea, a mere 1,000 miles away.

Or I could have gathered up lots of white stones and laid them out in the middle of the courtyard so they spelt H-E-L-P. I heard a story once of a soldier who got stranded in the Libyan desert when his Land Rover broke down. The RAF spent three days looking for him. They eventually found him because they spotted the black smoke after he'd set fire to his spare wheel. The RAF didn't charge him for the cost of all those aircraft-hours searching for him, but the Army made him pay for the tyre.

Even if I'd had something inflammable like a tyre, I couldn't have set fire to it as I hadn't any matches or a lighter. I'm not a smoker. I hope you're not; I can't bear the smell of stale tobacco.

Sorry to go on, but it's important I explain my state of

mind at that time because it had a huge bearing on what followed. I fell asleep and dreamed of bells, waking to a pungent smell, and the sound bleating sheep – perhaps twenty of them, overseen by a boy dressed in rags and leaning on a stick, watching me. He had a rifle slung across his body, nearly as long as he was tall. I guess he was about ten years old.

I stood up and smiled at him. "Salaam!" I said, as boldly as I could. He dropped his stick and unslung his rifle; I stretched out my arms, palms facing him to show him I wasn't armed. He gave me a shy smile and mumbled the Muslim greeting in reply. Then he slung his rifle, picked up his stick, shouted at his ovine charges and disappeared.

Got to go now and take my meds, then a session with Bob. Don't get me wrong; he's my trick cyclist. He's lovely, a real softy. And don't be too long getting back to me – please!

Regards,

Mel

Nothing wrong with her memory so far, he thought. But all that happened before the raid.

Chapter 3

He'd decided a gin and tonic and a packet of nuts would be in order, but when the tired flight attendant finally reached his row of seats, he was too engrossed in his reading to catch her eye. He wanted to find out more about Rand. He was curious to know how the man would reply to his daughter after she'd rumbled him.

From: Rand@djb9x2103i9.com
Subject:
To: Melanie55@gmail.com
26/08/19
>

I am not a Walter Mitty. Neither am I a lunatic. Nor am I ruthless. I work for an arm of the Government. Assignment is effected at the highest level and for good reason, often to prevent a major incident or to change the course of history for the good of mankind. Think of an assassination as being a surgical strike by one individual, usually against another, as opposed to an indiscriminate bombing raid, an inaccurate drone strike, or an artillery shell or a landmine which might cause collateral.

Think of the lives which would have been saved if Claus von Stauffenberg's plot had succeeded in its mission to assassinate Hitler. How millions would have been spared if Saddam Hussein had been taken out before the launch of Operation Desert Storm? Assassination is not permitted by international law, but that does not make every assassin a psychopath and a criminal.

You would be perfectly safe with me, but there is no question of us meeting, even if we lived in the same street.

Incidentally, I need to know where you live. Not the address but the type of accommodation you are in. You mentioned meds and psychiatry. Are you in a mental hospital?

I do not smoke. Your story is interesting and helpful. You are too modest. In some ways, you would make a good assassin. You are tough, and you have a brain. Tell me what you did next.

>

>

From: Melanie Green
Subject:
To: Rand
26/08/19

>

Good morning, Just Rand!

How are you today? Yes, I'm fine. Thanks sooo much for asking. Actually, I'm not very good at the moment. I'm going through a bad spell – flashbacks and things, headaches. I want you to cheer me up with lots of ways in which I could kill Mr Nasty. Then at least I could imagine me doing it, even if I didn't have the skill or guts to go through with it.

You want to know where I am. It's not a mental hospital, but a convalescent home specialising in the recovery of people who have suffered mentally. It has medical staff, but it feels more like a very select private hotel. And a few of the people here really do think it's a hotel! I'm undergoing an ITP (intensive treatment programme), but they try to treat us as much as possible as normal people in preparation for the eventual return to the outside world.

I have a lovely private room in the old part, but I think it's haunted. Sometimes at night, I feel a presence: a girl. It doesn't bother me, as I'm probably dreaming. And I have far worse images of real things in my head than to be worried about the supernatural. I've never seen her, but I hear her; her breathing, her sighs. And sometimes she cries. I wish I could help her.

There are public rooms – principally a dining room, coffee lounge, fitness suite with hydro pool, a hobbies room, library and a study centre. That's where I am now, in the study centre typing away at one of the three Windows 10 machines. And there's a guest suite so we can have visitors. Dad came soon after I arrived and stayed there for a couple of days.

As you would expect, we have a fully equipped medical centre. Sometimes I assist – when I'm not in there being treated. They don't let me do anything too serious, but I'm trying to get back into the swing of things. When I get out of here, I hope to resume my career.

Not too soon, he thought. Not until you are better. It worried him that she might be let loose on patients, but he accepted that a gradual return to a normal life was all part of the treatment.

Inmates like me can come and go as they please, although there's a secure wing if anyone fancies themselves as Hannibal Lecter. I referred to 'inmates', but the staff insist we are 'guests'. I think lunatics would have been a more accurate description, at least in my case when I first arrived. But I'm not mad now. Just mad at Mr Nasty.

Electric bikes are always on offer; they don't go far before you have to pedal, but you can reach the shops and just about make it to the nearest tube station. Staff are kind and wonderful, although sometimes I get some odd looks. I'm always nice to them, but some of them, some of the time, seem as if they're scared of me. Until I smile and say hi how are you today. Then they beam back at me, almost with relief. Strange, it's as if they think I'm someone else. I wouldn't hurt a fly. Except for you-know-who.

Being medically trained probably helps. Not that I've done much psychiatry. But they know that I know about things, and they're good at explaining them. Maybe they see me as one of them.

We're a mixed bunch, but mostly men. Some of us here have PTSD, in various stages of recovery, and there's a handful of alkies and other addicts who are rehabbing. We have a couple of bi-polar bears and a few odds and sods who are obviously here for something, but nobody seems to know what.

And they come and go. Actually, some never go; after recovering, they take a job here. It's like a big family. We all look after each other. The thing is there is always someone worse off than you, so you don't wallow in despair; you count your blessings.

The place must cost a fortune. The MoD is picking up my tab, thank goodness. And, would you believe it, I'm still getting my Army pay – and all that back pay. There's not much to spend it on, so when I get out of this place, I should have the wherewithal to do what I need to do. Which reminds me, whatever you suggest by way of a wet job, it must allow me to get away with it. It would give me no pleasure to imagine his lingering death if I had to worry about Mr Plod arresting me.

Life's okay here. I do look forward to getting out of the place, but they say it's important that I complete the treatment. They can't say exactly how long it would take, as everyone's different. To be honest, they look after you so well here, that it'll be a bit of a wrench to say good-bye.

Sleep is my biggest problem. Nightmares – and they say I sometimes sleepwalk. The injections knock me out, which is good, but then I have trouble waking up. I get a bit of exercise each day. Normally, after breakfast I go for a walk – if I don't have a session with my therapist. He's nice. He suggested I joined the bereavement support group.

Is that enough? Colour of eyes? Vital statistics? If you must know, I'm a lanky blondish, boring broad, but because I don't come from South Dakota I have all my pearly whites*. I'm a simple soul who doesn't really do make-up or false eyelashes and things. I used to be good at sport – hockey and swimming were my favourites.

*Did you know that the toothbrush was invented in South Dakota? Otherwise, it would have been called a teethbrush. Don't blame me; it came off the internet.

And, how about a nice greeting? And a friendly sign-off? Or don't they do that in SD?

Kind regards,
Melanie

>

>

From: Rand@djb9x2103i9.com
Subject:
To: Melanie55@gmail.com
27/08/19

>

Dear Melamine,

How are you today? Have you been in the dishwasher yet? Thank you for your explanation of where you are staying. It sounds as if you are in good hands. Please continue with your story. When you have completed it, I will decide on how I can advise you. Blue eyes do nothing for me and vital statistics are irrelevant.

Best

Just Rand

Michael found Rand's attempt at humour irritating. On the other hand, it was a relief that the two of them were able to exchange a bit of banter. All part of getting to know each other. Perhaps he was harmless.

From: Melanie Green

Subject:

To: Rand

27/08/19

>

Oh, we _are_ being funny today. Do you find me dishy? You seem very reluctant to tell me more about yourself, but it looks as if I'll have to keep going if I'm ever to receive the benefit of your professional advice.

Tell me if you get bored. I'll try not to wander off topic, which I know I tend to do. Actually, I find it quite therapeutic, committing it all to the computer screen. It makes me realise I did have to jump a few hurdles and navigate through some clashing rocks. I feel less like a failure. I don't hate myself so much.

It seems strange to Michael that two people could meet on the internet and have what was turning out to be quite an intimate exchange. Even though one of them was his daughter, he felt he was intruding. He was relieved to return to her story.

Netflix recap. Press OK to skip intro. There I am, in the courtyard in the back and beyond somewhere in Afghanistan. Little-Bo-Peep – with a rifle slung over his shoulder – has run off with his sheep, leaving me alone with my medicine chest as company. I cleverly deduced that he might have gone off to tell someone about me.

It was a strange feeling. I couldn't work out if I was pleased or worried. Was he going fetch his father? Would he come and rescue me? Would he bring food? Or would he simply kill me, a member of a hostile and much-hated invasion force? Or was the lad just going to leave me there to starve to death?

It was nightfall, and I was starting to shiver, thinking that I might risk moving into the ruins for the night. I heard the distant noise of an engine, going up and down in pitch. An unseen headlight jerked its beam in my direction, and finally I spotted the pick-up, silhouetted against the evening glow from the west.

It was making slow progress, which gave me plenty of time to slowly panic. But I took some deep breaths and stopped myself. Should I hide? Should I go and meet them? I decided to lie down next to my medicine chest with its big red crosses and pretend to be asleep, on the basis that they would not see me as a threat and start firing at me. All Afghan males seem to carry guns.

They soon found me with their torches, and I pretended to wake up, stretching my arms out so they would see I wasn't armed. I opened my eyes and lost all my night vision, but I slowly stood up and salaamed them, bowing my head in respect even though I couldn't see them. I think there were three of them.

They blindfolded me, tied my wrists behind my back and dumped me in the back of the pick-up, along with my medicine chest. The journey was terrible — three hours of bone-shaking purgatory. But I was pleased about the blindfold. Obviously, they didn't want me to see where we were going – not that there were many street lights and signposts in that neck of the woods. But if their intention had been to kill me, I reckoned they would not have cared if I found out where their secret hideout was.

Having carefully helped me down from the pick-up, they guided me into a building, took off the blindfold and untied my wrists; I massaged them, as they do in films. In the light of the Tilley lamp hanging from the ceiling, I saw a homemade bed against the far wall. In front of it was a crude wooden table on which stood a plastic bottle of water and a plate of what looked like biscuits. They were hard but delicious, and the water was wonderful; I gulped it down.

The door banged shut behind me, and I was alone. I looked around and saw my medicine chest, just inside the door. In a far corner, I saw there was a hole in the earth floor and a home-made wash-stand. Not quite the penthouse suite, but do-able.

I tried the door. It creaked open, and I looked out into the dark night. Stars above me, millions of them. It didn't take me long to realise what I had to do. I closed the door and crashed out on the bed.

And so began my new life, as a GP in a small village in rural Afghanistan.

Really? Michael was intrigued to know how that happened. Perhaps being a 'general practitioner' in the Hindu Kush was not quite the same as working under the NHS in Dulwich. Less regulation, but no support. And there must have been a language problem. How can you treat someone if they can't explain what's wrong with them? Then he remembered an argument he'd had at uni about that very subject – with a friend who was studying veterinary science. He looked forward to hearing directly from Melly how she got on and what she managed to achieve.

That room became my surgery, pharmacy, the local A & E department, field hospital (MASH to you) and maternity unit. Of course, my medical supplies were soon expended, and I had to fall back on other methods of treating the sick and wounded: magic potions and poultices, snake oil and charms – placebos, in other words. And they worked – along with a wee bit of mild hypnosis and a few tricks of the trade.

The village became my home. In my spare time, I taught English and learned the local dialect. The women were suspicious of me at first. They gave me food and clothes and things for my room, but it took time to win their trust and accept me, but two of them eventually became my full-time assistants.

I think it helped me not being religious, as I didn't care what they believed in. To me, they were just humankind – kind being the operative word. Hospitable, perhaps. They call it *Melmastia*, one of the main principles of their culture.

My first patient had been the son of the local warlord, for want of a better word. My job – and the reason they brought me there – was to remove shrapnel from a difficult leg wound. He was so grateful. We became good friends; he was about my age and was charming and fun. We became lovers, then a couple. Nothing was official, but his family made a big fuss of me despite the religious complications; I suppose it was the hospitality thing. So, in effect, Shahpur became my common-law husband. And the magic happened, and I became pregnant.

Michael could hardly believe it. His darling daughter had dismissed in a few lines what he had been hoping would happen for years: her finding a fella, falling in love, tying the knot and popping out a grandchild for him. Then he realised she was writing to Rand, someone she'd never met, a bloke to boot. He would not have been interested in chapter and verse. Michael would have to wait to hear the details directly from Melly.

We were so excited! My female assistants helped me with pre-natal, the delivery and post-natal, and they became like aunts to me. Jangi was just the most adorable baby you could ever wish for, and we treasured him. Dad's longed-for grandson. Shame he never held him in his arms.

Life was good. The people were marvellous, quite unlike how they portrayed the Taliban in the Western media. Why do we always demonise our enemies? I suppose it makes it easier for us to kill them. Anyway, the people in that village were kind, unselfish, honest and generous. At least most of them were, like in any other family, tribe, society or nation.

We lacked the comforts of modern living in the West, but we were free of many of the stresses which go with them.

In fact, life was too good. Something had to end it, and it did. I'll tell you next time. I'm going to have to stop. Sorry.

Kindest regards,
Mel
>

>

From: Rand@djb9x2103i9.com
Subject:
To: Melanie55@gmail.com
28/08/19
>

Thanks. Carry on when you are ready. And how are you today? Are your emails password protected? My concerns are not for me, but for you. I cannot be found. My email address is untraceable. I am a professional, trained in the art of being invisible, of remaining in deep cover until I am required to carry out a mission. It is my job.

Best
Rand
>

>

From: Melanie Green
Subject:
To: Rand
28/08/19
>

How kind of you to inquire about my health! Not too bad, actually. And thanks for replying. To be frank, the next instalment is challenging because of the memory losses. Anyway, here goes.

Then came Melanie's description of the massacre. Michael skimmed through it as if by avoiding the details it would lessen its importance. But he realised there was enough in there to support his case that a war crime had been committed. He wondered what a lawyer would make of it, whether it would in some way justify the killing of the man leading the raid. He would need to discuss that with his friend David Goodman.

By the time the captain announced they were making their final approach to Gatwick, Michael had read Melanie's file three times. The first time, he was cross she hadn't contacted him during her years of freedom in Afghanistan, to let him know she was alive. And he was upset she hadn't somehow managed to get word to him about her partner and their child, his grandson – his flesh and blood – who had lived and died without him ever being aware of his existence.

He was livid the MoD had lied in the letter, telling him she'd been imprisoned by the Taliban for those missing years. And he was angry she hadn't been there to share the grief of her mother dying. It was from breast cancer – two years after they had received notification that their darling daughter was missing in action, presumed killed.

On the second reading, he felt more sympathy

towards his daughter, realising for the first time the huge amount of stress she must have been under, getting trapped in that village under those extraordinary circumstances and then watching her partner and son being killed. And for a parent to lose a child, he knew from personal experience it could be an almost unbearable ordeal.

News of the sexual assaults was a shock, but he knew rape happened in war – rape and pillage. Even so, he found it hard to believe his Melly could have been violated in that way, and by someone on her own side. What a vile creature. Michael wasn't a vengeful person, but a little part of him secretly hoped the man's death had been a painful one.

He did wonder about where she had been in those missing months. She didn't say much about it, so perhaps she was amnesic for much of her stay. By the time she'd returned to UK, she was in reasonable physical shape. Whoever had cared for her knew what they were doing. He decided he'd quiz her on that – when the time was right.

The final reading of the email exchange was less of an emotional experience for him, as he realised he had a job on his hands. He had to submit her eye-witness account of the war crimes to the MoD. However, his main task – his mission – was to make sure his daughter didn't get involved in any court proceedings, let alone become a suspect in a suspicious death.

Chapter 4

As Michael drove through the grand gateway of Beechwood Hall, he recalled his first visit there; Melanie had not been in a good place. But if her recent emails to Rand were anything to go by, she had settled in well, made friends and was enjoying what the establishment had to offer.

He drove slowly past the lake and caught sight of a lone fisherman on the far bank. It reminded him of his attempt at sea-fishing during one of their holidays at Littlestone; the hook had caught on his bottom.

The main house came into view, a grand Victorian mansion in Gothic style with a brick and stone façade and mullioned windows, set in beautiful grounds. It was getting dark and the lights were on. As he approached the main doors, he saw her standing underneath the great arch, illuminated by the ornate cast-iron and glass lantern above her head. Her upright, proud figure reminded him of Dawn, and he wondered if his wife would somehow know that her beautiful daughter, her only child, was very much alive. Not that he believed in life after death – but his wife had, so perhaps her faith did enable some trick of time to take place. He hoped so.

Inevitably, the greeting was emotional. Father and daughter hugged each other and smiled and cried at the same time. Melanie spoke first.

"Come on, Dad, let's go inside. How was the flight? And how are all those wealthy widows doing down in La Manga?"

Michael was glad of the distraction and wiped his eyes with the back of his hand. "Fine thanks. The flight, I mean." He reflected on the second question. Nobody could ever replace his Dawn.

They both laughed as they walked arm in arm into the great hall. The girl behind the reception desk gave Melanie a big smile.

"Hi Siobhan," said Melanie returning the smile. "This is my dad. He's also Dr Green. He's booked into the guest suite."

"A pleasure to meet you, and to be here again. It's Michael, by the way." He signed in and hung his visitor's pass around his neck. Father and daughter made their way through the double security doors to the grand staircase. Melanie explained that she had arranged dinner in her room that evening, which would allow them to talk without any risk of being overheard. As they walked up the stairs, she asked her father if he'd managed to read the file she had emailed to him. His look answered her question, and they continued in silence to her room.

"Welcome to Maxim's," she said, extending a forearm towards the table for two, set in the centre of the oak-panelled room. He remembered the big bay window overlooking the forecourt and the lake beyond, but Melanie had closed the heavy brocade curtains. "Per'aps monsieur would care for an aperitif?"

"That would be nice." He thought a stiff drink at that moment would do him no harm at all. "Well, what have you got?"

"Everysing! Whatever your 'eart desires."

"A dry sherry, please."

"Sorry, luv. Sherry's off. I can do you a Tesco prosecco if you could do me the honours and open it."

The silly exchange had lightened the mood, and Michael found that the cool bubbly liquid soon relieved the tension in his stomach. He was amazed at how his daughter had changed since his last visit. She looked gorgeous – radiant, even. No dark circles around the eyes, the knot between the eyebrows had melted, the ready smile revealing her straight white teeth, and her short blonde hair was shiny and bounced around her head like it did when she was a teenager.

On the dot of eight o'clock, there was a knock on the heavy oak door. Melanie opened it, and there was a figure in chef's whites supporting a huge silver tray on one upturned hand at shoulder height. The other carried an ice bucket. All the stops had been pulled out for this important encounter. Michael noticed the look the man gave his daughter. It said I like you very much, and here, I've done my best for you.

"Dad, this is Luigi. He's the head chef. The best of the best. Luigi, my dad, Doctor Michael Green."

The two men exchanged a few words and smiles as Melanie looked on. At the first pause, Luigi backed towards the door and wished the pair, "Buon appetito!"

The meal was good. The two of them talked almost non-stop, but Michael steered well clear of the questions he had intended to ask his daughter. They could wait for another time.

Michael was the one to wilt first. Perhaps polishing off the bottle of prosecco was the reason, but his excuse was that his time-clock was still an hour ahead. Much to his surprise, Melanie had kept her bounce throughout the evening – probably because she'd stuck to the fizzy elderflower cordial. He reckoned that if some eligible young man had asked her out to a West End night club after the meal, she would have jumped at the chance. The improvement was impressive.

He did tell her he had an appointment in London the following day, but he didn't wish to raise her hopes by saying what it was about. He wanted to sound out David before discussing the subject with her.

Michael arrived at the offices of Matthew, Finch and Trowbridge at five minutes before mid-day and took a seat in Reception. At precisely noon, David appeared. "Sandy, my dear chap. How wonderful to see you!"

He was embarrassed when Sir David Goodman greeted him with his nickname from boat-club times. His straw mop had long given way to a thin covering of silver-grey wisps which barely hid the sun-spots on his scalp. "Great to see you, too. Thanks so much for seeing me at such short notice. And it's Michael nowadays, now the sand's gone!"

He had to admit to himself that the long-lost friendship had been lost a long time ago. They had never been really close, but having been crewmen together in the Jesus College winning eight at Henley forty-odd years ago, there was a bond, and it was clear to Michael it was mutual.

David led the way up the grand 18th Century staircase to his office on the first floor. He turned the large brass handle, and the heavy oak door swung open revealing a bright, spacious room overlooking a small courtyard. A grand crystal chandelier hung from the high ceiling, and the walls were lined with bookshelves fully laden with ancient tomes. He waved to Michael to take one of the faded leather armchairs by the window, and he took the other.

After the inevitable reminiscing and the 'whatever happened to so-and-so', he explained they'd be going to his club for lunch, which had been booked for one o'clock. Being just five minutes walk away, it gave them plenty of time to have a natter. Michael asked what particular field David had specialised in during his legal career, and with some pride he replied he was now Senior Partner of Matthew, Finch and Trowbridge, old Trowbridge having retired last year.

"As for my speciality," said David, "it's more a case of what I try and steer clear of. I won't be much help with conveyancing or family work, but if it's a driving offence that's niggling you, I can certainly see what I can do. And we do have a bankruptcy department, if..."

"No, David. It's nothing like that. Actually, it concerns my daughter. She's a doctor, too. And she could be in a bit of trouble."

"What, litigation? There is so much of it around these days – and we do have a team which can handle that."

"No, it's not to do with her job... I think the best thing I can do is to give you a file she has put together for me; it tells the whole story. And once you have read it, you'll know as much as I do." He put his briefcase on his lap and fished out the hard copy and passed it across."

"Michael, do excuse me." David returned to his partner's desk and pressed a button. Five seconds later, his secretary appeared, a slim girl elegantly dressed in a cream silk blouse and pleated dark blue skirt. David handed her the file and asked her to make two copies. Five minutes later she returned and gave the hard copies and the original to her boss.

"Thank you, Julia." David smiled as he watched her leave the room. "I always find it wise to have two copies. Would you mind if I kept the original in case we need more?"

Michael nodded, took the new copy offered to him and returned it to his briefcase. David sat down at his desk, put on a pair of horn-rimmed glasses and started scanning his copy at speed, clearly the result of much practice.

Michael wondered if he would have recognised his friend if he'd passed him in the street. The shock of wavy brown hair had been replaced by a few strands of grey, and the tight jawline had melted into a fleshy neck. The dark eyebrows had retained their colour and grown much longer, giving him an owl-like appearance. But the eyes were bright and still had that intelligent sparkle which Michael remembered so well.

He noticed David had slowed right down and was

following the print with his finger; he was frowning. Every now and then he paused, picked up his fountain pen and made a note on his legal pad. Michael heard the occasional sharp intake of breath; he saw the glasses coming off for a moment while David stared at the window, then going back on to let the reading continue.

Michael saw David's jaw drop with a noticeable click of the tongue a couple of times, and after about ten minutes he saw David's hands were shaking. Finally, he watched David carefully place the stapled wodge of A4 sheets on the tooled leather of his desk, as if they might explode. They lay there, folded back to one of Melanie's emails. Michael noticed his handwritten scrawl in the margin: WAR CRIME!! The harrowing details came back to him.

It must have been in my fourth year, as we had recently celebrated Jangi's second birthday. Early one morning, I woke up to the familiar sound of helicopters. Not that we got many, and if they did come our way, they were at high altitude.

I guessed there were three or four of them. The whopping got louder and then turned to whooshing as they landed. I jumped out of bed and looked outside. Dust swirling around, so I couldn't see much. I went back inside and closed the door so the dust wouldn't come in. Then I heard gunfire, bursts of it; and shouting. And screams.

What the hell? I thought. I rushed outside, livid, that someone was playing silly buggers. Men running, some bodies on the ground. A man in Brit uniform shouting orders. I noticed he had black crowns woven into the slides on his shoulder straps; a major. I ran up to him, shouting at him to stop. I remember saying, "what the hell do you think you're doing?" I think he was shocked I was English.

I ran back inside to find Jangi crying. Shahpur was leaning over his cot trying to comfort him. I picked up my baby, and Shahpur ran outside. From inside, I heard his voice shouting in broken English. I was worried for him and went outside to see what was going on, just in time to see the major raise his service pistol and fire twice. The first shot went wide, but the second one blew the back of Shahpur's head off.

The major saw me and shouted a command, something like, 'get the fucking bitch' but in a posh voice. Two soldiers in Brit combats came and grabbed me and dragged me over to the major, with Jangi still in my arms. One of them snatched Jangi away; he, my baby, was screaming, "mama, mama". The soldier holding him said, "What now, boss?" The posh voice bellowed "Kill the fucking thing, you bloody idiot!" There was a pause. "No, boss. No more," was the reply.

The major raised his Browning. I broke free and threw myself at the major, grabbing the straps of his flak jacket, pleading for my child's life. I heard a shot.

The major pushed me to the ground. I managed to look round, in time to see the soldier with Jangi still in his arms crumple to the ground. Blood was spreading on the dry earth beneath them. There was no way a two-year-old's young body was going to stop a 9mm magnum round.

I think I must have been hit on the head because I do remember feeling a very sore swelling just above my left ear after I'd come to in a helicopter – such a distinctive sound. The trouble is it's very difficult to say what was real and what I dreamed.

One of my memories was being in a room, like a prison cell, dark and musty. One light bulb, an earth floor damp to the touch. A distant chugging of a generator. Walls of rusty wriggly tin. I can still see the major's face, leaning over me, close up. Everything was blurred, but there was something about his hooded eyes which frightened me; they were like dark beads, deep in their sockets under a heavy brow. His stubbled chin jutted out below a thin upper lip revealing his lower front teeth; they were stained yellow. He smelt of smoke and gingivitis.

I remember him asking me lots of questions about military positions and deployments, types of weapons and sources of supplies. When I wasn't able to answer any of them, he called me a defector, a traitor, and much worse. I said I was Captain Melanie Green RAMC. He swore at me and called me a liar, an imposter. He said I was a nobody, that I didn't exist. He said I belonged to him, and nobody else knew about me.

Unfortunately, I had no means of identification. I'd long given up wearing uniform, much preferring the cool flowing clothes which the village girls all wore. I couldn't show him my dog-tags as I'd tied them above Jangi's cot as a distraction for him, a toy. He would hit them with his hand making them quietly jingle. And being stainless steel, they would reflect the light of the Tilley lamp as they slowly turned.

I think I was drugged. I can remember waking up and finding a cannula inserted into a vein on my right forearm. And I remembered the abuse. He raped me, a few times. Sometimes I would be conscious and feel the pain. At other times I'd wake up and find myself very sore, or bleeding.

God knows how long I was in that ghastly room – two or three days? A week? I did get food, chunks of stale bread, and water which was heavily chlorinated, and there was a bucket which served as a loo. It was so horrible. How could an officer in the British Army be so vile?

As for Jangi and my husband, I think I blocked it out of my mind. At least I tried to, but I could never forget seeing Shahpur's head blown apart. I watched it happen a thousand times in my dreams. My memory of Jangi was his screams, then the gunshot, then the soldier collapsing to the ground with my baby in his arms.

I wished so many times that it had been me holding him. I would have clutched him tight, and with my last breath I would have been able to comfort him – and let him know that Mummy was going to come with him and would be with him always. I've seen enough deaths to know they rarely happen instantaneously. I would have had time to whisper in his ear. I would have told him we were going together to join Daddy. I know he would have smiled. He loved it when the three of us were together.

I should have have left him in his cot. It was so stupid to take him out there. I'd heard the gunfire. I cannot forgive myself, ever. It was all my fault.

Got to stop. I'll try tomorrow.

Love Melanie

David looked up at Michael and frowned. "My dear chap... What can I say?... I'm so, so sorry. Poor girl! And you! It must be such a worry – what a bastard. Well, you've come to the right place. I'm sure we can help." He picked up the papers and continued reading, stopping occasionally to re-read parts. Michael could see his lips moving.

I must have had some sort of breakdown because I have flashbacks of a hospital bed in a private room. A proper bed, clean sheets, nurses in white uniforms who would come in and replenish my drip and bring me meals. Nobody spoke to me, nobody asked me any questions, and I can't remember ever speaking to anyone. But I would hear voices and sometimes music from hidden speakers – but maybe I imagined that.

There was a large window but the glass was frosted, so I had no view of any kind. In one of my lucid moments, I noticed an electrical socket on the white wall. The holes weren't like they are in England, more like slits, and they were upright rather than horizontal. I wondered where the hell I was – and how long I'd been there, as I spent most of the time sleeping and having wild dreams.

My next proper memory was waking up here at the convalescent home, here in leafy England, in my room. I felt good. A nurse was standing by my bed and she smiled. She said I'd done really well and that in no time I'd be up and about. She showed me how to work the bed, operate the nurse alarm and master the TV remote control. Actually, I felt fit and well physically, but getting my brain to work properly was difficult.

I've been here for just under six months. I'm now aware of the day, the date and the time of day. I've managed to work out that I must have spent about fifteen months in that other place, wherever it was. God knows why I was there for all that time. It's amazing I never got bedsores – or muscle wastage for that matter.

Shortly after arriving here, some kind man brought me my passport, driving licence, credit card and mobile phone. I say they were mine, but they weren't. But somehow they were all in my name, as if by magic, with my picture on the passport and driving licence, and my own signature on the back of the credit card. So, actually, I'm beginning to feel quite normal. Bob said it was a sign that I was making good progress.

And Dad came to see me. That was so wonderful. Since Mum died, he's lived full time in Spain. He was over the moon to hear I was alive but very upset to see me in such a state.

He came as soon as he got the MoD letter, but it had been sent to his Dulwich address and taken ages to find him at La Manga. It said I'd been held captive by the Taliban for four years. But they don't have electrical wall sockets with upright slits in Afghanistan.

I must admit I wasn't able to tell Dad everything. I don't think either of us was in a fit state to handle it. But I did mention the raid on the village led by a British Army major, of how I saw him deliberately shoot and kill Shahpur before taking me prisoner. Dad reckoned it was a war crime and vowed to report it. Next time he comes, I might show him these emails so he will have the full story. So thanks, Justy, for getting me to face up to things and put digital pen to electronic paper.

By the way, why did you join that Facebook group, the one on bereavement? It seems odd that a trained assassin would ever feel grief or care to console.

Love

Mel x

Chapter 5

He let David continue. Clearly, he'd grasped the enormity of the main issue, but Michael thought it was important he also read the rest of the emails. They showed Rand knew a thing or three about assassination.

From: Rand@djb9x2103i9.com
Subject:
To: Melanie55@gmail.com
30/08/19
>
I joined the support group because bereavement can be an unfortunate and unwanted side-effect of my work. An execution ends one life, but it can ruin several others. I need to understand it.

Thank you for telling me what happened. I think we can now start planning the project. Four factors need to be taken into account.

The first is purpose. Sometimes it is simply the

removal of an individual, so a carefully contrived accident, suicide, illness or other misadventure can achieve that. If the purpose is to send a message to others, perhaps as a warning, the take-out must be seen as man-made and deliberate. If the reason is vengeance, as in your case, the death might need to be long and painful to match the suffering caused. If it is for justice, the punishment should fit the crime.

The second factor is when. There might be a requirement to eliminate the target quickly before he or she can carry out some action which has to be prevented. Or maybe there is no rush.

The third is where. Do you lure the target to a place where the action can take place, or does the assassin go to the target's home, office, or wherever he or she might happen to be?

The final factor is means. These include arrow, bullet, bolt, blunt instrument, dagger, sword, kitchen knife, box-cutter, explosive, poison and garotte. Those are for deliberate executions. If the death is to be portrayed as an accident or suicide, one has drowning, fire, asphyxiation, electrocution, falling, RTAs and aircraft crashes to name but a few. The list is almost endless. The choice of means might be limited by what is readily available.

The assassin's craft is not just to carry out the deed, but to plan it in meticulous detail, taking into account all the factors. Failures are not permitted. It is not easy.

Tell me more about Mr Nasty.

Justy

It was also important that David read Melanie's account of how she discovered who Mr Nasty was and what she did about it. Michael didn't think she had acted wisely – but then she was a PTSD patient and could be forgiven for her lack of judgement.

From: Melanie Green
Subject:
To: Rand
30/08/19
>

Hi Justy – I'm glad you like the name. Thanks for the tutorial on assassination. It's got my mind buzzing with possibilities. How about fish-hooks? My dad once managed to get one stuck in his bum while sea fishing off the beach at Dungeness. I was a child at the time but I remember it was very painful for him, and he had to go to the local A & E to have it removed – and he's a doctor!

I can tell you more about Mr Nasty. About five weeks ago, I was watching Channel Four News, and they were reporting on an up-and-coming by-election. I'm not interested in politics, but as it was in our neighbouring constituency, I did prick up my ears. Then I heard that voice. A clipped upper-class accent which I had last heard about two years ago in a makeshift prison cell somewhere in Afghanistan. I shivered.

He was telling the interviewer how suitable he was to becoming an MP, having served his country as a major in the SABR – that's the Special Air & Boat Regiment – both in Iraq and Afghanistan before becoming a councillor for East Cheam or wherever.

He mentioned his talent with languages and how it would help him represent Britain on the global stage, and how his leadership qualities would qualify him for high office, should his colleagues at some time in the future plead with him to throw his name into the hat.

Something like that. My heart started thumping and my palms became moist. It was definitely him, despite his hair being smarmed down to one side and the pristine white collar and blue tie. The grey stubble had gone but not the same smug smile, the leer – except his teeth had been whitened. Andrew Bretton-Willis. I emailed Dad straight away, now I had a name, as that would obviously help with Dad's war crime investigation.

I couldn't sleep that night as I was so angry. I hoped he would lose the by-election, but he won. That made me fucking furious! The morning his victory was announced, I applied to join the bereavement group on Facebook. Bob said it was a good idea of mine – even though he'd suggested it! So sweet. I wanted to know how I could handle that bitterness, the heart-racing anger. And you responded.

That's it, really. I did take a trip to his constituency office a couple of weeks back, but he wasn't there. I asked for his home address, but they wouldn't give it to me. Just as well, as I think I would have gone there and thrown a brick through his window.

Then last week, after I got your email asking if I had explored bringing him to justice, I called in at the local police station. I said I wanted to report two crimes. A rather bored-looking Mr Plod took me into a windowless back office and sat me down in front of a desk. He slumped down behind it, plucked a ball-point pen out of his breast pocket, yawned and took a form out of one the desk drawers and started asking me questions. Name, madam? Melanie Green. Nature of crime? Rape and murder, I replied. His eyes rolled. Date? About two years ago. Place? Somewhere in Afghanistan.

A big sigh from behind the desk. Name of perpetrator if known? Yes, I do know who it was, I exclaimed. The new MP, Major (retired) Andrew Bretton-Willis. A sharp intake of breath, and he put his pen down. He asked how he could get hold of me. When I gave him my address, he gave me a patronising smile, stood up and said he would look into it. This way, madam, and can we give you a lift home? After rattling off a satisfying string of expletives, I stormed out. Bob said I should have remained calm.

What should I do now?

Love

Mel x

Michael wondered how he would have advised her

under the circumstances. With difficulty, he reckoned. Would he have told her not to worry and that everything would be fine? Or would he have frightened her, as Rand did?

From: Rand@djb9x2103i9.com
Subject:
To: Melanie55@gmail.com
31/08/19
>
Nothing. Stay inside. You could be in danger. Fishhooks. I'll see what I can come up with.

   Justy
>
>
From: Melanie Green
Subject:
To: Rand
31/08/19
>
Justy. You're frightening me. What's up? Can we not meet? You could then explain it to me. And I'd feel safe with you. Please? I just don't see how I could be in any danger.

   Mel x
>
>
From: Rand@djb9x2103i9.com
Subject:

To: Melanie55@gmail.com

01/09/19

>

Sorry. We cannot meet. I will tell you why you are in danger. Your father has instigated an investigation into a war crime. He would have submitted as much information about it as he knew, and we assume he has now updated said info with the identity of the perpetrator, a retired British major named Andrew Bretton-Willis, a newly elected member of the British parliament. We must also assume your father gave his own name, and the name of the only known witness to the crime: you.

You have submitted a report to the police accusing a British lawmaker of raping you in Afghanistan and murdering your partner. You stormed out of the police station uttering 'a string of expletives'. You are an in-patient at a mental hospital.

Do you not think there is a possibility that Andrew Bretton-Willis might have been informed of both the accusations against him, of committing a war crime and a sexual assault? Do you not think that he would have been given the name of his accuser, and the name of the only witness to his alleged war crime?

Does your British brain not tell you that the police might have made contact with said MP and warned him that a deranged woman by the name of Melanie Green, currently undergoing psychiatric treatment, was angry with him and might try to harm him?

The man has embarked on a new career in politics.

His success depends on his reputation as a law-abiding citizen and, as you Brits say, 'a pillar of the community'. Do you not think that he might wish to prevent knowledge of either of his crimes ever becoming public? Can you, little lady, think how he might achieve that? How he might use any means to protect his career and escape a life sentence?

Take care,

Justy

>

>

From: Melanie Green

Subject:

To: Rand

01/09/19

>

Justy, I'm so sorry. What a daft idiot I've been. Do you think he would really come after me? Should I be ready to defend myself? At least I know what he looks like. Perhaps I should think about killing him, before he kills me. I think I could come to terms with that if it were a matter of self-defence. Or should I go back to the police and ask for protection?

What would you advise? Please reply as soon as you can.

Love

Mel x

>

>

From: Rand@djb9x2103i9.com

Subject:
To: Melanie55@gmail.com
02/09/19
>

Do not go back to the police. Your credibility is too low. Give up any thoughts you might have about eliminating him. You would be the prime suspect in any homicide investigation. They would try to discredit you in any way they could, so your evidence of his felonies – weak as it is anyway – would be rejected. You would probably spend the rest of your life in an institution for the criminally insane.

Time is now of the essence. I'll do what I can. Keep safe.

Justy

>

>

From: Melanie Green
Subject:
To: Rand
02/09/19
>

Hi, Justy. Thanks so much for your email, and the reassurances. And the advice. I'll await instructions from you. Should I tell my father of the situation? Do you think he might be in danger, too? Are you sure we couldn't meet? Perhaps for a coffee, here. We could go for a walk and talk things over. It would be nice to meet anyway.

Love

Mel xx

He'd been touched to read of her concern for him. It had never occurred to him that he was in danger from anyone. All he ever wanted to do was to report Mr Nasty's war crimes – and keep his daughter out of trouble. On first reading that particular email, he'd been itching to find out if Rand did think he was in danger, and what instructions he'd given Melanie.

From: Melanie Green
Subject:
To: Rand
03/09/19
>
Hi, Justy. Did you get my last email, dated 02/09/19? I hope so. Do write soon.
  Love
  Mel xxx
>
>
From: Melanie Green
Subject:
To: Rand
05/09/19
>
Justy. I can't bear this. You say I'm in danger, and I can now see why. But I'm waiting for you to help me, to

advise me what to do next. Please reply. If you're short of time, just let me know you are still there and are getting my emails.

I understand if you don't want to meet me. It must be difficult in your profession to, you know, have friends, when you have to be in 'deep cover'.

I look forward very much to hearing back from you.
Love
Mel xx

>
>
From: Melanie Green
Subject:
To: Rand
07/09/19
>

Hi, Justy. Are you are there???? I thought I'd let you know I feel much better this morning. For the first time in ages, I slept really well. And I'm not all panicky about you know who. I think I'm a stronger person. I've taken your advice about staying in buildings, and I actually feel quite safe. There's always someone around, so it's not as if I'm alone.

It's funny, though. I no longer think someone's following me. Did I mention the ghost? I know it sounds stupid, but shortly after I arrived here, I often felt a presence, a girl, about my age, trying to speak to me. It just goes to show what tricks the mind can play – if one's suffering from trauma. Bob said it's very common with PTSD patients. Anyway, she's gone.

Lots of love,
Mel xxx

That first email to Rand on 7th September had puzzled Michael. She said she felt so much better, yet at that stage she was completely unaware that Mr Nasty had died. At least in theory. He didn't have much time for telepathy, but he did wonder if there was some magic at work, something which had told her subconsciousness that her abuser had died.

Whatever had happened, he'd been greatly relieved to read that his daughter had felt well enough to write to Rand telling him about it. The bombshell had come later the same day.

From: Melanie Green
Subject:
To: Rand
07/09/19
>
Help me, Justy. Please! The police have just called at the home. A man and a policewoman. To see me, and they asked me lots of questions about me and then about Andrew Fucking-Willis. How well did I know him? When did I last see him? I told the truth, but just thinking of him made me cross.

I asked them why they had come to question me. I thought it was because I had reported the rape and murder some weeks ago; I was pleased they were following it up because when I was in the police station they didn't seem very keen on doing anything about it. But I was wrong. The more senior of the two, a detective sergeant, said it was just routine.

She said that, tragically, the Shite-Honourable Andrew Bretton-Willis MP had been found dead in his apartment that morning, by his cleaning lady. I smiled. I couldn't help it. For a start, it was such a relief that I was no longer in the danger which you kindly drew my short-spanned attention to last week.

More importantly, the fucker was dead. Justice had sort-of been done, without either of us lifting a finger. It was a wonderful feeling. I just hoped it had been a long, slow, painful death, not a heart attack in his sleep.

But I didn't dare ask. That was the other thing I did wrong. Not only did I smile at the news of someone's death, but also I didn't ask how he died – which would have been the normal reaction. The detective sergeant and her side-kick looked at each other, and they almost imperceptibly nodded. The sergeant sighed and looked me in the eye. She was frowning. "Miss Green", she said. "We may have to come back and ask you some more questions. Do you have any plans to go away at all?"

I said I didn't. She suggested I notify them if my plans changed. She asked me if she could see my passport. I gave it to her. She asked if she could hang on to it for now, as I wasn't about to go anywhere. I didn't like to refuse.

They thanked me and departed, leaving me somewhat baffled. And worried what they might ask next if they returned. Obviously, if they do come back, I won't say anything about us, and the help and support you have given me. The last thing I want to do is get you involved. I mean, if he'd been murdered, we don't want you, with your background, becoming a suspect. It might blow your deep cover.

If they do question me further, do you think it's best to say nothing or to make it up as I go along? Do you think they suspect me? Longing to hear from you. Please write. Please!

Love you lots

Mel xxx

How's the fellow going to advise her this time? he'd thought. The answer was on the next page.

From: Mail   Delivery   System   Mail-Daemon@relay084mail.eu.net

Subject: Mail Delivery Failed: Returning Message to Sender

To: Melanie55@gmail.com

07/09/19

>

SMTP error from remote mail server after RCPT TO:Rand @ djb9x2103i9.com:

host   hotmail-com.olc.protection.outlook.com [108.32.5.92]: 565 7.5.1

Requested action not taken: mailbox unavailable.

Chapter 6

The Senior Partner of Matthew, Finch and Trowbridge placed the papers back on his desk and leaned back in his executive chair, elbows on the arms and his fingers clasped over a rather large tummy. He swung the chair gently from side to side.

"So he dumped her."

"It certainly looks like it. A great shame."

"Yes. And no. I'll explain later. A couple of questions, if I may. Do we know how the MP died?"

"No, David. We don't. I only arrived last night – from Spain – so I've not had a chance to do any delving. And last night Melanie had very little to add to what she'd put in those emails. She's doing okay. In fact, I think the man's death has helped."

"Well, that's understandable, if this chap Rand put the fear of God into her by suggesting she might be in danger."

"I think it was more than that. The MP was clearly a focus of her anger, and when he died..."

"I understand, but I must ask the next question. Look, I've never met your daughter, and you must think it preposterous of me to ask this, but do you think she and this friend of hers could have done him in?"

"Melanie? No chance." He lowered his eyes for a moment. "As you see from her emails, she liked the idea of revenge, and she asked Rand to suggest ways of finishing him off so she could imagine it. But she's a doctor. She's spent her career saving lives. She's a soft-hearted, lovely person. I cannot imagine her lifting a finger to actually hurt someone, let alone kill them."

"Of course. I was going to say that there are defences one can put up against a case of murder. Your daughter clearly went through some horrific experiences and as a consequence suffered PTSD, a recognised medical condition. And finding out about her attacker living nearby could have led to abnormality of mental functioning. This could have caused her to form an irrational judgement on her actions, and it does explain her conduct – if she had killed him.

"Alternatively, a person in her position could claim they killed as a result of a loss of self-control triggered by some factor, providing they can show a person of the same age and sex with an ordinary degree of tolerance and in the same circumstances would have acted as they did."

Michael listened intently as his friend rattle off the legal explanations. He was duly impressed.

"The fear of serious violence against them could trigger that loss of control. And if Melanie had killed him, I think the fear of the man who'd raped her coming after her to silence her for good would be sufficiently grave to qualify as a reasonable trigger. Mind you, neither of these defences would get her off the hook. She'd be charged with manslaughter, but at least that might avoid the life sentence which a murder charge demands."

"But she didn't do it. We don't want her on any charge."

"Sure, Michael. I agree. What about her friend, Rand?"

"You now know as much about him as I do. Melanie had her doubts about him initially, but she thinks he's genuine. Maybe a bit of a fantasist, but his later emails had a ring of credibility about them. I think he was trying to help her. And, as she said, she found it a help to share her thoughts with him. For her, the relationship was therapeutic. I think she became quite fond of him, actually."

"I'd go along with that. But did you get the impression he could've killed the man? Do you think he could've been what he claimed to be?"

"A trained assassin? Nope. Just some lonely fellow who befriends people on the internet. Perhaps he's read too many spy thrillers. Melanie would not have fallen for all that bullshit about CIA training."

"That's a shame."

"I don't follow you. Why should it be a shame?"

"Because if we can show that he could have done the deed, he might become a suspect and take the pressure of your daughter. At least the police might want to have a word with him – assuming we tell them about him. And if they can find him. Some of these social media trolls do cover their tracks pretty well.

"Now, we've got work to do. The way I see it is that we have four possible elements to deal with. First and foremost is the risk, dare I say the probability, that the police will wish to see her again. Let's hope it might just be to tell her he died of a heart attack and that's the end of the matter. But if the fellow died under suspicious circumstances, she might be in the frame, given she has a motive, namely that he allegedly raped her and killed her husband and son. And if so, they might wish to question her under caution, in which case we must prepare for that."

"What? They'd arrest her?"

"No. They'd more likely ask her in for a formal voluntary interview. It has three main elements: the caution itself which tells her she has the right to remain silent – but it warns her it may harm her defence if she doesn't mention when questioned something which later she relies on in court. A bit of a mouthful, but there we are. The second element is the right to legal advice. Finally, she'd have the freedom to leave at any time – although I wouldn't advise anyone to do that as it could force the police to arrest them.

"Having a lawyer present is a must, to see fair play and advise their client on what to say and what not to say. Some people think it's an admission of guilt, but it's not. Neither is remaining silent, providing your lawyer advises you to do so. If you simply refuse to co-operate with the police, that can arouse suspicions."

"David, is there something I can do?"

"Well, you can help by advising her that if she is asked in for questioning, she should agree. Obviously, she is entirely innocent and will want to co-operate with the police, but you must persuade her that it's best to do so with a lawyer present. I guess she doesn't have one at the moment, so she can either make do with the duty solicitor or, if you and she are happy, summon me. I would like to help. It will remind me of my early days, being called out in the middle of the night-"

"That's very kind, but your fees these days must be many times that of a duty solicitor."

"Fees? Nonsense, my dear chap. This one's on me. Remember the time you found me comatose on the buttery floor and put me to bed? You saved my life."

Michael thought very hard but couldn't remember the incident – he had always watched out for his mates after boat-club dinners. But he smiled and let David continue.

"And to be perfectly honest, I would enjoy the challenge. I would need to meet her so we could discuss the issues if she were called in for questioning. But, all being well, helping the police eliminate herself as a suspect will be the end of the matter as far as she's concerned.

"Next, we must be prepared for her to be charged-"

"Charged? For what?"

"I very much doubt if it would ever come to that, but the trick of the game is to stay one step ahead. By being ready, we might just stop it happening in the first place. If the charge were murder, she'd have to spend a night in custody before going in front of a magistrate. He would remand her for the Crown Court where the judge would decide on whether to grant bail, so we would need to have at our fingertips a good case so we could spring her straight away. Then we would have a few weeks before the fun starts.

"The third piece of the jig-saw is Mr Rand. Where do we fit him in? Is he a major player, or can we simply dismiss him as a crank who befriended her in that chat room? Should we track him down, or forget about him? If the MP was murdered, our Mr Rand could be seen as a lone suspect, or a partner in crime, or simply as a friend who could shine some light on your daughter's unfortunate mental state."

"She does seem so much better," said Michael. "Compared with my last visit some months ago."

"That's good to hear, but we might need a psychiatric assessment of how she was when the possible murder took place. If she can come through that as a perfectly sane person, it will obviously help her defence."

"But I thought you said her suffering from PTSD would help."

"Ah, yes! But only if she's prepared to plead guilty to manslaughter."

"David, you're confusing me. It's so complex."

"Good. It's meant to be. Otherwise, how would chaps like me earn our living? Finally, there is the matter of her file." David pointed to the papers on his desk.

"What's wrong with it?"

"Nothing. The question is, do we use it? It could be a two-edged sword. A prosecuting counsel might see it as evidence of her intention to kill the man, or we could use it in defence to show that this young lady is entirely innocent of any wrong-doing and is a victim herself. True, she welcomed the idea of his demise, but her emails show she was perfectly happy to imagine something awful happening to him, rather than do anything about it. My goodness! Look at the time. Come on, Michael, we'd better get our skates on."

The two men resorted to the comfort of small talk on the way to David's club, and it wasn't until the Dover sole arrived that Michael's mind drifted back to Melanie's file. He was touched she'd remembered the holiday at Littlestone. It had been a happy time for the three of them. Except, of course, for his attempts at beach casting at Dungeness.

At the time, he had felt such a fool, getting the hook caught – and it was a big one with a needle-sharp point, made of tempered steel. It didn't merely nick the skin under his chinos but buried its barb deep in the muscle of his right buttock. Of course, had Melanie been a son it would have been simple. He would have cut the eye of the fish-hook, downed his trousers and asked her to push the thing through, until the point and the barb reappeared. Not the sort of thing he would subject his six-year-old daughter to; they would have both been scarred for life.

David did not return to the subject of Melanie's predicament during the meal; Michael assumed that it might have been a breach of protocol to talk shop while eating. But after the crème brûlées, David leaned forward in his chair, and having made sure the waiter was not hovering behind him, he spoke quietly.

"I'm concerned about the rape incident.

Unfortunately, it provides a possible motive which could drive a victim to murder, but leaving that aside we must accept that rape of that nature in a war zone is a war crime and should be investigated as such. Others might have collaborated and they should be pursued."

Michael frowned. He hadn't had a suitable opportunity to ask Melanie about that aspect of her story. And he didn't like the idea of her violation becoming public knowledge.

David continued. "Then there is her allegation of the shooting of unarmed civilians by or under the orders of a British Army major. By the sound of it, not quite on the scale of the Mai Lei massacre, but a war crime nevertheless. Even though the alleged perpetrator is dead, there might be the matter of reparations. In any case, such crimes should be thoroughly investigated in order to show others that they will not be tolerated or condoned under any circumstances. But that's a matter for another day... So, as a medical man, what's your take on this new euthanasia bill?"

The friends exchanged business cards as they walked through the reception area to the exit. Michael couldn't resist asking his friend how he'd got his knighthood. David stopped and glanced around him, then mouthed four words, "The Hague – war crimes."

Then in a normal voice, he added, "Not for me, of course, but for my team. In recognition of their efforts."

Chapter 7

Michael was back at Beechwood Hall by tea-time. By then, the effects of the lunchtime brandy had worn off, and he felt ready to report progress to his daughter. He'd texted her from the tube with an ETA, and they'd arranged to meet in the coffee shop. After a cup of Earl Grey and a slice of banana cake, they agreed that a walk around the lake would be good, as they could talk in private.

Melanie had never met David – he was long before her time. So her father started by explaining how he knew him and why he had re-established contact with him. He told her he'd given David a copy of her file with the emails, as it could serve as proof of her innocence. He didn't tell her what David had said about it being a two-edged sword, as he didn't want her to become anxious about it being used against her. He need not have worried.

"No, Dad, I don't want it used. The last thing I want

is for Rand to be dragged into this. I know he's only some crank, but he did try to help me. He listened. All he was ever going to do was suggest how I could kill Mr Nasty so that I could imagine it. It wouldn't be fair. And if I did land up in court, I wouldn't need it. I would simply tell the truth. They wouldn't want to read all those emails, anyway. I'm sure they'd realise I'm innocent."

He smiled and said nothing. Innocence to be sure, he thought. A rape victim, innocent of killing the man who had carried out the assault and – allegedly – had killed her partner and son? She certainly had a motive.

Means and opportunity? He had no idea how the MP had died, let alone what the murder weapon was – if indeed he'd been murdered. As for opportunity, he couldn't imagine Melanie going up to Central London, seeking him out, then doing away with him in his own flat. How would she get in? A woman suffering from acute PTSD? She was hardly capable of such an act. Even though he rather liked the idea of little Melly taking revenge, he knew she couldn't possibly have done it; his darling daughter, a kind, compassionate, caring person who would not hurt a fly. Surely not.

Melanie confirmed she'd heard nothing further from the police during the day and said she'd let her father know as soon as they did. She assured him she was happy to have David advising her and liked the idea of someone by her side during questioning. She admitted that letting the policewoman take her British passport was a mistake, but at least it showed her the benefit of having a lawyer present.

They walked on in silence. It was a beautiful evening, still air, a clear sky apart from a couple of vapour trails – and pleasantly warm. A man jogged by and lifted a hand in greeting and smiled – a fellow 'guest', she explained.

Her father sensed it might be a good moment to tell her what David had said about the rapes, that they were war crimes which should be investigated. But he wasn't ready to quiz her about the details. However, she did yield to his questions about the shooting and filled in a few blanks.

When she first ran out of her hut to see what was going on, she saw three bodies on the ground. She wasn't sure who they were but from their clothes, she knew they were village women; they would not have been armed. As for them wearing suicide vests or being a threat in any other way, that was ridiculous. She'd heard bursts of gunfire and screams, so she assumed there were more casualties. The major seemed to be directing the operation, shouting orders.

Alongside him were two soldiers, also in combat dress. They were armed with sub-machine guns. The major had a pistol in his right hand and was waving it around. When she asked him what he was doing, he swore at her. She ran back to her hut to make sure Jangi was safe. He was in his cot, crying. Her husband ran outside to confront the major. He was not armed. She followed him with Jangi in her arms and saw the major fire at him, twice. The first shot went wide. The second caused the fatal head injury.

When Michael asked her what happened next, she clammed up. He wasn't going to push it. He knew she had a breaking point.

"That's John", said Melanie as a tall figure approached them carrying a large plastic box in one hand and a fishing rod in the other. Nice-looking chap, Michael thought – about Melly's age. John smiled when he saw Melanie approaching.

"He's a good friend," said Melanie. "And the head groundsman. When he's not fishing."

After the introductions, Michael asked him what he hoped to catch in the lake; he assumed it was stocked, possibly with trout. Sadly not, was the reply – just a few lucky roach and perch.

"Lucky? How come?" said Michael.

"It's Percy. About fifteen kilograms of carnivore. A pike. I've caught him twice in the last three years, but he's taken my line many more times than I can remember. He's a real fighter."

Michael saw Melanie stifle a yawn and thought it best not to relate his fishing tales to John. He explained they had better be getting back and he wished John good luck with Percy.

Father and daughter were strolling back to the main house. "He seems a pleasant fellow – and better at fishing than I'll ever be!"

Melanie laughed. "He's great. I've been helping him in the greenhouse – and planting out when things become ready. We get on well, but he's married with two kids, worst luck. Otherwise, who knows?... Dad? Don't give me that look. I'm not fourteen any more!"

They reached the main house and went their separate ways, Melanie up to her room and Michael to his guest suite. Supper was on him that evening, and he thought Melanie might appreciate being taken out to a local hostelry.

Siobhan recommended The Dog and Duck and offered to book a table. She reminded him that Beechwood Hall was an alcohol-free establishment and that his daughter may not be accustomed to liquor of any kind. It made him wonder how she'd got hold of the wine the night before, but he remembered that guests were generally free to come and go as they pleased. Perhaps it really was from Tesco's.

The Dog and Duck was typical of many inns in the South-East. The gently sagging oak beams and the original inglenook fireplaces confirmed its ancient origins, but the large menu cards, the uniformed waitresses and the soft piped music told the tale of its lucrative transformation into one of those gastro-pubs so favoured by the suburban 'haves' who secretly seek the rural idyll of yesteryear.

Melanie was happy to stick to soft drinks, and her dad was pleased she was enjoying the dish of the evening, an Asian curry with all the trimmings. Leapfrogging the worrying possibilities of subjecting her to further questions about Bretton-Willis' death, he gently steered the conversation to her plans for the future.

"Good question, but I'm really hoping to get back to work."

"That's wonderful to hear. You've made such good progress. Any thoughts about a speciality?"

"GP-ing. Dad. My old job."

Michael was surprised. "Are you sure? Don't you feel you have served your time in the Army? You don't have to stay, you know." He was worried. After what she'd been through, he'd hoped she'd settle down and join a good practice somewhere in the Home Counties. And meet someone nice.

"Army? No, Dad! They're discharging me when I leave Beechwood, hopefully soon. It's been very good of them to keep me on the books all this time, but I must get back."

Michael's heart sank. He wondered if his daughter

was still having problems – fantasies or flashbacks, he couldn't be sure. "Back where?"

"To my village. They need me. I belong there."

"What? In Afghanistan? You want to go back? After all that happened there?"

"I want to go back *because* of what happened there. A part of me died there. When the rest of me is ready to go, I want to go with it. I know it sounds daft, but I'll be a whole person again... And I want to see my friends – at least those who've survived. And my patients... And pay my respects to my two boys... It's a beautiful place, Dad. Really."

Michael sighed. He knew his daughter well enough not to try and change her mind.

"Tell me about it," he said.

"Ah! Where do I start? Difficult, because I'm not sure where it is. We just called it home – in Pashto of course. I know it's in the north-east of the country, and we – they, should I say – are feudal Pashtuns. They go back hundreds of years. I found the history hard to fathom, as it's not written down, nor is the religion or culture. It's all passed down by word of mouth, and not being very good at the language, I didn't really get it."

"What about the oppression of women? I mean, you of all people. You must have found that terrible. The Taliban are notorious-"

"Taliban, Dad? Who's talking about the Taliban?

Do you know what it means? Students! They're a bunch of students! It's a political and military organization about 50,000 strong who have taken over parts of the country. Not ours, though. Nobody controls our area, except us. The Taliban has only been going since the 1970s. By contrast, there are over fifteen million Pashtuns in Afghanistan, and they have been around since thousands of years BC. Many of them in rural areas still practice Pashtunwali-"

"What's that, Melly, a kind of yoga?"

"Shut up and listen! You might learn something. It's their way of life, a cross between a religion and a code of conduct. I admit it does expect men to be fearless and courageous and all that stuff, but they are also expected to protect women. And they do, from violence, violation and any form of abuse. We feel safe in Khuh Tabar – which is more than can be said for London. Pashtunwali encourages independence, justice, hospitality, love, forgiveness, revenge and tolerance."

She stopped to take a breath, and Michael jumped in. "Revenge, eh? Tell me more!"

"Dad, it's one of their main principles. It's called Nyaw aw Badal – justice and revenge. If someone wrongs you or someone you love or you're protecting, you have to seek justice or take revenge against the wrongdoer yourself. There's no time limit, and the punishment must fit the crime."

"I get that. An eye for an eye and all that. What are the other principles?"

"Bravery – that's for men, though. A Pashtun must defend his land, property, and family, and the honour of his name. If he doesn't..." Melanie ran a finger across the front of her neck.

"Loyalty. They owe it to their family, friends and tribe. Then you have righteousness. A Pashtun must strive for good in thought, word, and deed. Pashtuns must behave respectfully to people, to animals, and to the environment around them. Pollution of the environment or its destruction is against the Pashtunwali. Isn't that wonderful? They've been respecting the environment for all these years while we in the West have been ruining it.

"Then there is Pat, Wyaar aw Meraana which means respect, pride and courage. We must show courage and take pride in ourselves. We must respect ourselves and others, starting with family and relatives. If you don't have these qualities, you're not worthy of being a Pashtun."

"Darling, do you consider yourself a Pashtun?"

"Sort-of – because I married one. And I follow the code. Which reminds me, Naamus is the protection of women which I was talking about earlier. A Pashtun must defend our honour and protect us from vocal abuse and physical harm. So contrary to popular belief, we girls quite like being Pashtuns.

"And that's about it. But at the top of the list is Melmastia. Sounds like a horrible disease but it means giving hospitality to all visitors, regardless of race, religion, nationality or wealth and doing so without any hope of getting anything back in return. Good one, that. It saved my life."

Michael drained the last of the red wine into his glass. He felt so proud of his daughter and so ashamed of himself. There he was, comfortably ensconced in a false life in a Spanish resort, pandering to the hypochondriacal whims of rich holidaymakers. What was he really achieving? But he had the sense to realise he'd had his chance to do great things, change the world or stamp out forest fires. His time was over. All he could do now was to help his daughter achieve what she wanted in life – and she'd made it perfectly clear to him what that was.

"Dad?"

"Yes, darling?"

"When we've sorted out this, this load of bollocks about Mr Nasty, come with me. Come and see my home. See me at work. Then at least you can imagine me there, when we WhatsApp or whatever. Meet my friends. Spend a few days with me. We can sleep under the stars, trek up to the snowline, watch the sunsets. I know you won't be able to stay. You have your own life. Like I have mine... I'm sorry I've been a disappointment to you-"

"Disappointment? What on earth do you mean? Quite the reverse. I'm proud of you, what you've achieved, what you have coped with, and Mum would have been equally proud. You are a wonderful daughter..."

"Thanks, Dads. I'll get my violin! But you know what I mean. It all ends with me, your one-and-only-"

His hand reached out instinctively across the table to hers, but the arrival of their waitress trying to tempt them to an overpriced dessert stopped him before that precious contact was made.

"Darling. I want to hear about him. All about him."

"Who, Dad?"

"Jangi, my grandson."

A big sigh from Melanie – and a smile – as she launched forth, starting with the moment she thought she was pregnant. Every detail was there. What he ate, what he did, when he said his first word, 'Mama'; no surprise there. She re-lived the day when he learnt to crawl and made a beeline across the hut and out of the door, and described his first tentative steps. She mimicked his laugh – and his machine-gun-like crying when he didn't get his own way – and she described his handsome looks and his muscular little body in great detail.

Michael heard all about their adventures; the three of them, hiking up the mountains in the summer to the high pastures where the goats roamed free, Jangi in Shahpur's back-pack. His first winter and his fascination with the snow, Shahpur making him a little toboggan.

He noticed the sparkle in his daughter's eyes was fading, and she was starting to frown. He sensed she was coming close to the end of her tale, as he knew how it finished. He wasn't sure whether to stop Melanie before she got really upset, or to keep quiet and let her finish.

He was saved from the dilemma when their waitress-for-the-evening came with the bill, yawned and asked if everything was all right. Michael looked at his watch. It was close to midnight.

Chapter 8

Michael woke up the next morning at 6.35 when his phone pinged. It was a text from David:

> Times reports death of mp found in bath at his luxury apartment suicide not been ruled out police pursuing other possibilities have appealed for info phone me after 9

He was meeting his daughter for breakfast at 8.30, in the restaurant at Beechwood Hall. He thought it would be better not to tell her the news until he'd spoken to David. A cup of strong coffee with scrambled eggs on toast made Michael feel ready to face the world, and by the time he had returned to his room he was able to make the phone call.

"Morning, David, Michael here. Thanks for your text. Any further news?"

"No. They're trying to keep it below the radar. At least he hadn't taken up his seat. I could put out a few feelers, but I think I should wait until I've been formally appointed by your daughter. And I don't think she should do so at this stage."

"But surely, the sooner the better? As you said yesterday, we need to stay one step ahead."

"Absolutely, but we mustn't muddy the waters. It might send the wrong signals if it's clear that Melanie has signed up a lawyer already. If the chap had topped himself, why would she need legal advice? It's almost a confession."

"I see what you mean. Sorry. But what are your thoughts, about how the man died?"

"Early days... Found in bath is helpful. He could have drowned, deliberately or accidentally. Sometimes it can be the result of a sexual experiment that goes wrong. More people accidentally drown in bathtubs than through acts of terrorism. And many suiciders choose to do it in a bathroom, as it's a private place. They're less likely to be disturbed – or be discovered in time to be saved. Less mess; comfortable. And if you slit your wrists the hot water helps the blood run. Some say the warm water makes them feel like they were back in the womb and close to the comfort of mother."

"So, you're hopeful it wasn't murder?" said Michael. He heard David sigh.

"Of course, it could've been natural causes – heart attack, stroke, aneurysm, that sort of thing, but in a man of his age – and I would imagine having been in the Army he was pretty fit – I think it is unlikely. But you know much more about that kind of thing than I do."

"I'm familiar with many causes of sudden death, and I've had cases of drowning and near-drowning to deal with. But when it comes to murder, you're the expert."

"Michael. In my forty years of crime, I've rarely handled a case in which a murderer has killed his victim in a bathtub, or popped his corpse into one having done the deed. Mind you, that doesn't mean it doesn't happen. Do you remember that Welshman who worked for GCHQ?"

"The guy locked in a bag? Poor devil."

"That's the one. Ten years ago. Found dead in suspicious circumstances, in a bath at a Security Service flat in Pimlico. Still a mystery. The inquest found his death was unnatural and likely to have been criminally premeditated, but the Met reckoned it was probably an accident. The word on the streets was that he was assassinated."

"Assassinated? Why? And who would to that?"

"To keep him quiet. The Russians. He knew of a mole they had in GCHQ. So they say. Just speculation."

"But this MP. What's your take?

"Look, I'm guessing, and I could be quite wrong.

Suicides are usually obvious. So it is unusual for the police to say they are 'not ruling it out' and that they are looking at other possibilities. Perhaps they think it could be murder made to look like suicide. We are going to have to wait, I'm afraid."

"God, David. You're beginning to worry me. So what might have they found at the crime scene which would suggest other possibilities? I trust there was no locked bag involved."

"No, no bag. But there must have been something suspicious or unusual."

"And there is no way of finding out?"

"Not without arousing suspicion. It's not as if Melanie was a friend or relative. He allegedly shot her husband and child, took her prisoner and allegedly raped her-"

"What do you mean? Allegedly? Don't you believe her?"

"Steady on, Michael. It's just a legal term until an action is proven. I believe her, but it does not matter what I think. It's what the police think. And – if she's charged – what the courts think. We must think how they might think. It's a tricky one. I guess they questioned her straight after his death because she had only a couple of weeks previously reported him.

"Certainly, she had a strong motive, either for killing him or getting someone else to do it. Indeed, some might say she had moral justification in taking revenge herself or having him killed, even though his crimes were committed two years previously. Two years is a long time, but if she were in hospital for most of the time and physically unable to do anything about them, the justification would be stronger.

"On the other hand, if she knowingly falsely accused him, she would have no motive for killing him. If a young woman was intent on revenge, would she report his crimes to the police? I think it shows that she wanted him brought to justice. It was unfortunate that reporting him established a link between them just days before his demise. But on balance, I think she did the right thing."

Michael remembered last night, his daughter going on about the Pashtun code, revenge being one of the main principles. But now she's back home, he thought, she wouldn't do a thing like that. Not here. His daughter was innocent. It was simply a case of letting the police know she wasn't involved and the nightmare would be over. He was disappointed David hadn't come up with something more positive to report back to Melanie.

Then he had a thought. "David, I accept we've got to wait to see if the police want to question her again. In the meantime, would you like to meet her? I'm sure any doubts you might have about her would soon go – and I know you would get on well with her. She's a lovely girl-"

"Hang on, Michael. I'm very much looking forward to meeting her, but I still think it best if our first meeting is strictly between client and her legal advisor, and that should only happen if and when they decide to call her in for questioning under caution. To do my job well, it's probably better that I'm not seen to be a chum of the suspect.

"The relationship starts when she calls me, having received the police request to attend for a voluntary interview. Or, if she is arrested, when she makes that telephone call. Sometimes it's easier to be frank with an adviser who isn't a family friend or relation. Rather like Rand. They'd never met, but she felt able to open up to him in a way that a daughter might find it difficult to talk to her loving father. Do you see what I mean?"

Michael mumbled a yep. It was similar in his profession. You could be too close to your patients if they were good friends or relatives. Perhaps that's why she didn't talk to him about the rapes. He rang off, assuring David that he would let him know if there was any further news from his end.

Melanie had an appointment with her psychiatrist that morning. So after breakfast, they arranged to meet at 12.30 for a stroll before lunch. Michael reckoned he had time to catch a tube to Trafalgar Square, walk down to the Ministry of Defence and ask to see the major who had replied to his initial reporting of the shooting.

He thought it was wiser to do this without Melanie. He would take the copy of her file and show them the emails she'd sent Rand in which she described what had happened. He didn't expect to get very far, but a face-to-face meeting might give him an indication of their interest. If he felt there was mileage, he would ask David to handle it, although he'd rather David concentrated his time and efforts on looking after Melanie, at least until she was in the clear. By then, her evidence would have more credibility.

Throughout his career as a general practitioner, Michael had had much experience in meeting people for the first time and listening to what they had to say. He soon recognised those who were suffering from a medical complaint, who were reporting an injury or were concerned about a child or a relative. And it only took him a few minutes to recognise those other symptoms which revealed the true purpose of their visit which was not to receive advice or treatment, but something else. A sick note, a friendly chat, or confirmation that there really was something dramatically wrong with them having looked it up on the internet or read about it in the Daily Mail. He saw it as his duty as their general practitioner to provide whatever they needed.

At his meeting that morning at the Ministry of

Defence, the boot was on the other foot. He had been asked to take a seat in Reception while Major Birch was informed of his presence; it was like a dentist's waiting room. He became anxious about the time, but having consulted his watch on three occasions during the first five minutes, he realised time was not exactly rushing by.

After what seemed like an age, a man wearing a dark suit, collar and tie appeared, flustered and looking as if he'd run half a mile to be there. His jacket looked almost new, but his matching trousers were crumpled and shiny from a life of driving a desk.

"Dr Green? I do apologise for keeping you waiting." The two men shook hands. "I'm Major Harry Seymour. I took over from Major Birch about three months ago. Do call me Harry. Now, can I get you a coffee, or tea? And if you would follow me, we can find a room where we can sit and talk."

"Thank you. A coffee would be nice. White with no sugar." Michael noticed Harry was not carrying anything; no fat file stuffed with evidence, or an iPad on which several photographs had been stored.

Harry left him sitting in one of the two armchairs on either side of a wooden coffee table in a windowless room on the ground floor. There were no out-of-date magazines on the coffee table – except a copy of Soldier – and the only notice on the walls was one about security. He read it three times: 'Bored? Lacking excitement in your life? Like to meet some interesting people? Just leave your security cabinet open...'

The grey metal desk was bare and looked as if it had seen little use. Harry returned a few moments later with two paper cups which he carefully put down on the little table. It was not the VIP treatment.

"Now, Dr Green, how can we help you today?"

It was as good an opening as any, and one Michael had regularly used, but it left him not quite sure whether he needed to start from the beginning.

"As you know," he began. It was an old tactic he'd often employed, as it did not suggest lack of knowledge even when there was none there. "I first wrote five months ago after my daughter reported to me a rather disturbing incident which happened in Afghanistan a couple of years ago. She was serving out there as a doctor." Michael opened his briefcase and handed Harry a copy of his original letter.

"Ah, yes. And then Tom Birch replied. I've seen the correspondence."

Like just now, thought Michael.

"Then I wrote again about six weeks ago, giving you the name of the officer involved."

"Name? Of the person who committed this 'crime'?" Harry frowned.

"Yes. I have a copy of my letter here. I sent it on 1st August."

"1st August? That explains it," said Harry. He was

smiling again. "Block leave," as if that accounted for the loss of the letter. "May I see it, please?"

Michael handed it over. The smile on Harry's face changed to a frown. "Dr Green, do you have anything else you wish to show us? Any evidence that this officer was involved in a crime?"

"Crimes, actually. Apart from killing unarmed civilians, he raped my daughter repeatedly during interrogation. The only evidence I have is a statement from my daughter. But she would be happy to give evidence under oath, in court. Let me show you an email she wrote to a friend, as it will give you some idea of what she went through."

Michael extracted from his briefcase the copy of Melanie's file and flipped the pages over to the email she'd sent Rand describing the attack. He'd marked the passage when he'd first read it on the plane coming over. He passed it across.

Harry quickly read it and passed the stapled pages back. "And your daughter is where at the moment?"

Michael felt Harry's stare. "In England," he replied with a smile, "but there is one other thing you may wish to know – if you haven't heard already. This officer died last week."

Harry broke eye contact; his jaw dropped. "My goodness. What happened?"

"We don't know. There was a small piece in The Times this morning saying he'd been found dead in his bath. Obviously, the police are looking into it and have appealed for information. I expect they're waiting for the postmortem report."

"So why have you come to see us this morning? Surely, if the guy is dead, there's no point in us investigating any crime he might have committed."

"Harry. This officer did not act alone. He was commanding some sort of detachment. And he must have been under orders to carry out the raid. What were those orders? Who gave them? Had he, or others, carried out similar operations? Where did he send my daughter after he had interrogated her and assaulted her? Why was I told she was held captive by the Taliban for four years? Surely, the MoD wants to find out these answers as much as I do."

Michael took a sip of his coffee while he waited for Harry to respond. The officer ran his fingers through his hair and straightened his tie. Michael noticed that the bulging skin above the man's collar had turned red.

"Dr Green. I see your point. I think I'd better pass this one up the line. How can we get in touch with you?"

Michael gave him his mobile number, and the one for the surgery in Spain.

"France, eh?" said Harry, as the two of them made their way back to the main entrance.

"No. Spain. I live there, and work in a surgery, as a

GP. I'm not sure when I'll be going back, but probably sometime next week."

"I'll see what I can do. Goodbye, Dr Green."

Chapter 9

"No, Dad. Nothing. I would've have called you."

Michael was back at Beechwood hall. He was not sure if he was disappointed or relieved that Melly hadn't heard back from the police. He knew she'd be stressed if she were called in for further questioning, but on the other hand, the sooner the better. He wanted it to be over.

"So what about you? What have you been up to while I was being shrunk by my shrink?"

"Well, I thought I'd take the opportunity to pop up to the MoD and see if they'd made any progress with the war crimes."

"And?"

"Sadly, the matter was above the pay-grade of the man I was allowed to meet. He didn't even know Bretton-Willis had died. When I told him, he seemed to think that was the end of the matter, but I put him right on that. He said he would speak to his boss about it."

"Well done, Dad. You tell 'em. They've got to investigate it. It can't be right that such things can happen. I'll do whatever you need me to do."

"Thanks, Melly. If you feel..."

"Now, I've got a surprise for you. Luigi's given us a hamper, for a picnic. I thought we could drive somewhere, and have lunch away from here. Somewhere in the country, with views. It's such a lovely day."

"Sounds good to me!" Michael liked the idea of getting Mel away from Beechwood Hall for a few hours. Of having her all to himself and getting her to relax and talk.

He'd loved hearing at the pub the previous evening about her life in Afghanistan, and he liked the idea of visiting her village with her. It was a huge source of regret to him that he'd known nothing of her being there at the time. Surely, he thought, she could've got word to us somehow, just to say she was alive. She might have told him and her mother that she'd met someone, and had become a mum. Certainly, he believed that had Dawn known her daughter was alive and well, it might have given her more strength in her battle against cancer.

"How about Box Hill?" he said. "I once cycled up it – in my youth. Quite a climb, but great views at the top. And lots of picnic places. I guess it's changed a lot since then."

"Sure, Dad. Why don't I take the car and you could relive your boyhood by going on one of our electric bikes?"

"You must be joking! How about me driving and you working the sat-nav?"

"Dream on! Technology? Me? I'll borrow a road atlas from the library."

As they turned off the A24, Michael recognised Zig Zag Road, the 1.6-mile climb up to the summit, and he was relieved he was behind the wheel of a car rather than astride a bike. Not that it was any faster, as there were so many cyclists going up and coming down that it was almost impossible to overtake them. Melanie followed the route on her map and suggested they stopped at the National Trust Visitors Centre.

Having parked the car and looked at the board showing all the footpaths, they set off to find a good spot for their picnic. Melanie insisted on carrying the hamper. Not that it was particularly heavy, but Michael was amazed that his daughter was able to manage it with such confidence. For someone who had spent a long time in hospital, she was amazing: strong in wind and limb. He assumed that three years in the Army had helped, and village life in the foothills of the Hindu Kush couldn't have been cushy, to say the least.

The picnic table was wobbly and uneven, but once Melanie had put the white tablecloth on it and set out the plates of sandwiches, it looked respectable and inviting. It was one of those constructions which incorporated a seat on each side, but they chose to sit next to each other so they could enjoy the stunning view and the big sky above it.

After Michael had threaded his legs through the structure, Melanie joined him and poured out the elderflower cordial into the glass tumblers, grinning broadly as she did so.

"Isn't this wonderful? Look! That must be Chanctonbury Ring. I reckon that's over thirty kays away."

"And that town must be Dorking. Before the M25 was built, we used to have to drive right through the town centre on the way to your mother's parents."

"Yes, Dad. Was that by stagecoach?"

"Most amusing. But how did you get around in Afghanistan? You mentioned the pick-up, but there can't be many vehicles there."

"In our village, there was just the one. The trouble was there was no infrastructure to support them. No garages, no filling stations, and spares were almost impossible to get hold of. And the roads – if you can call them roads – were terrible. Rocky, precipitous in places, and liable to flash floods. And sometimes they would disappear completely."

"So how did you get around?"

"Me? I didn't. Not really. Shahpur and I would often go for a hike, but people in our village didn't really go anywhere. Shahpur did teach me to ride, and that was great fun."

"But you used to ride as a girl. I seem to remember you were pretty good at it, winning rosettes at gymkhanas."

"Dad, we're talking Afghanistan here. We rode camels, the ones with two humps. They're Bactrian camels and have roamed wild in Aff for donkeys' years." She giggled at her accidental joke and put her hand over her mouth. "Wonderful creatures, amazing. They can survive huge extremes of climate. In the winter they eat snow, and in the summer they can go for months without water – and when they do find it, they can drink gallons of it in one go."

"That's amazing. Is it like riding a horse?"

"Not really. You sit between the humps, so you feel more secure, even though your bum can be over two metres above the ground. Most obliging creatures; they kneel to allow you to climb aboard. And they never throw their riders. Some weigh nearly a ton, and they can happily carry a load half their weight, so they hardly notice a mere human astride them. They can run fast for short distances, but it is generally slow going. About two miles an hour, so you're not going to get very far. But it's fun."

"Melly, did you ever get itchy feet in that village? Or somehow want to make contact with the outside world? Did you ever try to...to."

"Oh, Dad! I know what you're going to say. I should have done. I should have let you know, somehow. But it was difficult... I got overtaken by events..."

Michael noticed the change. She was back in that village. He kept silent and let her carry on.

"I was woken early on that first morning at Khuh Tabar. They took me to the head man's house – hut, more like. His son was lying on a home-made bed in the main room, in a fever. I saw the dirty bandages around his left thigh and guessed what the problem was. Anyway, some guys brought my medicine chest over, and I went through the procedures. It was touch and go.

"The family watched, but I was all on my own as far as treatment was concerned. That evening, I got them to move Shahpur to my hut, so at least I could get my head down yet keep an eye on his stats. Three days it was, and voilà. He pulled through and was out of danger. And he kept his leg. Of course, he couldn't walk at that stage, so with the help of the village ladies, I nursed him and cared for him until he could hobble around on makeshift crutches.

"There was no way I was going to give up on him,

let alone abandon him. It never crossed my mind to leave the village. I suppose it's the duty of any prisoner of war to try and escape and return to his unit, but I wasn't a prisoner of war. I wasn't a prisoner of anything. And had there been a red telephone box in the middle of the village square, I don't think I would have used it.

"Sometimes I did wonder what would happen if the Army found out about me, whether they'd launch a rescue mission and descend on the village mob-handed and kill anything that moved. And what would they do with me? Would I be court-martialled as a deserter, or would they try and make out I was some kind of hero – like they did with Jessica Lynch in Iraq. Anyway, I was sure of one thing; if they did find out about me, they weren't going to leave me there.

"The days went by, and the weeks, and Shahpur got better. And I acquired more and more patients. He didn't really need me any more, but I needed him. His company, his smile, his gratitude for what I had done – it was just my job, but it was good to feel I'd achieved something. His family and the whole village were grateful, and they made a right old fuss of me, giving me presents and bringing me food, lending me pieces of furniture for my home, pots and pans and things. And clothes.

"I think if I had asked them to get me to Kabul, or at least get a message from me to the British Embassy in Kabul, they would have found a way to do it. But I never asked. There was a language problem, of course, and I was anxious not to be too pushy, so I just accepted the situation and got on with my job.

"I never asked how Shahpur got injured. To be honest, it never crossed my mind in the early days. But as his condition improved, I did wonder if I had 'assisted the enemy'. I imagined being tried for treason and locked up in prison, bringing shame on my unit, my country – and on you and Mum.

"I thought about you every day. I imagined your reaction when you first heard the news. I knew you'd grieve. Then I wondered what would happen if you heard I wasn't dead but alive and well, behind enemy lines in Afghanistan. You would've reported it and tried to get me back. Supposing something then happened to me. At first, I had no idea what they'd do to me – or whether I'd survive the tough life in a remote mountain village. I thought I'd wait before making contact, to see how things went. The last thing I wanted was to have your hopes raised, only to grieve again when you'd heard I'd fallen down a mountain or died of some unknown disease.

"Then the friendship between Shahpur and me grew. I tried to teach him English, and he helped me learn Pashto. We teased each other and shared jokes. A smile, a certain look, a touch – you know what I mean. I dreaded the thought of leaving him. We became a couple, and I sort-of didn't want you to find out. I thought you would be so disappointed in me. I thought he'd soon get fed up with me and want a local girl – he could well have done. So I reckoned it was better if you and Mum didn't know. If he'd finished it, that would have been the time to have made contact – somehow.

"Becoming pregnant wasn't part of the plan, and I would have done something about it. But Shahpur was so pleased. His family – and the whole village for that matter – were delighted. There was no way I was going to get rid of his baby, or bugger off with it, leaving him on his own. And after Jangi arrived, wild horses would not have dragged me away from my two boys. My life – my place in life – was with them, at Khuh Tabar.

"I thought of Mum, and how shocked she'd be. Her only daughter, brought up as a good Roman Catholic girl then marrying a Muslim. She was so old-fashioned about such things. I didn't want her to hear third-hand about it. I wanted to tell you both myself, and for you to meet Shahpur in person, and our gorgeous little Jangi. Mum's heart would have melted, and I know you would've got on famously with Shahpur and been a super Grandpa. I told myself that one day, it would happen.

"Dad, I'm so sorry-"

Michael put his arm around her and gave her a squeeze. "Shall we tackle those sandwiches?"

Melanie blew her nose and smiled. "Sure, Dad. Let's do that, then walk to the top."

Chapter 10

Michael found it hard to accept his daughter had not even tried to make contact during her years in Khuh Tabar. That evening, he thought long and hard about her situation, and he wondered if there was another way she could have handled it. He came to the conclusion there wasn't.

The trip to Box Hill inspired him to suggest another outing. He thought Melly would enjoy it, and it would take her mind off waiting for that call which might never come. Also, it would give him another chance to probe his daughter further about what happened under interrogation.

At breakfast the next day, he proposed they drove down to the sea. He wondered about Bognor, being almost due south of Beechwood Hall, but before he was able to suggest it, Melanie's eyes lit up.

"Dad! Can we go to Dungeness? It's so lovely, and it shouldn't be too crowded, now schools have gone back. John could lend you some fishing tackle and you could try beach casting again—"

"Yes to Dungeness, but if you think I'm going to make a fool of myself with a fishing rod again... It's quite a way, but if we left at about ten, we could have lunch at that pub. You won't remember it, but we had fish and chips there on the day of the Great Hook. Then we could go for a walk along the beach and see how it should be done."

"A snag. I've got an appointment with Bob this morning. You know, my psychiatrist? At 9.30, for two hours. Perhaps I could change it."

"Darling, why don't I come with you. I'd like to meet him, and perhaps he could switch you around."

"Sure. You'd like him. He's really nice. He's helped me enormously."

"Dr Green, what a pleasure! I've heard so much about you."

Michael wondered what Melanie had been saying during her therapy sessions, probably under hypnosis. "Nothing bad, I hope?"

"Not at all. I'm pleased you were able to get over for a few days. I think Melanie really appreciates it."

She smiled at the pair of them. "Bob, would you mind if we were to cancel today? My father wants to take his little girl to the seaside."

"Not at all," said Bob, "it'll give me a chance to catch up on a few things. I'm planning an expedition—"

"Bob's a famous climber, Dad. He wrote a book on it."

"Famous? Don't listen to her." Bob turned to Melanie. "If you want to go and get ready…"

"I get the message, you want to talk about me behind my back. Only joking. You have my consent. Seriously. I'm a medic, too, you know."

The men briefly talked about climbing, and Michael told Bob that he, too, loved the mountains, but his preferred option was walking rather than climbing – although he could handle the occasional scramble.

Bob told Michael that psychiatry could be like climbing a mountain. You need to set yourself a clear goal and work out a route, but until you start the climb you are never going to know every handhold. And you can find yourself in danger and have to reroute and find another way up. Naturally, there is risk, but you do whatever you can to mitigate it. Life without risk, he said, is just admin.

It made Michael smile. He then turned the subject to Melanie. "How's she doing, Bob? Really?"

"Well. All good, now. It was a slow start. I've never seen a worse case of PTSD before. But she's intelligent and strong. I think her war-zone experience toughened her up. She got used to death. It was part of her job. So in her good moments, she was able to remain rational about the loved ones she'd lost."

"And her bad moments?"

"First of all, there's the depression and the headaches. We can medicate those. Then there are what I call the difficult sessions."

"Difficult? In what way?" Michael remembered the broken stool, the crack in the door panel; just a four-year-old testing the boundaries. Then the occasional early-teenage tantrum.

"Normally, she is an ideal patient – co-operative, and she does exactly what I ask of her. She's great. A wonderful person. And forthcoming. I've heard her describe her traumas several times, and when she is her old self, she describes them as if she were commentating at a sporting event. She's very detailed, both in her description of what is happening and her feelings. She never gets it wrong or contradicts herself. She is frighteningly precise, which makes me believe that her account is close to what actually happened.

"But occasionally, the shutters come down. It's as if she's a different person. She takes no notice of what I say, and she says nothing. Perhaps she is giving her mind a rest. When it happens, I don't push it. I just let her walk out of the room when she's ready."

"Have you ever had to sedate her?"

"Sedate her? Good Lord no. Her anger is there, but under control."

Michael felt his shoulders relax.

"Then we have the guilt. That can be tricky."

"But how can she be guilty of anything? It was hardly her fault her orderly was killed in the helicopter crash, and she couldn't be blamed for the death of her husband and son."

"Absolutely, but the guilt comes in two forms. You wish you'd done something differently which might have prevented the deaths. That's not a logical guilt, but it can be quite real for some people. Then there is the guilt of having, shall we say, dark thoughts. Of wanting to take revenge. Of course, that's perfectly natural, but for someone like Melanie it can induce a feeling of shame."

"So how do you deal with that? How do you purge them of vengeful thoughts?"

"We don't. We let them have their revenge fantasies. Sometimes we encourage it. For most patients, it's cathartic, providing relief through the expression of strong emotions. They like the idea of revenge and sometimes find it amusing, but we are careful to persuade them that revenge is not the answer. The guilt can then kick in and they feel remorse that they had those terrible thoughts. And, believe me, some are horrific.

"The next stage is to persuade them how wonderful

they are that they have not taken any harmful action. Hopefully, this will make them feel good about themselves. I think the death of her victimiser has instigated a great change. It's released her from her revenge fantasies. She knows there's now no opportunity for her to avenge her husband and child. If you like, she's been let off the hook.

"You see, it wasn't just the revenge she felt. It was also a sense of duty. She tried to bring him to justice by reporting him, but I think she realised she wasn't going to get anywhere. We are talking about a man who deliberately killed her husband – and was possibly responsible for other villagers who died in the attack on that village. In her mind, she owed it to them, too. She reckoned she had to repay her debt to them, for all the kindness they had shown her. Which included saving her life."

"I go along with that," said Michael, "she does have a sense of duty, of fair play. Of wanting some form of justice."

"I think she can now feel that justice has been done, however he died. A life ended... and she's free from his threat. But I'm sure Melanie hopes there was an element of punishment in his death as well. Anyway, she has finally got closure, and I think she feels more secure. Are you aware of the sexual assaults she experienced?"

"Yes, but only vaguely. We've never talked about them."

"Well," said Bob, "I think she was frightened he might have come back into her life in some way, possibly to kill her. It is not uncommon for a rape victim to experience that fear. And in her case, her attacker had killed others."

"I understand a friend of hers had warned her that as she was the only witness of the killings and the rapes, the man might want to eliminate the evidence."

"Rand?" said Bob. He looked down and smiled. "He was probably right, but to what extent she was in danger we shall never know. I cannot say how real the threat was in the first place, but at least it's no longer there. She's safe, thank God."

"What are your thoughts on Rand? Was he a help to her?"

Bob stroked his chin. "On balance, yes. She always spoke fondly of him, but I'm not sure if she believed him. But he listened. I never saw their emails, but she'd often quote him. Sometimes a relationship of that sort can be helpful, one in which the patient feels they are in control. They never met. She was able to keep him at arm's length. Not like being on the psychiatrist's couch!"

"So, Bob. How much longer will she remain here?"

"If you'd asked me that question a few weeks ago, I would have said months – not before the end of the year. But there has a been a huge improvement, and I almost feel the summit is in sight. So maybe a few more weeks..." Bob looked down. Michael noticed the corners of his mouth sagged.

Bob sighed and continued. "She'll never get over the bereavement, but she will be able to handle the grief. As for the rapes, it is a good thing he's dead – whatever the cause."

Melanie bounced back into the room wearing a straw hat. "Here I am, complete with bucket and spade."

The two men smiled at her. Her proud father announced it was time to hit the road, and he and Melanie left.

The two rectangular silhouettes of the Dungeness nuclear power station broke the flat horizon ahead of Michael as he drove south along the coast road from New Romney towards the shingled headland.

"Are we nearly there?" asked Melanie, yawning as she slowly recovered from her doze.

Michael smiled as he wondered how many times that question had been asked by a child of its parents. He looked at his watch. "Fifteen minutes, at the most. I suggest we go straight to the pub and have lunch, then we can have a wander afterwards."

He was pleased she had nodded off, as it showed she was relaxed. He hoped he'd be able to ask his daughter about Rand. He was happy that Bob thought the guy had helped despite being a bit of an oddball. If Rand had really been a trained assassin, the police would surely want to question him about the MP's death.

He still found it hard to accept her relationship with Rand, of two strangers telling each other all about themselves, yet not really knowing for sure whether they were being fed a pack of lies. But that didn't seem to bother Melanie. She seemed to like him. Michael wondered if he'd come back into her life, and whether they might eventually meet for real. It didn't surprise him she wanted to keep Rand out of any form of police enquiry. Perhaps she was right not to want him involved.

"It's got to be fish and chips," said Melanie, casting her eye over the menu card. "I mean, you can't come to the seaside and have a steak, can you?"

"And mushy peas? Lots of tomato sauce? Or has age weaned you off the stuff?"

"No, Dad. You've got to dip your chips into something."

"Now, what about a drink?" Michael didn't want to encourage his daughter to have alcohol, yet he felt a small beer wouldn't do her any harm and might even help her on the road to full recovery. He would join her, on the basis that by the time they set off for home, the alcohol would have worked its way through his system. The beers arrived first, and a few gulps on an empty stomach gave Michael the push he needed.

"Darling, tell me more about Rand. Obviously, I've read his emails to you – and Bob seemed to think they helped. Would you agree?"

"Dad. The only contact I've had with Rand has been those emails. But Bob's right; Rand did help me, in a number of ways. I don't want to trivialise his role in my recovery, but I found him amusing. He made me smile. That stuff about his training! And his lack of a sense of humour. I enjoyed teasing him. And he tried to understand it. He never got cross – or if he did, he never showed it. But I must admit it was frustrating that he never replied until the following day – and sometimes his replies were so short. It would have been nice to have met him in person, and have a proper chat. I did find it helpful that he got me to talk about things, in a way that I could not have done to you – or any other person. Dad, don't give me that look."

"Sorry, Darling. I'm not cross or disappointed with you. I just wish I could have helped more, when I came to Beechwood Hall in April—"

"Listen. You were wonderful. I was in a bad way, and you were there for me. You helped enormously. Rand's help was different. I mean, you would never have encouraged me to take revenge, but just thinking about the possibility was good. It was amusing – and it got me thinking of nasty ways I could dispatch Mr Nasty. Like fish hooks. Are you sure you don't want to try again?"

"Try what again?"

"Beach casting! I'm sure we could hire a rod – and having become a dab hand at extracting shrapnel from human flesh, I could whip the hook out in no time at all should you catch yourself. I could do it then and there, on the beach, in front of everybody-"

"Melanie. Stop being ridiculous... Ah. Here comes the fish. My goodness, look at the size of them!"

Neither of them was able to finish the king-size portions, but both agreed the battered cod was perfectly cooked and the home-made chips were divine. No room for desserts, but coffees followed, giving Michael a chance to ask his next question.

"Just going back to Rand for a moment, have you any idea why he stopped replying to your emails? You don't think you might have overdone the teasing, do you?"

"No. I think he actually liked it. Rather like you, he pretended to be miffed, but wasn't really. Perhaps he thought I was getting too close. Actually, I did feel close to him. I felt I could confide in him. If he was a spy in deep cover or whatever, perhaps he felt he had to back off."

"Well, I think it was appalling the way he just

stopped. He could have at least answered your questions and been there for you after the police had called. And closing down his email address. That was a bit extreme, don't you think?"

"Yeah, but there must have a been a reason. He said he'd plan an assassination for me so I could imagine doing it. I don't think he'd go back on his word. But when Mr Nasty went and died on us, there was no need for any assassination plan, real or imaginary."

"At least he's got your email address. You never know, he might come back. Would you like him to? Do you hope to meet him one day?"

"I'm not sure. As I've said, I don't want him to become involved if the police investigate me. That would be so unfair."

"But you do realise the police might want to do a search on your phone and computer. It's what they do nowadays. And David says he might want to use your emails in the unlikely event of a trial, as proof that you had no intention of actually doing Bretton-Willis any—"

"No, Dad. As I've said, I'm not having him drawn into this. As for the police searching my computer, I don't have one. I use the Study Centre ones. There are three. I cannot imagine them taking all of them away for questioning. And I don't send or receive emails on my phone."

Michael decided not to push it. "So, how do you feel about a walk along the beach?"

"Great. You sit there, Dad. I'm getting this."

Michael watched his daughter as she extracted her credit card from her purse, rose confidently from her seat and went to the bar. He wondered if the roles were reversing. He noticed heads turn. And he remembered the look she'd got from both John and Bob. There was something there. Obviously, there was no question of her psychiatrist betraying his professional code – and John was married with two kids – but it made him realise that his daughter had inherited some of that magical attraction which had persuaded him, all those years ago, that Dawn was the one for him. It wasn't just looks.

Melanie said she remembered the railway carriages. It was a long time ago, but she was fascinated to see them, there on the shingles, turned into homes for fisherman. Now, twenty-two years later, many of them had been extended and refurbished, so much so that it was only their distinctive curved roofs which indicated their origin.

She also recalled the lighthouse, a black-painted circular structure about 50m high.

"Do you remember the steps, Melly? We went up it. I think there were something like two hundred of them."

"A hundred and sixty-nine, Dad. You made me count them. I guess it was to take my mind off my vertigo. But Mum was far worse than I was. Didn't she have to go down?"

She's right, thought Michael. He was amazed a six-year-old had recalled such detail of their visit in 1997. Was it time to ask his daughter about the rapes? If he were to feed them into the war crimes investigation, he would need more information.

He broached the subject as they were trudging along the beach, the pebbles beneath their feet giving way with a crunch at every step.

"Darling, you know you said yesterday that you'd help with this war crimes thing. Well, I just wondered if you would be prepared to give evidence about the assaults."

Melanie stopped. Michael turned around to face her. "Assaults, Dad? What are you talking about?"

Michael could hardly get the words out. "The rapes. Bretton-Willis raping you while he held you captive. You mentioned them in one of your emails to Rand."

Melanie walked on, head down. "Dad. The man's dead. I don't want to talk about it. But I do think it's important that his crimes against others are fully investigated and that reparations to that village are made and that anyone else involved faces trial. And, when they are found guilty, are suitably punished... I just cannot believe an Army unit could have behaved that way. They were like a pack of animals."

He noticed her breathing was getting faster. He tried to calm her down. "Rape and pillage, Darling. It happens—"

"Shut up, damn you! How many fucking times do I have to say it?" She stopped in front of him. She was shaking.

Michael saw her eyes had changed. They were deep in their sockets below a furrowed forehead and had lost their sparkle. Her fists were clenched. He knew from old that nothing he said would have any effect, or even be heard. He and Dawn had tried to get her to count to ten, when she was little, but it never worked.

He put his hands in his pockets, broke eye contact and looked out to sea. He remembered the advice: show no aggression. He heard her turn around and stomp off, stamping the pebbles down as she headed along the shoreline. He waited for a few minutes before following her, keeping a safe distance behind.

She stopped to watch a fisherman, and he caught up with her.

"Look, Dad. He's caught something!" Melanie pointed at the man standing near the water's edge. She was smiling as she watched him heaving at the stout fishing rod then reeling in the line as he lowered it.

"Goodness," said Michael, "it must be a big one. Cod, I guess, at this time of year."

He watched the fisherman land his catch on the beach and dispatch it using a rusty spanner. The man then wrestled with the large barbed hook which was well and truly wedged in the creature's lower jaw. Michael looked at his daughter. She was watching the grizzly sight, too. Her eyes were wide open, and she was smiling.

Chapter 11

To Michael's surprise, the large wrought iron gates didn't open automatically when he drove up to them. He was about to get out of the car when an MoD policeman emerged from the small side-gate and limped over to the driver's side.

"That's Ronnie, Dad. One of our security guards. He's nice. He used to be a patient. Ex-Army."

Michael lowered his window. "Yes, officer?"

"I've got an envelope for Dr Green, sir." He smiled across at Melanie. "I'll open the gates, and if you could pull up on the left by the hut…"

Michael parked and followed Ronnie into the hut.

"No, sir. It's for Dr Green."

"But I'm Dr Green."

"Dr M Green, sir. Look. It says here." He showed Michael the brown envelope.

"But I am-" Michael realised his mistake. "I guess it's for my daughter. I'll give it to her."

"Sorry, sir, but I need to give it to her personally – and she needs to sign for it."

By the time they had both returned to the car, Michael had realised what it must be.

"Is that David?" Michael was back in his guest suite, pressing his mobile to his good ear. "It's come. They want her to go in on Tuesday morning at ten. Would you be able to be there?"

"Yes, of course. But now she's had the call, it would be appropriate for me to meet her. I assume the police have decided his death was not suicide or natural causes, but at the moment I have no idea what they have on her. It may just be a fishing expedition so it needs careful handling. Would Monday afternoon suit?"

"Fine. Thanks so much."

"And Michael. Just one other thing. I would like to see her alone if you don't mind. It sets the relationship off on the right foot."

"No problem."

Over supper that evening at Beechwood Hall, Michael told Melanie about David's visit. He was pleased she seemed relaxed about it, and he felt confident that under questioning her complete innocence would become apparent. It could finally bring the matter to a close.

"Dad?"

"Yes?" He smiled as he remembered how his daughter had always asked him questions in that way, perhaps from the age of three.

"Couldn't you be there? I'm sure David's very nice, but I think there's a lot you could contribute. I mean, you know me and he doesn't, and you could give your side of the story."

"I honestly think it is better if I leave you two on your own. He will make up his own mind about you and the situation, just as a jury would – not that it would ever come to that, but you know what I mean. You don't want your old dad holding your hand, do you, chipping in and interfering?"

"You wouldn't do that – but I get your point. I'll be fine."

On Monday morning at nine, Michael's phone rang. The Director of MoD Public Relations, a Major General Rupert Smedley, would like him to attend a meeting in his office that afternoon at 1400 hours. The general's PA was polite and professional, but the tone of her voice made it seem less like an invitation and more like an order. He confirmed he would be there at two. Next, he texted David with Melanie's mobile number and explained she would be there to meet him in Reception.

Michael liked the idea of being out of the way, as

he wasn't sure he could trust himself not to interfere while the two of them discussed the situation. Of course, he was anxious to know how David would ensure that his daughter did not get dragged into some false accusation of murder. He guessed that if the police decided the MP's death was not suicide or natural causes, they would be under enormous pressure to find who was responsible. Or who could be blamed for it.

Major Harry Seymour was waiting by the reception desk just inside the entrance. He was wearing the same jacket but with beautifully pressed trousers which were clearly kept for special occasions. And his black brogues were gleaming.

Michael thought his greeting was effusive; the man was trying too hard to be friendly, perhaps because he knew the greeting from the General might not be so welcoming.

The Director of Public Relations had a spacious office on the first floor overlooking The Thames. It boasted a thick fitted carpet, reproduction antique furniture and oil portraits in gilt frames on the walls, no doubt of famous predecessors. Michael guessed the office had been allocated to that appointment in order to impress visitors from the media and indicate to them how much importance the Ministry attached to wooing the general public. But he realised he was not there to be wooed when the large figure in shirt-sleeves slumped behind the mahogany desk did not rise to his feet.

"Afternoon, Dr Green. Take a seat." He pointed to the hard chair in front of the desk. "Now, I don't have much time, so I'll get straight to the point. You wish to raise a complaint against Major Bretton-Willis, sadly deceased—"

"No, General. I don't." Michael heard Harry take a sharp intake of breath; he was standing to attention behind the desk next to the seated figure of his boss. "I have already done so, four months ago, but it seems that no progress has been made."

"Progress, Dr Green? Exactly what progress did you expect to achieve?" The general opened a thin file on his desk. "You allege that this officer, this fine officer with an unblemished record committed some 'war crime' while on operations in Afghanistan?"

"No. It wasn't a war crime. It was several. He shot and killed an unarmed male civilian, a two-year-old child and one of his soldiers who was holding the child in his arms. Other civilians – unarmed women – were killed during the operation led by Bretton-Willis."

"And you were there at the time and saw this happen?" The general looked at his staff officer and smiled. Harry smiled back.

"No. I wasn't. But my daughter was. She saw the male civilian shot. It was her husband-"

"Husband, you say? Husband? And I suppose the infant was her child?"

"Yes. As a matter of fact it was. But that's not all. Bretton-Willis struck my daughter, rendering her unconscious, and he abducted her. He took her to some makeshift prison for interrogation-"

The general held up his hand. "Stop right there, if you please. Before we go on with this... this 'account', can we first establish exactly what your daughter was doing in that village, and indeed who she was?"

"Is," said Michael. "She survived. She's here, in England." The general stiffened and leaned forward in his chair; he frowned at Michael, then glared at Harry.

"She's recovering from PTSD at Beechwood Hall. At the time of the incident, she was serving in Afghanistan in the RAMC as a captain. She got left behind on a casevac mission; the helicopter was shot down over the mountains miles from anywhere, and everyone assumed she was on it. The village took her in, and she looked after their sick – until the raid."

General Smedley sat back in his chair and sighed. "How unfortunate for her. But you must realise that it is the duty of every prisoner of war to escape and return to their unit. And, if they 'give aid and comfort' to the enemy, they are actually committing high treason. Not that your daughter will be 'hanged by the neck until dead', as they say, but she could expect a life sentence – if we pursued it."

"She was NOT a prisoner of war! She was giving aid and comfort, not to 'the enemy', but to members of a small rural community in the foothills of the Hindu Kush. They had nothing to do with the Coalition's invasion."

Michael could see where the conversation was leading to, and he felt his neck go red. But he wasn't going to give up. "I should also point out that while she was being interrogated by Bretton-Willis-"

"Remember, she was a suspected deserter," said the general, "a defector during wartime and Major Bretton-Willis was doing his duty by taking her prisoner and interrogating her. That's hardly a crime, is it?"

"No, but raping her a number of times during her so-called interrogation is!"

"Come come, Dr Green. Do you really believe British Army officers go around raping their prisoners?"

"General. I believe my daughter. But I don't expect you to believe her, or me. I expect you to at least investigate the matter."

"But, if this fellow is dead, tell me, what is the point?"

"As I've explained to Major Seymour, my daughter and her family weren't the only victims. And the officer didn't act alone. He was in command of others and must have been under orders. Perhaps there were similar raids on other defenceless villages. Surely, the MoD wants to find out what happened as much as I do. And I want to know what happened to my daughter. I want to know where she was sent once Bretton-Willis had finished with her, and why I was told she was held captive by the Taliban for four years."

"Excuse me, sir," said Harry, turning to his boss, "Can we speak in private for a minute?"

The general nodded. "Dr Green? Would you mind waiting outside for a moment?"

It was ten minutes before Michael was called back in, but to him it seemed more like half an hour.

"Dr Green. We understand that the police believe that Major Bretton-Willis might have been unlawfully killed. Are you aware of that?"

Michael nodded.

"And do you realise that they are anxious to find out who might have been involved in his death?"

"Of course. I understand that."

"I believe, Dr Green, that your daughter could become a suspect, on the basis that she has accused him of raping her. You see, if she is telling the truth, she has a motive for murdering him. It's not unheard of for a rape victim to seek revenge. But if she imagined it all, the alleged attack on the village and the sexual assault – if she admitted it was all a fantasy in her mind created by the enormous stress she was under at the time – she'd have no motive for killing him, would she? The police would have less reason to suspect her. Do we understand each other?

"As for the other 'crimes', do you honestly think people would believe her? After all, she is in a mental home, under treatment for post-traumatic stress disorder. You're a doctor! Surely you recognise the symptoms of PTSD. The memory loss? The anxiety and depression? The nightmares? The fantasies? It doesn't exactly make her a reliable witness, does it?"

"I believe the Ministry of Defence should carry out a full investigation. My daughter was not the only witness to what was an illegal act of war carried out against a small unarmed village. I intend to go there, with my daughter, as soon as she is well enough, and I will gather what evidence I can to back up her account. If you do not investigate it properly, I'll go to the media."

Smedley smiled. "I'll be honest with you, Dr Green. The British Army maintains a zero tolerance to war crimes, and when they come to light, we do investigate them thoroughly and go to great lengths to bring the culprits to justice. But it does our public image no good at all if we are seen to fail in finding the perpetrators or in meting out appropriate punishment; we could be accused of a cover-up.

"Sometimes it is better for a crime not to be discovered than to come to light as an unfounded rumour with no hope of subsequent prosecution. Conspiracy theorists have a field day, the Press love it, the Opposition tear into the Government, the Sec of State tears into us – and if people think that they can get away with such crimes in the future, any deterrent effect of an investigation is lost.

"To deter others from committing such acts, justice must be seen to be done. And if the perpetrator cannot be punished, as in this case because he's been murdered, justice cannot run its course. Do you not agree?"

"I see what you mean. But there is a principle at stake. This officer—"

"Let me tell you, this officer had an exemplary record, having been awarded the MC as a lieutenant and been mentioned in dispatches twice. Not a public hero, but within the Army and his unit, he was highly thought of. His family were immensely proud of him. Do you really think we should add to their grief by accusing him posthumously of being a war criminal? Damn it, man, he's no longer here to defend himself! Should we tear him down from his pedestal for the sake of principle?

"And if it's justice you're after – assuming this officer had committed the crimes of which you so readily accuse him – don't you think his death at such a young age, on the verge of his new career, is justice enough? May I suggest you have another word with your daughter, and possibly with those treating her, with a view to persuading her to drop these wild accusations of hers which could well be mere figments of her imagination. It could be in her best interests. And yours."

"General. Let me tell *you* something." Michael felt his heart pounding and his nostrils flare. "My daughter is not going to drop her accusations. And if you are not going to investigate the matter, I certainly will."

The general stood up. Harry quickly moved out behind the desk and towards the door.

Michael remained tight-lipped. He stood and looked at the two men and realised he was not going to get any further. He was more convinced than ever that he should take Melly up on her offer and go with her to Khuh Tabar. He would conduct his own investigation out there and bring back the evidence and place it on the general's desk.

Michael shook the offered hand and thanked both men for their time. Harry opened the door and lightly put his hand on Michael's back.

"A word of advice, Dr Green," said the general. Harry stopped in the doorway, and Michael turned around to listen.

"Don't go out to Afghanistan looking for trouble. You might just find some."

Chapter 12

Melanie had booked a small room in the Study Centre for her meeting with David. They were still at it when Michael returned at four-thirty, just in time to help himself to a piece of Luigi's banana cake from the plate on the table between them.

"Dad!" Melanie gave him a big smile. "Let me get you a cup of tea, then tell me about your day."

"Later. A tea would be great, thanks. But I want to hear how you two got on, and whether you think you're ready for tomorrow."

"Michael, I can assure you that you have nothing to worry about concerning your charming daughter. It's a pleasure to have her as a client, and she's totally clear in her mind. I think we can safely say that the police will be quite satisfied, as indeed I am, that Melanie had nothing to do with that man's unfortunate death. They have no grounds at all for detaining her – unless, of course, they are able to come up with some magical evidence which links her to the crime, and I very much doubt if they'll be able to do that."

"Dad, David's been wonderful. He's explained to me exactly what's going to happen. I know I've got nothing to worry about, but I'm very pleased he's going to be by my side tomorrow. As for evidence they might have linking me to the crime, the only thing I can think of is me reporting the man to the police. And they knew that before they questioned me last time."

"Can you remember if they mentioned me at all, last time?"

"No, they didn't. Why would they?"

"Only because I reported the attack on the village to the MoD when you first told me about it. Then I wrote again at the end of July after you'd told me the officer's name. I suppose I'm a link of a sort. I just wondered if the MoD would have informed the police."

"At your meeting," said David, "did they give any indication that they had done so?"

"None at all. I got the impression they had little information about anything, but maybe they were just not letting on. The purpose of the meeting seemed to be to persuade me to drop my complaint. To warn me off. And they did not think it was a good idea if Melly and I went to Afghanistan when she was better."

"Really, Michael? What did they say?"

"Just that I shouldn't go looking for trouble there. The general said I might find it."

"What?" said David. He was frowning. "That almost sounds like a threat to me."

"Sounds like a typical general to me," said Melanie. "All bluff and bluster. Goes with the rank. When you get to know them, you find out it's a bit of an act. It's what people expect of them, so they become a bit like Melchett in Black Adder. You know?"

"Well, in that case I don't think we'll initiate legal proceedings against them for harassment just yet," said David. "You do know harassment is a crime as well as a civil offence? Protection from Harassment Act, 1997!"

Michael asked David about the procedure for the following day.

"I'm going to make my way back to the office this evening, then tomorrow morning I'll arrive at the police station at nine sharp so I can have a word with the investigating officer. I'll introduce myself and see if I can sound him out before Melanie arrives. They're going to pick her up from Reception here at ten.

"I don't know how long the process will take, but it could be over by lunchtime. As you know, she would be free to leave at any time, but I think we ought to allow them to ask all the questions they need to. You know, 'help them with their inquiries' as their media briefings used to say. We don't want her to be arrested, do we!" David laughed at the thought.

"Thanks for that," said Michael, "can I give you a lift to the station?"

David looked at his watch. "Are you sure? That would be awfully kind."

Once they were safely in the car, Michael said, "You were very optimistic in there. Was that for Melanie's benefit?"

"I'll put it like this. We don't want her up half the night worrying. But to tell you the truth, we have no idea what evidence the police have managed to come up with. They should've had the PM by now, and they've had the time to make lots of inquiries, so you never know. I'm not suggesting they'll have anything specifically on Melanie, but they might want to be absolutely sure before eliminating her from their investigation.

"If it's a case of murder, they will, of course, be under great pressure from the CPS to come up with a solid case. And as he was a politician – Conservative at that – there could be a groundswell from Westminster to get the case solved before the end of the summer recess."

"Murder," mumbled Michael.

"What's that?"

"Sorry, David. It's just that the general I saw this

afternoon said Bretton-Willis had been murdered. Perhaps he was jumping to conclusions... I assume I'm not allowed to sit in on the interview?"

"'Fraid not. But they'll record the whole thing and give us a copy. I suggest we wait and see when it ends; then we can decide whether the three of us can talk about it over lunch. I hear there's good eating at a pub called The Dog and Duck. Do you know it?"

"Actually I do. We went there a couple of nights ago. It's good. Why don't I go there anyway, and you two could join us when you can. Give me a ring when you're on your way."

Michael wished his friend good luck as he drove up to the Underground station. He felt lucky David was dealing with the matter; his daughter was in good hands.

It was nearly half-past midnight. Michael was wide awake lying on his bed in the guest room. He tried all the tricks, but he couldn't go to sleep. Just as well it's not me being grilled in the morning, he thought.

He had to admit that his meeting at the MoD had left him confused. He didn't doubt that Smedley meant it when he said there was a zero-tolerance policy towards any form of war crime. Yet he felt the general was not exactly keen to investigate what happened at Khuh Tabar.

Michael could understand his reluctance, bearing in

mind the main culprit was dead, and he guessed it was not the sort of thing a Director of Public Relations would want revealed to the general public. It made him wonder just how far they would go to keep such an incident under wraps.

At precisely five to ten the following morning, Michael and his daughter walked down the stone steps of Beechwood Hall main building onto the gravelled forecourt to await the police car. By the time it arrived a few minutes later, Michael's heart was pounding – despite Melanie's attempt at small-talk to distract her anxious father.

As the car rolled to a stop, a woman in plain clothes emerged. Michael reckoned she was in her forties – slim, thin-lipped, dull eyes. She went up to the pair with a smile and a boney outstretched hand.

"Good morning. Dr Michael Green? I'm Detective Sergeant Simmons."

"That's me – and this is my daughter Melanie."

"Yes. We've met. Good morning Melanie. Well, shall we get underway? If you would like to take a seat in the back..."

Michael wanted to hug his daughter. For him, it was as if she were departing for some foreign land for an unspecified number of years, rather than going down to the local nick for an hour. He tried to be brave and simply shook her hand. Having done so, he immediately felt like an idiot. And to compose himself, he reached into a pocket and extracted a visiting card.

"Detective Sergeant Simmons?" He found it a bit of a mouthful. "Here is my card. Do give me a ring if... if I can be of any assistance. I have a car so if you would like me to collect Melanie when, when..."

"Thank you, Dr Green. We'll let you know."

Michael waved as he watched the car leave until it disappeared through the main gate. Melanie didn't wave back, which he took as a bad sign – then he told himself not to be so stupid. Having got a grip of himself, he decided it would be fun and distracting to re-live his youth and go for a cycle ride.

On his way back to his room, he met John, the groundsman, and asked him where the bicycles were kept.

"No probs, Dr Green. Come with me. I can show you how to fit the batteries."

John pushed the shed door open, revealing a cycle rack holding a dozen or so bikes.

"No lock on the door, John? Don't they ever get pinched?"

"Ah, but there is a lock. My pass – or yours – lets you in. It's a proximity pass. You need to be within a few feet of the door for it to work. When you leave, it's as well to make sure the door clicks shut behind you."

John showed Michael how to fit the battery, adjust the helmet strap and raise the saddle.

"Many thanks, John. Just one question, how far can I go on one battery?"

"Depends on how hard you pedal and how fast you go. But these bikes are not too heavy, so if you do run out of juice, you can pedal it back home without too much of a problem. You should get about ten miles out of a battery before you have to do that. And there's nothing to stop you taking a second battery. Just make sure you put them both on charge when you come back."

"Thanks. And by the way, thanks for looking after Melanie. I gather you've set her to work with some gardening."

"Don't thank me! She's been wonderful; such good company. We'll miss her when she leaves."

"Glad to hear she's been behaving herself. And good luck with that pike!"

Chapter 13

The Dog and Duck was about eight miles away. By the time Michael was ready to set off, it was nearly eleven, but he decided to take his book with him in case David and Melly were running late.

At ten past one, several pages later, David walked into the saloon bar alone. "Michael, I'm sorry to be so late-"

"Where's Melanie?"

"At the police station."

"Without you?"

"The interview has been paused for lunch. It'll restart at two-thirty. Melanie was quite happy to remain there. She said she didn't fancy lunch and might go for a breather. I've told her to be cooperative but to say nothing – except please and thank you. I thought I'd take this opportunity to come over and let you know what's going on."

"Thanks. I appreciate that. All this waiting! Now, can I get you a drink or something?"

"Let's get a table, then we can talk. I won't have a drink, thank you, as I'm back on duty after lunch."

The pair chose a table in the corner farthest from the entrance. They sat opposite each other, with David facing into the room. He leaned forward on his elbows.

"Michael. Bad news, I'm afraid."

"You mean more bad news. What's happened?"

"Firstly, they managed to get hold of her posts to that bereavement support group. God knows how they do these things. But I managed to get a copy. Here we are. Have a quick read."

Melanie
New Member
29/07/19

Hi everybody, thanks for letting me join. To be honest, I'm really angry. Which is unusual for me, as I'm quite a mild person. My bereavement happened some time ago, but the pain doesn't seem to be getting any better. I've recovered from the trauma of the loss, but I can't seem to handle the anger. So, any tips would be gratefully received. And if there's anyone in the group who suffers in a similar way, perhaps we could chat about it and help each other.

Jenny

Member for four months

30/07/19

Hello, Melanie. Welcome to the group. I'm so sorry to hear about your loss. My dear husband passed away five months ago, so I know how you feel. He had struggled with cancer for a couple of years. I felt angry that The Lord took him away from me, at the age of seventy-two, but I remembered that God has a reason for everything, and that helped me get over it. Perhaps He has a plan for you ... (more)

Melanie

New member

31/07/19

Hi Jenny – thanks for your reply. I'm sorry to hear about your husband, but it must be a great comfort for you to believe there's a master-plan for us all, controlling our destinies. I'm not sure I agree with you, though – free will and all that. My position is slightly different, in that I'd only known mine for three years. Despite that, we were very close and planned to spend the rest of our lives together. As I'm only twenty-nine, that could have been quite some time.

Alison

Member for three years

02/08/19

Melanie, you poor dear, but a warm welcome to the group. Let's see if we can help. Anger is a natural emotion when someone is taken away, especially when it is by some awful disease like cancer. Why him? My Jonny was gathered when he was seventy-five, and we had been married for fifty-three years. It's a comfort to know I'll soon be joining him in Heaven, and that we will have a wonderful time up there. We might see you and your late husband there.

Melanie
New member
03/08/19
Hi Alison. Thanks for your kind words. Mine died suddenly at the age of 27. The shock was unbearable. I don't know about joining him in Heaven. Presumably, he won't grow old up there, but I will down here if I don't pop my clogs too early. Then when I get up there – if I ever do – he might not even recognise me. I'd be covered in wrinkles, and he'll still be 27. I mean, I couldn't expect him to remain faithful to me, could I?

Careful, Melanie, he thought. She was inclined to air her views at inappropriate times, especially when it came to religion.

Helen
Member for eighteen months
02/08/19
Melanie. A warm welcome to the group. I'm so sorry to hear about your bereavement. My Robbie died two years ago. I was angry with him for leaving me, but then I made myself remember all the good times we had together. After a few weeks, I did find it helpful to talk

about him, how we met and our wedding day, the birth of our lovely daughters, now both married with families of their own! It helped to share that burden. Perhaps it might help you if you told us more about yourself, and about your hubby. Do you think you could do that?

Melanie
New member04/08/19

Hi Helen. Thanks for your kind words. Sorry about Robbie, but it must have been a comfort to have so many happy memories of him. I don't have many of those, as I only knew my man for three years.

I guess having children and grandchildren is a great help. Not something I've done yet, produced a dynasty, as much as my father would want me to. He's been a help, but was terribly upset and still is, even though he'd never met my husband.

Michael looked up at David who avoided eye contact. He couldn't remember ever saying to Melanie that he wanted her to have children. Of course he was was upset when he heard the news about her man, but he'd got over it.

I know he would have got on well with him. Shahpur would have been a great son-in-law, as well as a wonderful father and husband – kind, caring, beautiful (at least to me). Always making jokes. Noble. One of the good ones. Anything else you want to know about him, other than him being dead?

As for me, I'm perfectly normal – was, rather. Trained as a doctor, joined the Army for a bit of fun and to save a few lives, or delay a few deaths. I made a stupid decision some years back and got captured/went awol – whatever. Shacked up with the enemy, met Shahpur, fell in love with him, and we had a boy, Jangi.

Adored them both, my darling boys. Until someone came to take me away and screw up my new life. I lost the two of them, within the space of about three minutes.

When I got back to UK, two years later, I was nearly straight. I was about four months into rehab when I found out who their killer was – and that he's walking free!!! The anger welled up. I have an almost unbearable desire to kill him. Otherwise, I'll have to live with my rage forever. Any tips?

Melanie
New member
04/08/19
Sorry, Helen. I got cross. I didn't mean that, about killing him. That's the trouble. I couldn't do that, unfortunately. Not if you spend a lot of your working life keeping people alive.

Richard
Member for One Year
10/08/19
Hello, Melanie. Welcome to our group. I was so sorry to hear about your partner. I lost my wife last year, so

I know how you feel. Perhaps you and I could meet up and exchange notes. I'm not looking for a relationship, but I do enjoy the theatre and eating out, and I would be happy to share such occasions with you. Please leave a private message in my inbox if you are interested. I'm fifty-three and in good health... (*more*)

There's always one, thought Michael.

Clarissa
Member for two years
12/08/19
Hi, Mel. Sorry to hear about your loss, but a future without a man can be rewarding. So, honey, don't give up. I can understand the anger, but if you're not already vegan, I would urge you to become so. If we purify our bodies and purge out the toxins, we find that all the pent-up anger goes and we become more at peace with ourselves. Did you know that men eat 28% more meat than women? And that's why they are so much more aggressive than ... (*more*)

Rand
Member for one month
13/08/19
PM me your email address.

"Nothing too obnoxious there, David. Are you worried about them?"

"Only the bits about her wanting to kill him. They

confirm her feelings towards him. I'm afraid it's a murder investigation."

"Because of those posts?"

"Partly. At one stage they thought it might have been some sexual experiment gone wrong, but the postmortem apparently found two puncture wounds, one in the front of the left thigh, the other in the spine."

"God! So he was poisoned?"

"No. Neither caused death. The thigh wound was caused by an auto-injector – like an epi-pen. Traces of fibre from his trousers were found in the wound. As for the chemical injected, they are waiting for some test results. They guess it was some sort of incapacitant – fast-acting – because there were no signs of a physical struggle."

"And the one in the spine?"

"Possibly to anaesthetise the victim, like an epidural – but you know more about those things than I do. Could have been done while he was incapacitated."

"But why would a murderer do that? Why not just inject him with a lethal dose of poison and be done with it? It seems a strange way of going about things. So how did he die?"

"Blood loss."

"What? From two injections?"

David sighed. "No, there were other wounds..."

"Okay. What were they?"

"Let me start at the beginning. When I arrived at the police station, I was able to meet the investigating officer, a policewoman, a sergeant-"

"Yes, David. I met her, too. When she came to collect Melanie. Seemed nice enough to me."

"She was helpful. Showed me the pictures. Thank God she warned me! I've never seen anything like it. The corpse was naked. Nothing unusual about that. And he was in the empty bath-tub – I've seen that before. But the corpse was facing upwards, suspended by two wires tied onto the shower fittings high up on the wall at the end of the bath. Only the feet and hands were touching the bottom of the bath. The weight of the rest of him was hanging on the two wires."

"Bloody hell!" said Michael.

"The police reckon the killer, having incapacitated his victim, heaved him into the tub then filled it up with water. The bath plug was one of those you operate by turning a knob. It was in the up position, but a sheet of cling film had been placed over the hole to stop the water draining away.

"The killer then attached the floating body to the wires and pulled them tight. They believe his next move was to make a tiny hole in the cling film, probably with a syringe, to let the water slowly drain away. I should add that although the bath was empty by the time the photographs had been taken, the walls and bottom of the tub were stained with blood. The tide mark showed the bath had been filled up to the overflow."

"Good grief! So if the police are correct, he died a slow and painful death as the water drained away. How gruesome! Did they show the photos to Melanie?"

"Yes. Unfortunately..."

"I wouldn't worry too much about that. She's seen some horrid deaths in her time. I think she's learned how to block out that kind of image. It must have been strange for her to see the dead body of her attacker lying in that bath. Did she react at all?"

"Yes, Michael. She did. It wasn't good."

"Why? What on earth did she do? What did she say?"

"She was very good in that she didn't say anything. Those were my instructions to her, to say nothing unless I nodded my head. And I didn't nod my head."

"So, what happened?"

"Your daughter laughed. Giggled, rather. As if it were amusing. The policewoman and her side-kick were shocked. I'm sorry, Michael, but it wasn't a sensible thing for Melanie to do. No normal person could have found those photos in the least bit funny."

"I agree. I can't imagine why she would laugh. You haven't explained the injuries which caused the bleed-out. Or how the wires were attached to the corpse."

"Well, there were two wires. This is the gruesome bit, so brace yourself. One wire was attached to the end of his penis, the other wire to his tongue. They reckon the main blood loss was from the penis, as the flesh had been ripped – a long rip through the blood vessel, so there was no chance for it to close. The wire to his tongue had obviously torn the ligaments and muscles in his mouth and neck, as about six inches of tongue was protruding outside the mouth; but there was not much sign of blood from that end, just a trickle out of the corner of his mouth... Poor bastard... He would not have been able to shout... "

"My God!" said Michael. "What a way to go! I suppose the killer arranged it so the incapacitant would quickly wear off and the victim would regain consciousness, but not before the epidural had taken effect so he couldn't struggle. The killer certainly knew a thing or two. And he must have planned it in advance. How did he tie the wires around the tongue and the penis?"

"He didn't."

"What do you mean? He must have attached them somehow."

David looked around the room and leaned forward. He spoke very quietly. "He used fish-hooks – big ones. In each case the hook had gone right through, so the points were projecting."

The two men looked at each other.

Chapter 14

"Good morning, gentlemen!" The waitress handed over the menu cards and a wine-list and asked if they wanted to drink.

"Tap water will be fine," said Michael.

Once the waitress had moved safely away, Michael asked his friend if he had any further information of interest concerning the murder.

"Time of death is puzzling. The PM says between six and seven on the Monday morning – but if the police are right about the bath draining away slowly, we have no idea of when the killer did the deed. Damn clever, if you ask me. It could have been any time, the evening before or during the night. Or the day before. Or the day before that."

"But what makes them suspect my daughter?"

"At the moment, very little. But they piled on the pressure hoping she'd slip up and reveal something. They do reckon the killer was medically trained, and they believe the motive wasn't simply to kill the bastard but to make him suffer—"

"That's why she laughed, David. She was pleased he'd died in that horrible way. I'm pleased, too. He raped my daughter."

"Which does give her a strong motive. Revenge is a powerful emotion, not only to dispose of the person who wronged you but to exact punishment. It's often planned months in advance, and clearly this murder wasn't committed 'in the heat of the moment'. It was a well-thought-out, deliberate act of vengeance by someone who knew what they were doing. I'm afraid Melanie fits the bill."

"David, for God's sake, you know as well as I do she couldn't possibly have done it." Michael quickly looked around the room. For him, it wasn't a point for discussion.

"I know that. But you have to look at it from their point of view. I mean, who else had the motive, for a start?"

"If you mean who would have wanted to punish the guy, you must include me. Have you a daughter? How would you feel if some bastard raped her and was walking free?"

"Michael, I don't have a daughter – just two sons – but I do understand how you must feel. I guess you're not the only person that adores her; she is a lovely girl

– woman – and possibly someone took revenge on her behalf."

"You mean someone like Rand?"

"Exactly. Someone who had a strong sense of justice, who was prepared to act outside the law if they believed the law was failing her. But did Rand have the medical knowledge?"

"We don't know," said Michael, "and neither does Melanie, and frankly we know very little about him except what he wrote in his emails to her. That was her only contact with him. And we don't even know if he was telling the truth."

"What about you? As you said, you would have wanted to punish the man who raped your daughter. And you have the medical knowledge, as well as a motive."

"Are you suggesting—"

"Not for one minute." David smiled. "In this job, you must think like a policeman. You have to consider all possibilities, however remote. It's not so much a case of finding who the culprit is, as eliminating who the culprit is not.

"Quite often a suspect will be cleared if they have an alibi. That is if they can show that by reason of their presence at a particular place or area at a certain time, she or he was not or was unlikely to have been at the place where the offence is alleged to have been committed at the time of its alleged commission."

"Surely, that's the answer. If Melanie can prove she was nowhere near the man's home when he was killed, she'll be in the clear."

"But we don't know when the bloody man was killed. We know roughly when he died, but not when the act which led to his death took place."

The waitress returned with two glasses and a large jug of water. Ice cubes danced on the surface, and two slices of lemon glided gently around in the water beneath them.

"Sorry. I get it. I'm being a bit of a lemon, I'm afraid. I'll try not to think like a doctor... Talking of possibilities, you don't think the military would want him out of the way, do you? Put it this way, with him dead, there's really no point in them investigating his ghastly war crimes, is there? At least they made that clear to me yesterday."

"Possible, but it's not their thing. Anyway, why would they want to go to such trouble to punish him?"

"To make it look like a revenge killing by my daughter? They could make out she was some sort of psychopath, get her put away for good. She's the only witness to those war-crimes – at least the only one in this country."

"Two birds with one stone? Possible, I suppose," said David, "But the last thing they would want is Melanie on public trial telling the world what he did to her – and what he did in that village. I guess they would prefer to kill both birds rather than have one squawking in a witness box."

"You think they'd do that?"

"Michael. I don't think so, but we are looking at possibilities. Perhaps the plan was to get rid of 'Mr Nasty' then follow it up by suiciding his murderer before she's brought to justice."

"Suiciding? What on earth do you mean?"

"Just looking at all possibilities. They bump off Mr Nasty so he doesn't spill the beans. Then they bump off his alleged killer so she can't give evidence of his crimes in court. Problem solved."

"Bloody hell!"

"The use of the fish-hooks is odd. Melanie mentioned them to Rand, but God knows how some shady government outfit would have got hold of that information."

"Could they have intercepted those emails?"

"No. Not the sort of thing the MoD would get involved in," said David, "but Counter-Terror might, or MI5, or GCHQ, but only if they were flagged up."

"What do you mean 'flagged up'?"

"The computers," said David. "They listen in. It isn't illegal, because no human listens and no record is kept unless they pick up key words."

"Such as?"

"Oh, the usual, anything that might give them a lead on terrorism – Muslim names, weapons for sale, how to cause mayhem, references to terror. Works like Alexa. She only listens when she hears her name."

"Oh right," said Michael frowning. "So she's not listening unless she hears her name. So how does she hear it?"

David smiled and slowly shook his head. "Don't ask."

When the waitress came to take their order, neither man had even looked at the menu. Michael didn't feel like eating but settled on a Caesar salad while David went for the steak in a baguette. Both stuck to water.

"David, did they have anything else on Melanie?"

"Not to my knowledge. No DNA apparently – except his own and the cleaning lady. Unusual, that. It's quite hard for a criminal not to leave some trace at a crime scene. No finger prints either, but that's easy. You just slip on a pair of surgical gloves."

Michael groaned.

"Hey! Chin up, old man! I have some good news. Although the police have a video of people entering and leaving the building, they admit it is not clear enough to give them a positive ID. It shows one person of similar build to Melanie – about the same height, slim – but they have no idea what flat they were visiting. I think they're hoping the test results on the injected chemical will provide a lead. We should know that this afternoon."

David tucked into his steak sandwich while Michael picked at his salad. David chuckled, and his friend asked what was so funny.

"Very interesting. I've attended a few interviews under caution in my time and seen a few tricks. But Simmons used one I'd never seen before. She was pressuring Melanie and, at a certain point, she banged her fist on the table in frustration. A moment later, a constable entered the interview room and placed a file in front of her. He whispered in Simmons' ear, just loud enough for Melanie and me to hear, 'the results of the DNA test, ma'am.'

"Slowly she opened the file. From our side of the table we could both just about read the upside-down heading on the piece of paper inside. We could make out the capital letters, DNA. Simmons pretended to read it, then lifted her head and looked at Melanie. She took a deep breath and smiled. 'Dr Green,' she said, 'don't you think it's time to tell us the truth? You know, you could make it easier on yourself. With your medical record, the charge could be reduced to manslaughter which might mean a lesser sentence for you'."

"God! What did Melanie say?"

"She came straight back without flinching. 'I've already told you *four fucking times* I didn't do it, damn you!'. You should have seen Simmons' face."

David asked the landlord to summon a taxi to take him back to the police station. Michael was saddled with the electric bike, but fortunately for him, the battery held out until he reached Beechwood Hall. As he was putting it away in the bicycle shed, his phone pinged. It was David. He asked Michael if he would mind coming down to the station.

"Sure. I'll be there shortly. Is Melanie ready to come home? I'll have the car, so it's no problem for me to collect her. And I could drop you off at the tube station on the way back."

"I think it's best if we discuss it when you arrive. Also, the investigating officer, DS Simmons, would like a word with you."

"I'll be right there." Michael wondered if they were after a character reference, or wanted to know more about Melanie. He was pleased he'd offered his help earlier, and he made up his mind to be as co-operative as possible.

"Ah! Dr Green, do come this way please." It was Detective Sergeant Simmons, full of smiles. Michael thought this a sign that all had gone well.

He followed her along the corridor. "So how's my daughter doing? I hope she's behaving herself."

"She's being very helpful." DS Simmons led the way into a small interview room. "Do take a seat. I'll be back in a moment."

She returned, carrying a file. "First, a few formalities, if I may. Your full name?"

"Dr Michael Lawrence Green."

"Permanent address please?"

"I live in Spain. The address is on my card, the one I gave you this morning."

"Ah. Of course. We just need to establish your identity. Do you have your passport with you?"

"Yes I do." Michael handed over his British passport. He rarely used his Irish one, but having lost his passport as a teenager back-packing through Europe, he always travelled with them both.

"That's fine. Thanks. Do you mind if I take a copy?"

"No, please go ahead."

Sergeant Simmons pressed a button on the wall. Michael heard a distant buzzer. A moment later, a young constable appeared, and the sergeant gave him the passport.

"It must be quite hot in southern Spain at this time of year, Dr Green?"

"It certainly is, but it's beginning to cool down at last."

"I suppose it's nice to come to England, especially during the summer months."

"Absolutely. It's a much nicer climate," said Michael. He was beginning to relax.

"Except when it rains! When did you arrive?"

"I flew over last Monday. My daughter emailed me

to say you had interviewed her about... about the... death, and I thought she needed my support. She's a—"

"You didn't come a few days earlier, by any chance?"

"No, not until I heard about the death. Why would I? The whole point of me coming was to help Melanie, to be there for her-"

"Quite so. But we have to check these things, to eliminate you from the investigation. It's routine. So you were in Spain during the period 5/6 September, the weekend Mr Bretton-Willis was allegedly murdered?"

"Yes. You can ask my secretary. She can confirm that I flew over on the Monday, the seventh. She arranged the tickets. You can phone her if you like. The number's on my card."

"Dr Green. We have already spoken to Daniela. This morning. She was very helpful. When we asked about you, she said you were taking part in a golfing tournament, in Marbella. Why would she do that, Dr Green?"

Michael gulped. He felt himself going red as Sergeant Simmons' eyes bored into his.

He remembered David's advice. Admittedly concerning Melanie, but he reckoned at that precise moment it was he who needed David right there beside him.

"I'm not answering any more questions until my lawyer is present!"

"Fair enough. I assume he's Sir David Goodman, the same expensive and renowned criminal solicitor who's acting for your daughter? Something to hide, have we?" The woman pressed the button on the wall.

The constable took Michael to another room, an office with a desk and an easy chair. David was behind the desk reading a copy of the Police Gazette. Once the constable had left the room, Michael explained what had happened.

David was horrified that he'd handed over his passport, as a matter of principle, but he assured him he would get it back. As for the informal grilling, David put his mind at rest and said that it was indeed routine to ask where certain people were at the time a serious crime was committed.

"But surely they don't think I'm the murderer?" Michael was indignant that he should suggest this. Yet again.

"Of course not. It's just police work. Remember, you do have a motive, even if the thought of doing him in had never crossed your mind. And you do have the medical knowledge. Which reminds me. They've had the results back from the lab on the substance injected into the man's thigh. Interesting. It's a mix of two drugs, sufentanil and naloxone. You'll know about these things, but I did Google it. Sufentanil is

500 times more powerful than morphine. It's very fast-acting, and they now use it for subduing – wait for it – aggressive patients in psychiatric hospitals. I don't know what the naloxone does."

"Strange, that," said Michael. It took him back to his days as an anaesthetist, his speciality for many years before he returned to general practice. "Naloxone is an antidote to sufentanil, but it takes longer to act. If you use them together, you can control the duration of the tranquillisation. And you could use a higher dose of sufentanil to get an even faster response. It's got a high therapeutic index-"

"A what?"

"Sorry. If you like, it's the gap between having any effect at all and killing you from an overdose. In other words, it's quite a safe drug when used as a tranquilliser. It would be safe to use on a mental patient, especially if the slower acting antidote was administered at the same time. They wouldn't be out for too long, just enough time to restrain them from harming themselves, or the staff."

"Or just long enough for the killer to administer the spinal, I guess."

"Sure. But you'd have to know exactly what you're doing. And getting that ratio right would be difficult."

"Yes, the ratio. Michael, I'm afraid I have some more bad news. The auto-injectors are undergoing field trials at the moment – it's quite a new technique –

and packs have been issued to our three high-security hospitals – Ashworth, Broadmoor and Rampton – and to Beechwood Hall. Each pack has a different ratio, and it would seem that Bretton-Willis received a dose from a Beechwood Hall epi-pen."

"But that's ridiculous. How can the lab be so positive? And I'm sure at Beechwood Hall they don't leave these things lying around. They'd keep them under lock and key. Sufentanil is a Class A drug, for Heaven's sake. And just because the thing came from Beechwood Hall does NOT make my daughter guilty of murder!"

David let him go on.

"I mean, there could be other people at Beechwood Hall – patients and staff – who could have stolen one of the pens. Or someone from outside could have known the place was doing trials and broke in and stole a pen. Easy enough to do. They're the size of a fountain pen. Or someone is trying to deliberately put the blame on my daughter. David, you've got to do something. I'm not having Melanie suffering like this. Have you told her this latest piece of evidence? Does she know she's being set up?"

"No-one is saying she's the murderer. No-one is even accusing her. But the evidence to date does appear to indicate that the police do have *reasonable grounds* to suspect her. Of course, whether they also have enough evidence to charge her is an entirely different matter."

"And me! They think I had something to do with it. The world's gone mad. My secretary, bless her, told them I was at a golfing match in Spain. Not her fault, though. She's a bit of a gossip, so I'd asked her not to let on that I'd come here to see my daughter—"

"Calm down. We can sort all that out. They can check your flight. You'll be on the manifest – if you are telling the truth."

"David, for God's sake!"

"I'm teasing. Remember, think like a policeman."

There was a knock on the door. "Yes?" said David.

It was the constable. "Sir. Sergeant Simmons is ready for you in the interview room."

"On my way," said David. And then to Michael, "why don't you wait here? This shouldn't take too long."

Michael forced out a smile.

Chapter 15

It was after six when David returned to the small office at the police station. He looked tired, and his shoulders were drooping. Michael sprang to his feet.

"What's up? Where's Melanie? Is she okay?"

"She's okay – but they want her to remain here-"

"You mean they've arrested her? How can they do that? She's not guilty of any crime."

"Michael. All they need are reasonable grounds to suspect her of a crime, and I'm afraid they do have those – motive, means and opportunity. They're not saying she is guilty. That's up to the courts to decide."

"But why arrest her? She came here of her own free will. Surely they'll allow her out on bail? Have you tried that? It's not as if she's a threat to the general public. She's hardly likely to go and kill another MP, just for the fun of it. Or abscond, for that matter. Where the hell would she go?"

"My dear fellow, in serious cases, such as murder,

manslaughter or rape, the individual will automatically be taken into police custody. They have no choice."

"So how long will they keep her? What's the next stage?"

"In a case like this, the police will seek guidance from the Crown Prosecution Service who will examine the evidence and decide whether the suspect should be charged. They will take into account lots of factors and will only prosecute if they think there is a realistic prospect of conviction, and if it's in the public interest to do so. I have to say that the fact the victim was an MP – a public servant – does make a prosecution more likely.

"I think it will all hang on the evidence. At the moment, it's thin, and I guess the CPS will urge the police to come up with some direct evidence which irrefutably links Melanie to the crime. Or a confession, of course."

"But they're not going to be able to do that," said Michael, "because she didn't do it."

"True, but to be honest, we are struggling to put forward evidence in Melanie's defence. She has no alibi covering the wide time-frame of the commissioning of the offence, and we cannot say she had no motive for killing him – unless she drops her accusations of rape, claiming the assaults were merely a fantasy of hers."

"You know Melanie. She's not going to do that."

"I fear you're right. In that case, I think there is the possibility of her being charged."

"My God... And then?"

"The police will continue their investigations hoping to firm up their evidence and they will inform the CPS accordingly. The CPS will then apply a stricter test; if the case fails, the charge will be dropped."

"And if it passes the test?"

"She'll go before a magistrate. If she pleads guilty-"

"For Christ's sake, man! She's not guilty. She's hardly likely to plead that she is."

"I know. So after her plea of not guilty, the magistrate will remand her for the Crown Court where she will be tried before a jury. They'll be guided by a judge, but it'll be their decision. Bear in mind that in nearly half the cases that come before the English courts, the jury acquits the defendant. And I believe, on the evidence we know of already, they will not be able to find her guilty beyond reasonable doubt. They might *think* she did it. They might think she *probably* did it. But to find her guilty, they must be satisfied that they are *sure*. Remember the Blackstone ratio."

"What on earth's that?"

"William Blackstone was the man who said in seventeen hundred or whenever, 'it's better that ten guilty persons escape than that one innocent suffer'.

Unless they can come up with some sound, direct evidence, I'd put my money on them finding her not guilty. She'll be free."

"Phew! So there is some hope..." Michael slumped down onto the easy chair in front of the desk.

"Certainly," said David. "I'm going to see if I can find anything out."

"Good luck." Michael took out his phone and checked his emails. There was just the one, from Daniela, explaining how she'd cleverly been fending off callers from England by telling them he was in Marbella.

Ten minutes later, David was back. Michael could tell it was not good news.

"I'm sorry, Michael. They've charged her-"

"What? Actually charged her? With manslaughter?"

"No. With murder. Which means they'll hold her here and put her up before the magistrates, hopefully in the morning. They'll remand her for the Crown Court, and unless we can put up an exceptional case for bail, she'll be sent to Bronzefield as a remand prisoner."

"Not Holloway? Where the hell is Bronzefield?"

"It's a women's prison, near Ashford in Middlesex. It took over from Holloway when it closed a few years ago. It's modern, privately run – and you'll be able to visit her."

Michael was stunned: his lovely daughter going to prison in spite of being entirely innocent of the charge. "What tipped it over the line? Have they further evidence?"

"Apparently, yes. There is a record of Melanie having access to the trial auto-injectors. Do you remember in her emails she said she was helping out in the medical centre at Beechwood?"

"But it's a Class A drug. They have to account for every one of those pens."

"I agree, so your guess is as good as mine until I find out more, but obviously the CPS thinks they've now got enough evidence to go ahead with the charge. Perhaps they are taking a bit of a flyer, in that they might be hoping for a confession before it comes up for trial in the Crown Court. I would imagine they have strict instructions from on high to get this case done and dusted. They might try and persuade her to plead guilty to manslaughter, on the grounds of diminished responsibility-"

"Please don't go down that route again. She didn't do it."

"Fair enough. I was just advising you of how they might handle it."

"Sorry. I'm a bit frazzled at the moment. More than a bit, actually."

"Hey, come on, man! We are going to win this! And I'll tell you how. Now, we both know the defence case is not very strong – very weak, actually – but fortunately we don't have to prove Melanie's innocence."

Michael frowned. "Surely, that's the whole purpose of having someone like you fighting her corner, to prove she didn't do it."

"It would be nice if we could, and by golly we'll try, but in this case I don't think we can."

"So how the hell can we win it?"

"Not by proving her innocence, my dear friend, but by casting doubt on her guilt. Remember, neither a judge nor a jury can convict an accused unless they are satisfied they're *sure* an accused is guilty. All we have to do is show there *is* reasonable doubt."

"All we have to do? Okay, how do we do that?"

David smiled. "Not as difficult as it might seem. You see, we can turn our problem around. For example, Melanie cannot come up with a cast-iron alibi because no-one knows when the act of murder was commissioned. But there could well be others who cannot account for their movements during the whole of that weekend. And if the prosecution tries to persuade the jury that Melanie managed to get her hands on a sufentanil auto-injector, we say that, if it were so easy, what's to stop someone else getting their dirty little hands on one as well."

"What about motive, though? How can we prove someone else wanted to kill him?"

"We don't have to. Remember, all we have to do is cast doubt. Melanie wanted him dead. Why shouldn't others feel the same about him? He raped Melanie – perhaps he raped other women. He killed an unarmed civilian in Afghanistan. Who's to say he didn't kill others whose loved ones had equally vengeful thoughts?

"Clearly, in his new career, he was ambitious. Perhaps he had rivals who wanted him out of the way. Or was he silenced because he had carried out illegal orders in mounting what could have been a punitive raid against a small rural community in a third-world country? Could he have incriminated someone higher up the chain? Did he know where the bodies are buried?

"The prosecution cannot prove Melanie was the only person to have a motive. Neither can they show that nobody else could have obtained a trial auto-injector. You see, although the circumstantial evidence does point to Melanie, it can point towards others. It'll be our job to make sure it does. Enough to cause that little bit of reasonable doubt in a jury's mind. She's innocent until proven guilty. The jury has to be sure she did it before convicting her."

"Thanks. That gives me hope. What happens now? Can I see her?"

"She has to remain here tonight..." David looked at his watch. "I guess it's a bit late now to get her to the court in the morning, but on Thursday morning she'll appear before the local magistrates' court. If she pleads—"

David stopped and corrected himself.

"As she will be pleading not guilty to a charge of murder, the case will then be sent to the Crown Court for a bail hearing, hopefully also on Thursday. Next is the plea and trial preparation hearing where she will again enter her plea. The court will set dates for the service of prosecution evidence and any other issues of law that may be required, and hopefully, fix a date for the trial. As I've said before, we'll try and get bail, but it will be difficult. As I'm a high court advocate, I'll be representing her."

"So she could be in prison for weeks, even though she's innocent?"

David sighed and raised his eyebrows. Michael got the message. "I want to see her."

"I'll see what I can do. Hang on here."

DS Simmons led Michael to the cells, explaining that this was very irregular, and she was only allowing it because he had been so co-operative. She emphasised that Melanie was not being punished but was merely on remand, a routine procedure in cases of this nature. This allowed her certain privileges like wearing her own clothes and having three meals a day and drinks whenever she wanted them.

"There you go, Dr Green," said the DS, as the custody officer swung the cell door open.

"Melanie! What can I say? I'm so, so-"

"Cut it out, Dad. I'm fine! Really. I've been in much worse than this. You should have seen the tent I had in Aff, at the base. And I had to share it. At least here I'm on my own. Then there was the dungeon, after... you know. This is luxury compared with that.

"And I'm really pleased about Mr Nasty. I feel he got what he deserved, yet I don't have to bear the guilt of having done it myself. I have a clear conscience, which is worth much more than any five-star hotel suite... It's an adventure, Dad! And the people are very nice. Tim's given me a jig-saw puzzle to do – he's the custody officer, by the way. It's 2000 pieces, so I hope I'm here long enough to finish it."

Michael found it hard to get a word in. When he finally asked her if there was anything he could do, she didn't say 'get me out of here'.

"Dad, could you possibly bring me my washing things and a change of clothes? And the photos on my bedside table? And anything else you think I might need. That would be great."

"Sure. Back soon."

"Hey, Dad. You'll need this." She handed him her pass. "Can you do me a favour? Don't tell anyone I'm

here. I don't want them fretting. Bob will hit the roof
– and Luigi, you know what he's like. Typical Italian!
And John will worry about the roses I'm meant to be
pruning. Tell Siobhan I'm fine and not to worry. She's
a real sweetie when you get to know her. She was in
the WRAF."

Michael thanked the custody officer and made his
way to the main entrance. A raised female voice
behind him stopped him.

"Dr Green?" It was DS Simmons. "You can't leave
just yet."

Michael looked around him, hoping to see David
appear from somewhere. He felt his heart pumping in
his chest.

DS Simmons smiled. "Let me get you your
passport."

Having completed his delivery mission later that
evening, Michael returned to Beechwood Hall with a
heavy heart. He didn't feel like eating, so he watched
the TV in his guest suite until he felt ready for bed. A
hot bath helped him relax, and shortly after his head
hit the pillow, he fell asleep.

Chapter 16

At breakfast the following morning, Michael nodded to the 'guests' he recognised. One of them asked where Mel was, and he explained that after all their exhausting activities, she was having a lie in.

Next on his agenda was a brisk walk around the lake. By the time he bumped into John he was puffing.

"Are you okay, sir? Sorry, you're a doctor. I shouldn't be asking that question."

"Fine, thanks, John. Just wanted to clear out the cobwebs."

"No Melanie?" asked John, lifting his eyebrows.

"Not this time. She's got things to do."

John's eyebrows descended into a frown.

"Thanks, by the way, for sorting out the bike for me. Worked a treat... Have you caught that pike yet?"

"Nope. I need to replenish my supply of fish hooks. You need special ones for pike – big ones, strong enough not to bend. I've lost a fair few, but now I make the leaders out of wire, as it gives better bite protection. Otherwise, a pike will cut straight through a normal line. Percy and I enjoy our spats. You fish?"

"Hah! Not really. As a boy, a bit, then I tried beach casting and got a hook caught-"

"Melly told me about that. I've had one in my finger. I tried to push it through, but the tip got caught on the bone."

Michael didn't like John using his special name for his daughter. It implied a degree of intimacy which made him feel uncomfortable.

"Do you see a lot of... Melly?"

"Sometimes. When she's not in one of her moods. We help each other – share our problems. We get on well. I'll miss her."

"Ah well," said Michael, not sure of how to reply. "I'd better be getting on. Nice to talk to you."

After lunch, he thought he would take the opportunity to have a quiet professional word with Melanie's psychiatrist while she was safely out of the way. He'd been impressed by Bob and felt he could talk with him in confidence, although he decided he would respect his daughter's wishes and not let on she was in police custody. Fortunately, Bob was free and welcomed Michael into his office.

"Thanks for the briefing the other day. That was useful. I'm afraid my knowledge of psychiatry is very limited, but I am anxious to understand exactly what my daughter's going through."

"Wouldn't we all? To be honest, none of us knows exactly how the human brain works. Or should I say the mind? We are making big strides, but we've still got a long way to go. When it comes to PTSD, I find the best way of explaining it – or understanding it myself – is to think about it as a computer, which in reality it is, with the various functions and components you have on your desktop machine.

"Let's start with the memory. Like a computer, the human mind has different types of memory—"

"Short-term and long-term?" ventured Michael.

"Yes, that's true, but I also see a distinction between memory of real things – things which have actually happened in the real world – and one's memory of thoughts and fantasies, of dreams. We all know it's hard to remember dreams; it's as if we are being locked out of them, but we know they are only dreams."

"'It's only a dream'. I can remember my mother saying that to me if I woke after a nightmare."

"That's right, and as we grow up, most of us don't worry too much about them. Now, if in real life we experience something really terrible – traumatic – which upsets our emotions every time we recall it, our central processor might do us the favour of shifting it across from our real memory to the dream memory. It's still there, but it's easier for us to handle; we treat it as a dream. The trouble is if we continue to have dreadful and disturbing experiences, such as continual abuse in childhood, our dream memory can fill up."

"And over-write our dreams?"

"Possibly, but the central processor doesn't want us to lose anything, so it might transfer some inconsequential dream records into our memory of real events."

"That's confusing," said Michael, scratching his head.

"Exactly right. Confusing. We can't tell fact from fantasy. One indication it's happening is sleep-walking. The person is out of bed and physically walking, but their mind records it as a dream... And that's why it's so important in handling PTSD patients to make sure the traumatic experiences cease. Eventually, the brain sorts it all out and the patient recovers, but it takes time and therapy. Much of my job is listening, allowing the patient to talk through their experiences and put them back in the right slots, sometimes with a little bit of guidance from people like me. Not rocket science, but in most cases it works."

"So was this Melanie's problem when she first arrived?"

"Yes. She exhibited all the signs of fact-fantasy confusion. The trouble is, so often we couch-quacks don't know what's happened to them, so to begin with we simply can't tell what's true and what isn't."

Michael wondered if Melanie's account of the war crimes had been the truth. "Bob, you say to begin with you can't tell, but can one eventually get to the truth?"

"Yes. In most respects. In Melanie's case I reckon most of her story is fact. I know she was gazetted as PKIA following the loss of a helicopter, and of course you must have received notification yourself. How she survived for three years in that village beats me, but the proof she did is right before our eyes. And I think the raid on the village did take place, and her capture and subsequent treatment, as it does explain her anger."

"In your opinion, is anything in her account suspect?" Michael had to ask.

"Not really. But I do wonder about her being married to the man she saw shot – it's almost unheard of for a European to marry into a tribal Pashtun community. As for having his child, I suppose it's possible, but..."

"But what?"

"I think Melanie – like many women of her age – yearn to become a mum, and it's not unknown for them to fantasise about it. She wanted to give you a grandchild, and maybe the dream became a reality, but only in her mind. There is an alternative explanation."

"And what's that?"

"Well, she felt very guilty about remaining in that village and not letting you know she had survived. Perhaps having an imaginary child to keep her there – one who conveniently gets killed off by the raid – was a way relieving that guilt."

"You mean an excuse? That's not my Melanie, at all!"

"I'm sorry. It may seem unlikely to you, but believe me, I've come across much worse deceit than that. It's not that the patients are liars, but often because they believe the fabrication themselves. They are self-deluders. Perhaps now she is so much better she might realise the truth but is too embarrassed to tell you she made it all up. She thinks the world of you, you know, and perhaps she worries that you'd be disappointed."

"Thanks. I see your point. Are you able to tell when a patient is lying?"

"Interesting one, that. Hypnosis is a useful tool. You see, people don't lie under hypnosis. You're tapping directly into their memory, not into some consciously processed version of events. And the version you get is generally more accurate and more detailed than the version they would tell you if they were fully conscious. A patient under hypnosis will remember things they think they've forgotten."

"Interesting," said Michael, "although colleagues of mine have used hypnosis as an anaesthetic, I've never got involved. As for hypnosis in the wrong hands, it worries me that a subject might be persuaded to do something bad, like kill someone."

"Let me put your mind at rest. A subject under hypnosis will never do something against their deep-down sense of right and wrong, their moral compass. Although we think morality is a conscious thing which is taught, we all have a herd-animal instinct of how to behave, and most of us follow the code, even under hypnosis.

"What I can say is that hypnotised people can do things which they never thought themselves capable of; like drawing an accurate picture, or speaking in front of an audience. As for the therapeutic effects, they can be valuable in curing PTSD, not only in finding out what caused the trauma but also in explaining it to them in more gentle terms rather than them having disturbing flashbacks."

"Sounds good to me. I hope it has worked on Melanie. Was she a good subject?"

"She was, actually. Of course, you can never be sure about these things, but she has over the months she's been here given me a reasonable account of what happened to her in Afghanistan."

"Glad to hear it. I'm really grateful to you for looking after her. Thanks so much for... everything."

"It's my pleasure."

"Thanks again. I'd better let you get on."

Michael was upset at the suggestion that his

grandson had only been a figment of his daughter's deranged mind, especially as he'd heard so much about him from Melanie a few nights previously. In case it was just a delusion, he made up his mind not to stress her further by ever mentioning it.

At about half-past one the following morning, the wail of a siren woke him from a deep sleep. That's the great metropolis for you, he thought. Someone's not going home tonight. Flashing blue lights seeped into his room through the drawn curtains. He heard shouting. He wondered if he was dreaming. When he realised he wasn't, he forced himself out of bed and went to the window.

His heart plunged when he heard the crackle and saw the orange glow coming from the main building a couple of hundred metres away. For a second or two, he thought the worst, then remembered with huge relief that his darling daughter was in custody at the local police station. But the thought of others trapped in there jolted him into action.

Having quickly put on a shirt and trousers and pushed his bare feet into his shoes, he raced to the scene, relieved to see the fire engines already in action. An ambulance was standing by. A man wearing a red fire helmet was giving orders. Michael rushed up to him and explained he was a doctor.

"Nothing for you, mate. Looks good. Only the

centre section. Sprinklers did our job for us – almost – but we need to check it out. And the alarms woke most of the patients up in time." He pointed with his chin towards the band of humanity gathered on the croquet lawn, dressed in an assortment of nightwear, gasping at the sight in front of them.

"All but one accounted for. But that doesn't mean they're inside. Sometimes they go walkabout, especially here. Not that we've ever had a live fire, but during our practices it happens. But we must check. Got a man in there now... Lucky it's just the centre section."

"That's where my daughter lives – but she's not there."

"Blimey, mate. I was told the missing person must be in there. It's the system they have. All inmates have passes, and it shows she's there."

"It's my fault, officer. I came back to get some things for her, and I must have left the pass in her room."

"Are you sure?"

"Absolutely, officer."

"Thanks, mate." The man spoke on his radio, "Wayne, it's clear. All accounted for. Building's empty. Stand down."

A few minutes later, a fireman wearing breathing apparatus emerged from the main entrance of the building. Michael could no longer see any orange glow or flames, just smoke and steam billowing out of the bay window of Melanie's room.

"Officer, it looks as if the fire's out. Is there much damage?"

"Out? You must be joking. Things will be smouldering, like; underneath the floor boards. But it's under control. Damage? Not much from the fire. You see the sprinklers did their job. Water damage, yes, but I reckon no serious structural stuff. It'll have to be checked out. The main thing is no-one was hurt. That's what we like, no casualties."

"Do you know how it started?"

"It's these old buildings, mate. Modern central heating dries out the woodwork, and it's like a tinder-box. Your daughter's room, all that panelling. All you need is a spark. Normally it's the wiring. It's all meant to be in steel conduit, right? But if they add a circuit, they might run the cables through plastic. Rats or squirrels eat the plastic, then tuck into the insulation and bingo."

"Did it start in her room?" Michael was concerned that he might have done something while he was going through Melanie's wardrobe, looking for something suitable for her to wear.

"Nah. Fire travels up. The room below was a linen store. My money's on one of those DIY heaters you can get, to air sheets and things. But forensics will look at it in the morning."

"Why's that? You don't expect it was deliberate, do you?"

"Arson? No chance. This place? They keep them all happy here. Topped up with happy juice. An outsider? What would they gain? You see it sometimes when an owner wants the insurance money rather than the building, but these days that's rare."

"What if it was an attempt to kill someone?" Michael had to ask the question while he had the chance."

"Struth, mate! You're a suspicious one! Mind you, it could have killed your daughter, that fire. Not so much the fire, but the smoke, especially if she'd been given a sleeping pill or three and all tucked up in bed, like. But who'd want to do that?"

Good question, thought Michael. Someone who didn't know she was in custody. Someone who doesn't want her blabbing in a court of law. He thought it best not to tell Melanie.

Chapter 17

He arrived at the courthouse promptly at ten – the opening time – to be sure of not missing Melanie. David had explained that in a case like this, magistrates don't have the power to consider bail; all they would do would be to confirm her identity, hear her plea and remand her for the Crown Court. Once Michael had checked with the ushers that his friend had not yet arrived, he decided to wait at the entrance to be sure of not missing him.

He smiled at the sight of him, emerging from a taxi carrying a very full-looking briefcase. He told him about the fire.

"Good Lord, Michael! That's dreadful! But what a stroke of luck Melanie wasn't in her room. Much damage?"

"Fortunately not. I'd taken a few things into her on Tuesday, her night things and washing kit – and luckily her book and photos of her mum which were on her bedside table. They let me inside this morning. The place was wrecked and smelled awful, but surprisingly her things in the drawers and wardrobe were not harmed. I don't think we should mention it to Melanie, at least not just yet."

"Agreed. Look, I've had a few thoughts. Mainly about Rand. I'm worried that the police might get ahead of us if they check him out first."

"Is there anything I can do?"

"Actually, I think there is – if you don't mind going to South Dakota. I'd like you to verify Rand's background."

"Rand? I thought we weren't going to involve him. Melly wanted him to be kept out of all this."

"Just in case. It would be helpful for us to know how real he is. As senior partner, I can't abandon the ship, and with holidays coming to an end we'll be getting very busy."

"David, it's the opposite for us, at La Manga. Holidays are the busy times. So I'll do whatever."

The men quietly discussed the plan just inside the main entrance, David swivelling his eyes around to make sure they weren't being overheard. They were interrupted when an usher came to tell David his client would be on in about five minutes. Michael wished him luck and followed the signs to the public gallery.

Melanie spotted her dad up there as soon as she was led into the courtroom. She smiled at him and waved. God, thought Michael, I hope she's not going to treat this thing too lightly.

The procedure began with the court establishing her identity and the charge being read out. Then the chair asking her how she pleaded. The two words, followed with a deferential 'sir', were spoken with her head held high and not the vestige of a frown or any other sign or gesture which indicated she was in trouble. And considering her night in the cells, she was well turned out, thanks to the smart light blue summer dress which he'd brought her for the occasion. The procedure was rapidly gone through with Melanie being remanded for the Crown Court next door.

David had explained this second hearing was simply for the judge to grant or refuse bail. He had also said Melanie was very fortunate her case was so serious, as the procedure was being bounced along in quick time, rather than having to wait weeks.

Michael wasn't so sure about Melly's good fortune, but he was relieved to hear that the political pressure would ensure the case would be prioritised.

If the judge didn't know Sir David personally, he would certainly know his reputation. Michael hoped that the fact this eminent lawyer was even applying for bail would convince the judge that there must be a case for granting an exception for this smart and intelligent young lady.

Michael settled himself into the Crown Court public gallery. After a few minutes, Melanie was led into the dock, and David took up his position in front of the bench. The court rose and in walked the judge. After the preamble, it soon became clear to Michael that the judge was anxious to hear what David had to say, but first on was the junior counsel for the CPS who made a case for refusing bail. She simply said, quoting Schedule 1 to the Bail Act 1976, that as the case was a serious one, the general right to bail did not apply.

It was David's turn. He began by agreeing that murder was indeed a serious charge, and that the law was right in removing the *general* right to bail. The reason was that a serious charge – like rape or murder – might encourage the accused to abscond before trial rather than risk a long prison sentence. But the removal of the *general* right to bail did not *deny* that basic human right to freedom to which the innocent are entitled: the seriousness of the offence is obviously just a consideration to be weighed in the balance and not by itself a ground for refusing bail.

He went on to say that the UK justice system is founded on the principle that a person is innocent until proven guilty, and that innocent people should not be locked up unless there were very special reasons for doing so. He then went through the special reasons – the risk of the accused absconding, committing another serious offence or intimidating a witness, proving in each case they were entirely irrelevant.

He urged the court to look at Melanie, a qualified doctor in the Armed Forces who had served her country in combating terrorism in Afghanistan and thus making our streets safer. A young person who had dedicated her life to saving others, someone with an exemplary service record, no previous offences, who is accused of murdering the victim because she had a strong and powerful motive: he had allegedly killed people she loved, taken her prisoner and repeatedly raped her. If this drove her to kill him, she was hardly likely to go around murdering other people. If she had not had this motive, perhaps the balance of evidence would have pointed to her innocence rather than her guilt, and she would not have been charged in the first place.

David continued by repeating each and every one of the grounds for refusing bail, pointing out that Melanie posed no risk to the general public and was hardly likely to interfere with any witness or disappear. He explained that she was undergoing the final stages of her treatment for PTSD at Beechwood Hall, where she was assisting in the medical centre.

Any interruption of that treatment could have an irreversible effect on her recovery, and her incarceration would deny Beechwood Hall the benefit of her valued services.

He concluded his application by offering the condition that Melanie should be held in the secure wing of Beechwood Hall from ten o'clock at night until six in the morning. To deny her freedom any further would be tantamount to declaring her guilty before her trial had even begun. And finally, he quoted Section 114 of the Coroners and Justice Act 2009 which allows bail if the court is satisfied that there is no significant risk of the person committing an offence that would be likely to cause physical or mental injury to another person. He said it was patently absurd to think this fine young lady, this public servant, this officer of the Crown would put the general public at risk in that way. Not to grant bail in this particular case would be a travesty of justice.

David had done a splendid job, and Michael was impressed. He wanted to go down to the floor of the court to congratulate him, but the usher in the public gallery indicated that those there should remain seated while the judge retired to deliberate on the case.

Ten minutes later, the court rose as the judge returned to deliver his judgement. David's application for bail had been turned down. Melanie would be remanded at Her Majesty's Prison Bronzefield until her trial.

Michael could not watch as Melanie was taken down. He leaned forward and supported his head in his hands, his elbows resting on his knees, his shoulders slumped; a proud man broken by a devastating and entirely unexpected outcome, a loving father having failed his daughter.

The floorboards of the public gallery creaked. He looked up to see an extended hand offering him a Kleenex. It was David. He sat down next to his old friend and put an arm around his shoulder. Neither spoke, but after a minute or two, they got to their feet and left the public gallery. Michael was grateful for David's support. He guessed he'd done it hundreds of times, put his arm around a family member following a bad outcome.

Once they were outside, David spoke. "Fancy a quick one?" He didn't wait for an answer but led his friend across the road into the King's Arms. "What's it going to be? It's my shout."

Michael settled for a medicinal whiskey and a few minutes later found himself nursing a double. They sat in the window, away from the bar. There were no other customers, but the girl behind the bar was busy cleaning glasses.

"The first thing to remember is that we might get

another bite at the cherry. If there is new evidence, we can apply for bail again – and I think we'd stand a good chance. There's always an element of randomness in these matters, as it depends on who is presiding, and I think this morning we were unlucky."

"You did a great job. Thanks. Anyway, you convinced me she deserved bail. It was such a shock when..."

"I know. But remember, Melanie is strong. She'll cope. Now, let's talk about Rand. We may have to involve him. You see, the police might be able to get into Melanie's email record, and parts of it do suggest he encouraged her. They will use that as evidence of her intent. Also, between you and me, it might help her if we can show that Rand is real.

"Let's be honest, he could have done it; for Melanie, to protect her. I think there was something between them. Okay, they never met, but perhaps he was concerned that the bastard would go after her. And if he was a trained assassin, who's to say he didn't do it? On the other hand, if we cannot show that Rand is real, the prosecution could claim your daughter made the whole thing up: a fabrication, from start to finish."

"Christ! I'd never thought of that."

"Well, it's happened before," said David.

The barmaid had emerged from behind the bar and was cleaning the tabletops, working towards the pair.

David continued. "So may I suggest we proceed with the plan we talked about this morning?"

"Sure. I'm happy to go ahead. If you could keep an eye on Melly..."

"Of course. Let me know when your flight is. We'll touch base before take-off. Chin up, old chap!"

Michael's phone sounded on his way back to the car park. An agitated voice said it was Harry Seymour, and would it be possible to meet that afternoon. Michael agreed and said he could be at the MoD Main Building by three. No, no, was the reply. By the Millenium Wheel, next to the merry-go-round; please.

Harry was pacing up and down and looking at his watch when Michael arrived a few minutes late. He was wearing a trilby pulled well down over his eyes.

"Sorry, Harry. Just missed a train and—"

"I haven't got long, but I need to tell you something. The shit has hit the fan." Harry was constantly looking around him and avoided eye contact.

"Okay. Tell me. What's happened? I assume it's about Bretton-Willis."

Harry winced at the mention of the name. "Look, they don't want your daughter in court. They cannot afford for all this... this thing about what happened to your daughter to come out. They're going to stop her."

"God-fathers! What do you mean 'stop her'? How are they going to do that?"

Harry rolled his eyes and looked around him. "Just get her out of here. Away. I don't know. As far away as possible – as soon as possible."

"Harry, I can't. There was a fire last night at Beechwood hall, and-"

"Oh God, no!" said Harry, then added to himself rather than Michael, "SHIT!"

"It's okay. She's not hurt. She's in a safe place." Michael smiled at the irony of it all. "She's in-" He stopped just in time. "As I say, in a safe place."

Harry's shoulders lifted, and Michael heard the sigh.

"Dr Green. Keep her there. Until we can find another way through this... this cluster-fuck. And you. Take care. These people are professionals. They're under orders. And for God's sake, don't tell anyone about this meeting. Get a new phone, a pay-as-you-go one. Otherwise, they can track you. I must go."

"Harry, a question—" but Harry was gone, speed-walking his way through the crowds towards the footbridge which would take him back across the Thames to Whitehall.

Michael returned to Waterloo underground station, booking his flight on-line as he went; it wasn't as difficult as Daniela made out. Having listened to Harry's warnings, he was relieved to get the confirmation of his reservation for the Friday evening flight out of Heathrow to Washington DC. Just twenty-six hours to go and he'd be aboard that aircraft and out of the country.

Chapter 18

Michael wasn't sure if it was the excitement of crossing the pond for the first time or the lingering daylight which kept him wide awake as the Airbus flew over the icy wastes of Greenland. The TV screen on the back of the seat in front confirmed the route, an arc crossing the North Atlantic and ending up at the US capital.

He was lucky to be by the window, bearing in mind he was a late booking in economy class. When the woman to his left craned her neck to admire the view, he leaned back to make it easier for her see it. Her perfume seemed familiar to him, but he couldn't put a name to it. She thanked him and they started chatting, firstly about the cramped seats and the dreadful meal, then about why they were on the flight.

"Me?" said Michael, "just a tourist, but I am hoping to trace some distant relatives – for the family tree I'm working on." The lie came easily to him, as he had rehearsed it in his mind several times. "I've only got a week, so I'm going to have to limit my sight-seeing. But as I'm on my own, I have only myself to please."

His fellow passenger expressed interest which encouraged him to continue. "The relations I hope to meet are in South Dakota, so I might be able to fit in a trip to Mount Rushmoor, but as my onward flight isn't until Monday, I'll have a wander around Washington over the weekend."

The woman explained she was spending two weeks with her son in Baltimore. He'd married an American girl and they had two lovely children. She asked him if he had a family.

"Well, my wife died a few years ago, but I'm lucky enough to have a wonderful daughter." For a moment he pictured her languishing in a cell at HMP Bronzefield; he felt himself frown. He wished he'd been able to visit her that morning, but he had to make do with a phone call. "She's twenty-eight, unmarried, but... I hope one day, Mr Right will come along."

His companion smiled and assured him that nature does find a way of making these things happen and that one day, he would wake up and find he was a grandfather. Talking of waking up, she said – if he would excuse her – she was about to do the opposite as her melatonin was starting to kick in. She covered herself with her lightweight blanket, put her seat back as far as it would go and left Michael with his thoughts for company.

He decided that if anyone ever again told him he'd become a grandad, he wouldn't believe it until he had seen the child. Not likely to happen, he thought, not while Melly was incarcerated. He dreaded the thought of something going terribly wrong and his daughter ending up with a life sentence. Then he remembered David's words, chin up old chap, and he reflected on his situation and the mission ahead of him.

His mind drifted back to that morning. It had all gone well, despite not visiting Bronzefield. He'd bought a pay-as-you-go phone and transferred his numbers across. With his old phone, he'd been able to speak to Melanie and hear how it was going. As he'd expected, she was taking it in her stride saying it was no worse than basic training. He'd explained he'd be out and about visiting friends but asked her to email him when she could to let him know how things were progressing.

Next, he'd phoned David on his new phone to tell him his flight times and report in veiled terms on what Harry Seymour had said. David had asked who was calling, but when he recognised Michael's voice, he'd said he was 'in the picture' and 'would take care of the goods' and wished his friend bon chance on the task ahead. After feeling more relaxed about his trip,

Michael had gone to the Study Centre and booked his accommodation in Washington DC and South Dakota.

On returning to his room, he'd packed just his cabin bag, on the basis that he'd only be away for the week. Nevertheless, it was a tight squeeze so he'd emptied the contents of his briefcase into one of the drawers in his wardrobe and replaced it with his washing kit and his kindle reader, leaving enough room for a daily paper.

He'd put his old phone on his bedside table, switched it on and plugged in the charger. And he'd decided to leave his British passport in his bedside drawer. When the time came for him to depart for Heathrow, he'd ordered a taxi, leaving the rental car in the visitors' car-park. His final act had been to close the door on his guest room and carefully slip his visitor's pass under it. He'd given it a good push so it would slide on the lino and disappear from view.

It had made him feel safe, knowing that if someone were to track his phone, they would think he was at Beechwood Hall and in his guest suite. And if they did a search of his empty room, they'd find the passport in his bedside drawer and assume he was in the country. Using his Irish passport to check in for his flight had completed the deception as his details would not appear on the UK Border Force computers. No-one except David would know he was on his way to meet Rand's parents. At least that was the idea.

It was evening when they landed in Washington, but Michael's body clock told him it was well after midnight. Checking into the hotel next to the airport seemed a good idea, and within fifteen minutes of settling into his room he was asleep. A few hours later, his eyes were prised open by the early morning sun streaming through a gap in the curtains.

It was only six o'clock, but having done his ablutions he went down to the restaurant and ate a hearty all-American breakfast, washed down with two large cups of coffee. He was duly impressed with his first taste of the US of A, and, suitably fired up and with tanks full, he booked into the first hop-on-hop-off city tour of the day which would take him around the great sites. By nine that evening, he was whacked and ready for bed.

He dedicated Sunday to visiting some of the famous national parks in 'DC' as he had learned to call the city; he found the colours stunning. Seeing couples strolling through the trees, arm in arm, reminded him of the woman he sat next to on the plane. Funny, he thought, that he didn't even know her name. Not that he was interested, but he liked her bright eyes with just a hint of naughtiness in them. No doubt at this moment, he thought, carrying out her grandmotherly duties in Baltimore.

Monday was the day of his flight to Pierre, the state capital of South Dakota. He'd read up about it and was surprised it was so small – for a state capital – with a population of only 12,000. That should make it easy to find them, he thought, given that Rand had kindly included their names in the bio he'd sent Melly. Not that he had time on that first day to do any searching, as the flight was five hours long with an hour's stop at Denver. By the time he arrived in Pierre, he had cottoned on to the fact that the locals called it 'Pier', with the accent on the first syllable.

The hotel did not disappoint. Cheap and only three-star, it boasted a swimming pool and a gym, and the staff were friendly. The Receptionist wanted to know how long he was staying – fair enough, he thought – but then asked why he was visiting 'Pier'. He could have said, 'Just some private business' but decided to return the hand of friendship.

"I'm compiling a family history, and I'm hoping to trace some distant cousins. Their name's O'Brian, with an 'a', the same as my mother before she was married. I wondered if there was a public records office in the city-"

"No sir, you don't want to do that! Not in Pierre. Hire a PI, we have lots of them, and there's not a great deal for them to do here, being that we have little crime. Give them a name, and they'll find out where they live, what they eat for dinner and anything else you want to know. Here," she opened a drawer and extracted a card, "try Sam. He's okay."

Michael thanked the good lady and took the card: 'Sam's Searches', and it gave an address. He turned it over:

Let us help solve your case!
Missing Persons – Auto and Trucking Accidents
Custody Matters – Cohabitation Verification – Asset Recovery
Hard Service Subpoenas – Heir-ship Clarification – Wrongful Death
Identity Verification – Finding Biological Parents – Genealogy

Yeah, he thought, Sam should be able to handle it. He would drop in and see him first thing in the morning.

Sam did not disappoint. He met Michael's expectations to a tee, from the droopy moustache down to the cowboy boots resting comfortably on the top of his desk. As Michael entered the inner sanctum, Sam jumped to his feet, pumped Michael's hand and offered him iced tea or coffee. Michael wondered if all Sam's walk-ins got the same treatment, but his query was soon answered.

"So what can we do for you today, Dr Green. Rosie said you were working on a family tree."

"Rosie?"

"Yep! From the hotel. Said you checked in yesterday."

Michael was taken aback and obviously looked shocked.

"Aw, Dr Green – can I call you Michael, by the way? She was just makin' sure she'd get the commission. No hard feelings, Michael? So, take a seat, my friend, and let's roll!"

Michael sat down on the wooden chair in front of the desk while Sam returned to his seat behind it and placed his boots back on the top of it.

"Well, my wife's maiden name – ex-wife, to be precise-"

"Sorry to hear that, pal. It happens to us all. Most of us, anyway. They just don't get the male psyche."

"Actually, she died, a couple of years ago."

"Michael, you have my deepest condolences. But I expect you've got over her by now. What about her?"

"Her maiden name was O'Brian, spelt with an 'a', but most people think it's just a spelling mistake. There are not many of them, and I thought it might be interesting to map out how the name spread. Her father came from Kinsale, in southern Ireland, and married an English girl, but I remember him telling me he had an older brother who emigrated to the States.

His family came over to stay with Dawn's parents – that's my wife – and I seem to remember they came from South Dakota..."

Michael was improvising. He hadn't worked out the fictitious relationships, and he hoped Sam wasn't paying too much attention.

"Poor thing!" said Sam, "marrying someone from SD! Only joking, Michael. Just my sense of humour. Quick, eh?"

Michael managed to chuckle. "Well, apparently they had relations in the capital city of SD, and I thought I'd come here and see if I could track them down. I want to find out if they had children which I could add to the family tree. I'd love to meet them. I think her husband's first name was Joe."

"Joe O'Brian?" Sam scratched the scraggy skin underneath his chin. "Gonna be hard, Michael. You're gonna have to give me a coupla days. Say, what about coming back Wednesday? I might have something for you. I'm proud to say we are a 'no glee, no fee' outfit – but I'd need something for expenses, Michael, in advance of course."

"Certainly," said Michael, and he fished out his wallet. "Will this be enough?" He handed over a hundred dollar note.

Sam leapt to his feet. "Jesus, pal! That's just mighty fine. So, see you Wednesday, eight a.m.?"

So far, so good, thought Michael, as he wandered

back to his hotel, not sure what to do with his time over the next two days.

The leaflet in Reception claimed that Mount Rushmore was South Dakota's main attraction. You mean there are others, thought Michael. So, very early on Tuesday morning, he joined the queue – line, rather – for the tour bus which would take him the 150 miles to the famous national memorial.

For the third time in two days, he wasn't disappointed. The presidents' heads were better than the postcards, and the Visitors' Centre was excellent. By the time the bus was due to return to Pierre, he felt he was a veritable authority on the monument. As he turned around to take one last look of the sculptures, he recalled the Hitchcock film he'd seen as a boy, *North-by-North-West*, about Cary Grant being chased across America pursued by agents of a mysterious organisation trying to prevent him thwarting their secret plans.

The thought jolted him back to the reality of his own situation, but somehow he felt safe in SD. The hotel receptionist had said there wasn't much crime in the state, and nobody except David – so he hoped – knew he was there. He hadn't put his email address on his new mobile, as it might compromise his new-found anonymity, so he was looking forward to getting back to the hotel and using one of their desktops to check his emails.

Apart from the spam, there were two. The first was from Daniela, hoping all was going well with his daughter's problem and that a Mr Smith had phoned up to ask when he would be returning from England. She took great pains to assure Michael she had not told a soul he was there, so she assumed it must have been a friend of his who he'd let in on the secret. Accordingly, she said she would find out and get back to him. When she asked for his number, he said he was phoning from a call box but would phone back in a day or two. He needed to see Dr Green specifically for some medical reason which he was not willing to disclose.

She also mentioned that a previous caller had called back twice to ask if Michael had returned from his golf tournament in Marbella. Daniela had told him not yet.

The second email was from Melanie.

Hi, Dad. How are you? Well, I hope. And I hope Beechwood Hall is looking after you properly in my absence. If you need anything, Bob will help. If he can't sort something out himself, he will know a man who can. Or woman, of course. John's good too, but more on the practical side. You've met Luigi. He's lovely, but unless it's to do with food he might make a pig's ear of it. Unless he's cooking it for the table.

Life here is a complete eye-opener. It's not the first

prison I've been in, if you count the army detention centre at Colchester which we visited during basic training. And I'm NOT comparing it to the hell-hole I suffered in Aff. No way.

Apart from being the biggest female prison in Europe, it's the most expensive to run and probably – in prison terms – the most luxurious. I have my own cell which is clean and comfortable, and as a remand prisoner I can wear my own clothes. Also, I don't have to work, but here is the thing. I've volunteered myself, and I'm helping out in the mother and babies unit. It's entirely unofficial, because they don't normally allow suspected murderers to do so, but I think they checked out my army record. It's wonderful. Okay, I did enjoy patching up squaddies in Aff, but to be working with birth rather than the other end of life is so much more fun. And the mums – new ones and old ones – are so appreciative.

Actually, we're lucky, because most of the prisoners are pretty benign, at least compared to the average customer in male establishments. It's so sad. Many of the girls here are in for things like shoplifting, breaching their licences or failing to pay fines. If you're well off, you don't have to shoplift. And if you get a speeding fine – like I did at uni – you just pay it. If you're poor and can't pay it, they stick you behind bars. It's so UNFAIR.

Sorry to bang on. I must tell you about my boss, the prison doctor. She's wonderful. We hit it off right from the interview. She's a fantastic inspiration to me, and if it wasn't for my commitments in Aff when I get out of here, I think I would like to follow in her footsteps. She's been in men's prisons, too. And believe me, she has some tales to tell.

Bob's been great. He comes most days, on the basis that I am still his patient, which means he doesn't have to stick to visiting hours. I think he swung it with my boss. I think she thinks there's something's going on. Honestly! How wrong some people can be.

And David's come in twice now. It's so kind of him. He's up to his eyes in work, but he still finds the time. He's working on the Defence Statement for the trial, and bless him, he's trying hard to secure an early date. I've told him not to bother, but he says he cannot leave me festering in this awful place. He should try Camp Bastion. Not that it's there any more, but in the early days...' nuff said.

Can't be too long typing this thing, as I've got my rounds. One of my girls is close, and I've assured her I'll be there. So sad, she doesn't have a mum; not a proper one, just a series of foster jobs.

Will write again soon.

Lots of love,

Melly xxxxx

It was a great relief to Michael to hear that his daughter was doing fine – and to know she was safe. The irony of it all struck him again. Bronzefield was probably the safest place in England for her at that moment, even though it had been designed to keep criminals in rather than criminals out.

Chapter 19

"Hey Michael, how're ya doin'?" It was Wednesday morning. Sam was standing in the doorway of his premises.

"Very well, thank you, Sam. How are you? Any success with the O'Brians?"

"Gee, pal. It's been hard. But I think we're there. Got an address, way out of town. But say, let me drive you there."

"Thanks, that's awfully kind of you. Are you sure you don't mind?"

"Happy to – but I'll have to put it on expenses. I tell ya, it'll be cheaper than a cab."

Michael climbed into the 1952 Chevrolet pick up. Before he had closed the door, Sam had let out the clutch suddenly and put the pedal to the metal. The tyres squealed and the door slammed shut of its own accord, just a moment after Michael had lifted his right foot clear.

A bumpy, dusty twenty minutes later Sam screeched to a stop outside a lone homestead, sitting in its own derelict plot. A woman was standing on the veranda with a witches' broom in her hands, frowning at the new arrivals. She had grey hair done up in a bun and wore a long dress covered by a grubby apron.

"If it's eggs you're after, Sam," she bellowed, "we don't do them no more."

Sam looked crestfallen, but the great showman continued unabashed.

"Just wanted it to be a nice surprise for you, Michael." And to the woman, "Hey, Martha. I've a man from England to see ya."

"England? That be England in Europe?"

"Sure is. He's a doctor."

"I don't need no doctor, Sam. You can take him right back where you found him."

"No. ma'am. He's come to see you about a pers'nal matter, your family tree!"

"He better come right on in, then... Come on, son. You come sit here, in Joe's chair. And Sam. You can just wait in that truck of yours. We're goin' to discuss pers'nal matters, d'ya hear?"

Michael and Martha sat next to each other on the veranda. He was flattered to be called 'son' although he reckoned he must be about the same age as Martha. He explained what he was trying to do. Having gone

through it with David, the hotel receptionist, Sam –
and several times in his own head – he had become
quite enthusiastic about the subject. He took out his
new phone to make notes, mainly to impress Martha
but also to note down anything which could be a help
to David.

He listened patiently to her childhood, how she'd
met Joe, why they settled in 'Pier' and how the coyotes
had had the last of their chickens. Michael asked if
they had a family and Martha replied one son. Michael
did a stage yawn and asked if she might be good
enough to give him his name.

"Jack. He's a good boy, but we don't see much of
him no more. Went east, he did. Works for the
guv'ment, he does. Clever boy..."

Michael waited for her to continue, but she seemed
to drift off into her memories. Sam sounded the pick-
up's horn. Michael felt he'd better move it on.

"Martha, does the name Randolph mean anything
to you?"

"Rand?" She looked at Michael, as if she was sizing
him up – or steeling herself for a confession.

"Not any more..." Her frown turned to a smile.
"Now he was quite something! Jack's elder brother.
Did well at college. And my! At military school, he
made us real proud. Won the sword, he did..."

Michael wanted to leap off his seat and hug Martha.

Melanie had not been making it all up. Rand existed. He was a real person. Michael let Martha continue.

"Then he got himself selected for special training in some university in Florida. We were so proud. He was happy there. Then he got posted... and never came back." She bit her lip.

"What happened, Martha?"

"Like many young men in the military, he went to Afghanistan, in Asia. Wrote to us every week, he did. He was a good boy. Then the letters stopped... "

Michael guessed what was coming next, and he recalled the shock and horror when he and Dawn were confronted by the Families Officer. He nodded to Martha and gave her that special look which doctors are so good at, the smile and frown at the same time which says I understand and I sympathise.

"Weeks went by. Joe and I sensed something wasn't right. Then the man called and told us the news... Our boy had gone missing..."

"Martha, let me tell you something." Michael moved his chair around so he was facing her, and he recounted how his precious daughter had also gone missing in Afghanistan, presumed killed, but by some miracle she had survived and was now back in England. He didn't want to raise her hopes too much for her own child, but he said it was possible that Rand could still be alive.

"Listen, son. We don't have no death certificate, but

mothers can tell these things. I know my boy is up there, and one day me and Joe will see him again – but not down here we won't."

"I'm so sorry. My condolences, to you and your husband. How long ago was it?"

"Years. It was two weeks before his twenty-fourth birthday. 2014. There. I've answered your question... Jack has no kids. No wife. Just us left."

"Thank you, Martha, that's been a great help. I'll put it on the family tree, so Rand won't be forgotten."

Michael knew he was getting carried away, but he thought it kinder not to rush off with the news and leave this brave woman with her sad memories. He was suitably rewarded.

"Now, son, I've got work to do, but if you need any papers, just ask Sam to get copies from our lawyers in town. They have my marriage certificate and the two birth records of my boys, Jack and Rand... Sam! Come on over here. This gentleman from England is making a family tree. Make sure he gets what he needs. Tell that lawyer to come and see me if I need to sign something."

"That's so kind," said Michael. "Those would be very useful. Thanks so much. Have a good day." Michael felt slightly embarrassed using the American expression. It didn't roll off the tongue as well when he said it.

That evening he phoned David, explaining in coded terms that he'd got more than enough to declare the mission a success. Hopefully, he'd have the paperwork in a day or two and would be back at base next week. He asked David to tell his daughter he'd got her email and was very grateful.

Unfortunately, his optimism on timings had been misplaced. The following morning, Sam explained to him over his hotel phone that in 'Pier' they didn't rush around like they do in New York. These things took a little time. Thursday was Sam's fishin' day, and come noon he'd be gone.

On Friday, Sam left a message for him in the hotel reception. The O'Brian's lawyer would see the couple on Monday to get their permission to release the certificates for copying. The copies would then be made and delivered to Sam Tuesday. Michael should pick them up Wednesday.

Postponing his flight to 'DC' to the following Thursday wasn't the problem Michael thought it would be, but getting one out of DC to Heathrow was more difficult. In the end, he settled for a take-off from Pierre on the Thursday with a flight out of Washington on the Friday evening. With any luck, he could make visiting hours at Bronzefield on the Saturday afternoon.

He was pleased with his progress until he read David's email with the bad news.

great news – – ptph has been brought forward very pleased for ms sake and well done for getting docs make sure u r at court tomorrow morning monday with them sharp at 830 am so we can have a discussion prior to start of proceedings at 1030 am

Simply not possible, thought Michael. He phoned David at home and they talked it through. David explained that if they lost the slot for the preliminary hearing, the trial could be postponed indefinitely as the prospect of a verdict before Christmas would be zero. It would have to go ahead on Monday. He'd have to wing it until Michael returned with the certificates and then ask special permission to submit them as evidence if they were needed.

He repeated his concern that the Prosecution might try to show that Melanie had fabricated Rand's emails – and his very existence – in order to escape justice. The marriage certificate would scotch this by showing she could not have invented the names of Rand's parents which appeared in the bio he'd emailed to her.

He then explained that Rand's birth certificate would – obviously – prove he was born. As for his death, David had listened to the sad tale, then asked him if the mother had offered a death certificate.

"No. If it's the same as it is in UK, one wouldn't have been issued until his death had been confirmed – or seven years had passed."

"I'll be straight with you, Michael. The *last* thing we want is his death certificate."

"Why? Are you suggesting he might still be alive?"

"I'm not suggesting anything. I'm merely pointing out that the evidence we will submit to the court will show that he was born and he *could* still be alive, and he *could* have sent those emails to Melanie. More importantly, if he is still alive, he *could* be the murderer. Remember, we don't have to prove it. All we have to do is convince the jury that someone other than Melanie *could* have killed Mr Bretton-Willis. And I think Rand fits the bill very nicely."

"But what about Melly? Assuming he did survive and had gone into deep cover, the last thing she wants is for him to be incriminated."

"Michael. I don't think either you or Melanie need worry about that. If he's what he said he is, his cover is very deep. I do have an IT specialist trying to trace him, but so far she's drawn a blank. He's covered his tracks well, and I don't think the police stand a chance of finding him."

"Is that good or bad?" asked Michael.

"Depends whose side you're on," said David, making it sound like a game.

"David, could you fix up for me to see her? I'll be landing at Heathrow on Saturday morning, so that afternoon would be great."

David assured him that he would arrange the visit with the prison staff and Melanie.

Michael felt terrible. The wheels of justice were beginning to turn, and there he was, trapped in the American Mid-West, with no way of getting back in time. But he was pleased he'd got the vital evidence, and he reckoned that the only secure way of getting it to David was delivering the documents himself. If he could present them in person, at least he could recount to the court how they came to be in his possession.

He was sorry he would not have the chance to talk to Melly before the hearing, to reassure her and tell her not to be afraid – like he used to when she was little, on winters' nights when it was dark outside. Christ, man, he said to himself, she's a grown woman. If anyone was apprehensive it was him.

Chapter 20

Sam said a 'logistics error' had delayed the copying of the vital documents. Fortunately, Michael was able to pick them up early from his office on the Thursday morning before checking out of his hotel.

In the cab on the way to the airport, he opened the envelope and perused the contents. All three documents were there, Martha's marriage certificate and her sons' birth records. They were stamped and signed by the O'Brians' attorney as being true copies of the originals. Also in the envelope was an invoice for $124.50, less the $100 on account making a total of $24.50. Michael made a mental note to settle it online as soon as he got back to Beechwood Hall.

In the departures lounge, he had time to read the early morning email from David which he had printed out at the hotel. It was a report on the plea and trial preparation hearing. Much to Michael's relief, it had been written by David's assistant who had been there taking notes. She knew about things like punctuation.

It began by saying that on the first morning, after the customary introductions and identifications, Melanie gave her plea of not guilty in a clear voice. For someone who had just come from prison, she looked remarkably well turned out, with freshly brushed hair, manicured nails, clean and ironed clothes and just a touch of make-up.

Then it outlined the main points made by the junior counsel for the CPS in her opening statement. She began by describing to the judge how the newly elected MP had been found murdered in the bathroom of his apartment. There was no sign of a break-in, and the only window open was four floors up. Either the victim knew his attacker and let her in, or they had a key.

She believed the crime had been planned in great detail, well in advance and carried out with the intention not only of killing the poor man but also of making him suffer in the most horrific way. There was no sign of a struggle, and the defendant had taken great care not to leave any fingerprints or traces of DNA.

She pointed out that none of the accepted forms of defence was valid. Evidently, self-defence could not be cited, and to carry out such a meticulously planned killing the defendant could not claim she lost control or had diminished responsibility. And both sides had ruled out any form of a failed suicide pact.

She told the judge the defendant had a strong motive and had spoken of her intentions to kill him to a number of people, some of whom would be called as witnesses. She would provide written evidence of how she was driven by rage to take the law into her own hands and commit this most horrible of crimes. The prosecution would call witnesses who would testify as to the defendant's medical knowledge and ability which were needed to carry out the deed, and witnesses who will give evidence that the accused had access to the medical and other paraphernalia required to carry out the crime.

She said Sir David might try to claim the evidence was 'merely circumstantial', but she assured the judge that when all of it was put together, it would point to one conclusion only, and that was the guilt of the defendant.

The counsel ended her statement saying that one might be tempted to conclude a deed of that nature could only have been committed by someone who was criminally insane. But the CPS would be calling an expert witness who will testify that the defendant was perfectly responsible for her actions and, although she had experienced trauma in the past, she was mentally fit enough to be tried and convicted of murder.

Michael had to stop reading. It sounded to him as if

the whole thing had got off to a bad start. But he was pleased Melanie was confident and looking smart. He returned to the email, hoping for some good news in the Statement for the Defence.

David had begun it by echoing the Prosecution's revulsion of the crime, agreeing it was indeed an especially cruel way to finish a life. He would not be contesting the forensic investigator's report, nor the postmortem's findings. He agreed his client had a strong motive for killing the man and that he would be explaining this in detail to the jury during the course of the trial. He agreed she had the medical knowledge needed; she was a doctor. He agreed she possibly had access to the medical devices the murderer used and the hardware required to carry out the killing. And he agreed that although she had suffered serving her country in the war in Afghanistan, she was mentally fit to stand trial.

But he told the judge that wishing someone dead was not the same as killing them, and his witnesses would show that his client would not hurt anyone, let alone kill someone in cold blood. Through the course of this trial, he would show that all the evidence for the Prosecution was circumstantial, and while the Prosecution might claim it all pointed to his client, he would show it could equally well point to others. A jury could not be sure it was her. They would have no option but to find her not guilty.

David ended his statement by telling the judge that the Prosecution was grasping at straws and had no DNA, no fingerprints, no positive ID, in fact nothing to link his client to the crime And he respectfully asked for the case to be dismissed at this early stage, rather than waste everyone's time and money, bearing in mind the pressures on the justice system. His client was at that moment – despite being innocent of any crime – behind bars at Bronzefield costing the tax-payer over £200 each day.

The judge said no. David didn't look surprised, but Michael reckoned it had rattled the junior counsel for the prosecution and dented her confidence.

The report finished by citing the two main issues of the case identified at the hearing and agreed by the two sides: whether the defendant had an intention to kill the victim, or merely wanted him dead; and whether there were others besides the defendant who had the means, motive and opportunity to carry out the crime. A trial date of 16th November had been proposed.

The other email waiting for Michael was from Melanie. Like the first one, it was a long one, so he decided to print it off and read it on the plane during the five-hour flight to Washington.

28/09/19
Hi Dad – this is your daughter, writing from Her

Majesty's Holiday Camp Bronzy. It's Sunday, and they've told me I'm due in court tomorrow to tell them I'm not guilty – for the umpteenth time – so I thought I'd dash off a few lines now to let you know how things are moving.

David's been great, and yesterday we had a conference here with Mark, the chappy David has chosen to defend me. Nice guy, tall, dark hair, imposing with a strong stare. Public school, loud voice and over-confident. Mum would have called him dashing. All I can say is I'm pleased he's not persecuting me, as I could find myself going down for a very long time.

Mark and David both think the case for the Prosecution is weak, despite seeing the statements from the witnesses. Of course it's weak, I told them, because I didn't do it. Apparently the witnesses are mainly testifying to what I have said, or written in my emails to Rand, or moaned about to that Facebook group. God knows how the police got hold of those, but David did warn me they might. We're leaving Rand out of it, at least for the moment.

Bob's been coming every other day. He's been helping me relax, and taking me through my meditation exercises. They really work, and according to his Lordship my anxiety level is at an all-time low.

It's strange to think I'll be in court again tomorrow – exciting in a way. It'll only be for a day, but David says the CPS is trying to get an early trial date. Apparently, they are under a great deal of pressure to lock me up and throw away the key. Actually, I'm looking forward to it as it will be a new experience.

Having said that, I'm not looking forward to leaving here. Stupid thing to say, but it's my work. I'm still under supervision, but I'm being kept busy. If someone gets an injury of any kind, they call me, as they think I know it all, having patched people up in a war zone. Little do they know I'm bluffing half the time. We have a saying in the Army that to be an officer, you have to 'talk cock with confidence'. So that's what I do. People perform better if they think the person in charge knows what they're doing. Not that I'm in charge, but sometimes they ask me for my opinion. Even if it's little-old-me who doesn't really have a clue.

I get on well with the prisoners. When I first arrived they'd ask me what I was in for. I'd say, 'I'm on remand'. Then they'd usually ask what the charge was, and I'd look them in the eye and say, 'for murdering the slime-ball who killed my husband and baby, kidnapped me, drugged me and raped me'. You can imagine the reaction. Some would ask me if I'd done it, and I would just smile, raise my eyebrows and walk away.

Nobody asks me any more. I think the word must have got around. And I never get any aggro. People are nice to me. Even the screws are pleasant, despite the terrible industrial relations which seem to dog this place. You know it's privately run? I'm not sure that's a good thing for something like a prison.

I've only been here a week or so – and I'm no authority on our justice system – but I wonder if we've got it wrong. I know we send people to prison for different reasons, to punish, to reform, to rehabilitate, to deter and to protect the public, but in trying to do all of these things we fail miserably to achieve most of them. Okay, we protect the public by banging up violent criminals, but most of the girls here are not violent and are no threat to society at all. They're just unfortunates who for one reason or another have fallen foul of the law. Many of them have a drug problem when they arrive. And some aren't here long enough to have it cured. Sad, that. Ironic that for them a longer sentence would be in their best interests. Some don't want to be cured. Drugs help them handle it, the claustrophobia and insomnia – double time, they call it, if you can't sleep.

The inmates here have warm and dry accommodation, security, good food, clean water, rest and friendship – Hertzberg's hierarchy of basic needs – then some: TV, good medical care, an opportunity to work, and a chance to better oneself through education and training. Not surprisingly, some of the girls love it here; it's the best thing that's ever happened to them. They're safe from abusive partners, and from the horrors of sleeping rough. But for others, the picture can be very different. Some are self-harming and suicidal because they've lost their job, their home, their partner, their children, their reputation, their friends or their self-respect. Or in some cases the lot. Prison has ruined their lives. It's so sad.

This is the point: you could have two girls who get

the same prison sentence for the same offence. Seems fair, but for one, it's a life changing opportunity for the better, the chance to get clean, learn a skill and return to the big wide world and survive or even thrive without breaking the law. For the other, incarceration could drive her to take her own life. How can that be a just punishment when its effect on the individual can be so hugely different?

Take deterrence. I'm told nearly half of all prisoners re-offend. In a place like this, life's so easy that for some the thought of coming back here is no deterrent at all. For them, it's like putting on a warm overcoat on a cold day, like coming home. They lose their liberty, but who cares about liberty if all it means is freedom to choose which doorway to sleep in or litter-bin to rummage through?

I'll tell you what deterrence is. It's chopping off the hand of someone who steals. Barbaric and brutal. But during my time in Aff, did I ever see someone without a hand? No. Not once. Why not? Because nobody steals.

Lots of girls here are in for nicking of one sort or another. If they lived in Afghanistan, many of them would not have become thieves in the first place.

In my village, there's virtually no crime – and I'm sure that's true in any Pashtun rural community. It's because under the Pashtunwali code – remember? – anyone who commits a crime can expect retribution from the victim or his family to match the harm done. Which can be the payment of compensation, or death. Revenge is very much a part of the justice system. And it deters, believe me.

I'm not sure about the 'turn the other cheek' philosophy in Western societies. I can understand its merits, in that it stops feuds and tit-for-tat crimes, but if you literally turn the other cheek you're likely to get it Stanley-knifed as well. And if nobody casts the first stone, at either guilty party, male or female, adultery inevitably becomes rife with all its tragic consequences; it was forbidden by the Ten Commandments for a reason.

Don't get me wrong. I'm not saying everything about the Pashtunwali is right or good, but it's been going for thousands of years and sort-of works. In my view, the justice system here in the UK sort-of doesn't work. It's broken.

I'm about to try it, so wish me luck.

Your loving daughter,

Melly xxxx

P.S. A gorgeous baby girl, by the way, just under 3kgs. Absolutely lovely. Both doing well.

Chapter 21

Two thousand kilometres of rolling prairies later, Michael landed at Dulles International Airport in good time for his ride into the jaws of possible death waiting for him in his own country. At least they can't get at Melanie, he thought, as he recalled Harry's warnings. Perhaps the man was being over-dramatic, or he'd been sent by Smedley merely to put the frighteners on Melanie's dad in the hope he'd persuade her to deny all knowledge of the attack. True, her denial would remove her motive for killing the major. More importantly for Smedley, it would also prevent news of the massacre leaking out into the public domain.

As he checked into the gate, he recognised the woman immediately, even though her head was buried in a book. It was the Baltimore grandma whom he'd sat next to on the way over. With two hours to kill before take-off, she was a welcome sight, sitting there on her own with an empty seat beside her.

His heart missed a beat as he approached her. She raised her head and looked at him, then broke into a broad grin. For him, it wasn't the smile so much as the eyes – the windows of the soul. They gave him a funny sort of feeling he hadn't had for a long time. He dismissed it as the last vestiges of some primaeval urge which had no business to be there in a man of his age.

"Hi, on your way back to London, then?" Such a stupid question, he thought, as the words tumbled from his mouth.

"Yes," she said, "I am, actually," and she smiled and closed her book. "And you? Or have you come to the wrong gate?"

The laughter from both of them broke the ice, and she patted on the seat next to her to indicate he was welcome to use it. They exchanged notes on their respective holidays and swapped stories of their experiences of all things American, including the people – as if two weeks in the country had made them experts on the subject. When the tannoy announced the two-hour delay, they both groaned without meaning it, and Michael suggested they should go and find something to eat.

By the time they boarded the plane, they had crossed the line between acquaintance and friendship, so it was with some mutual regret that they parted company on entering the aircraft to take their respective seats at different ends of the economy cabin.

Half an hour into the flight, the pilot asked on the PA system that dreaded question which no doctor wants to hear: is there one of them in the house? However, there was nothing to keep him shoe-horned into his economy seat, so he unfurled himself and went to report to a flight attendant.

It had been a simple procedure, re-inserting a catheter into an elderly gentleman, but the patient was much relieved in both senses of the word. The captain of the aircraft was also relieved, as Michael's intervention had saved him from having to return to Dulles Airport after dumping much fuel into the Atlantic Ocean. He expressed his appreciation by asking Michael if he and his partner would like to move to the front of the plane as there were two empty places in First Class.

They felt like naughty children who had sneaked into some forbidden sanctuary, quietly giggling at their good fortune as the immaculate flight attendant led them to their seats-cum-flat-beds. There was no way they were going to miss it; they'd have to pretend they were together. But after a couple of aperitifs, they relaxed into their roles and made the most of the hospitality on offer.

They agreed the meal was first-class without realising the double meaning, and talked well into the night, determined not to waste a moment of their new-found luxury by falling asleep. But fall asleep they did, eventually, side by side and head to toe, with the privacy screen stowed, each wrapped in their own blanket and being extra careful not to intrude on one another's space as the cabin lights dimmed and the personal reading lights around them were switched off one by one. It was nevertheless a highly intimate situation in which they found themselves – for a couple who hardly knew each other.

As they stepped out of the aircraft into the jet-bridge leading to the terminal building, the flight attendant, immaculate in her full uniform-for-landing, overheard Michael say to his attractive and elegant partner: "By the way, my name's Michael."

"And mine's Celia" was the reply. The flight attendant just looked at them with her head slightly to one side and smiled, as if to say, it's okay, I've seen it all before.

The cold and damp of a grey September morning jolted Michael out of his energy-sapping, east-about dose of jet-lag, back to the reality of his situation as he climbed out of the warm taxi at Beechwood Hall. It was Saturday, so nothing much would be happening trial-wise. His daughter would be back at Bronzefield for the weekend having endured the preliminary hearing on a charge of murder. He had read David's report of the opening statements but had no idea of how matters had progressed from then on. He would hear David's version of events on Monday, but he looked forward to visiting Melanie that afternoon and hearing her side of the story.

He was relieved to find his guest suite had not been broken into, but was frustrated when he realised he had no means of getting in. Following the mini-fire, Reception was back up and running in the main building, and Siobhan smiled as he stumbled through his improvised explanation before giving him a temporary pass.

On returning to his room, he emptied his cabin bag and briefcase, showered and changed, and after lowering his consciousness level for a quick forty, he went out to the visitors' car-park. His rental car was there, and having checked there were no bombs underneath it – like they do in films – he set off for HMP Bronzefield.

He arrived in good time for his four o'clock appointment, ahead of the statutory half-hour in advance. He reported to the Visitors Reception

Centre, only to find that they required two forms of identity and proof of address. He just had his Irish passport with him, but a few heartbeats later he remembered his driving licence was in the glove compartment of the rental car and he quickly went back to get it.

"Hi, Dad! Good to see you. Did you get my emails?"

"Good to see you, too. Yes, I did get them. Many thanks, they were fascinating. You seem to have settled in all right."

"Sure. I've been in much worse. But tell me about your trip. David told me you'd swanned off to the States. How did that go?"

"Did he tell you why I went?"

"No. He said once you got back, you'd report to me. I liked that!"

"Well, I tracked down Rand's parents. In South Dakota. Or at least his mum."

"Wow. What's she like? Is she a trained assassin, too?"

"No, Melly. Just a mum who's lost one of her two sons, sadly."

"Let me guess which one. Rand?"

"First time. But the good news is he is – or was – a real person and not a figment of your imagination."

"Figment of my imagination? You mean you didn't believe me?"

"No, Darling. I mean, yes, of course I believed you.

We both did, David and me. He was worried the Prosecution would try and persuade the jury that you'd made it all up."

"Why would I want to do that?"

"Remember, they're trying to prove you killed the MP. It's their job. And we've got to stop them. Anyway, how did it go? I had a thing from David's office about the hearing, and I thought it finished rather well. Were you happy with it?"

"Yeah. I suppose so. I'm new to all this. To be honest, I took an immediate dislike to the Prosecution's attitude. Then having heard David lay into him at his summing up, I realised that both sides are liable to be, shall we say, combative.

"Now, that's enough about me, let's talk about you. Tell me about Rand's mum." Melanie glanced at the wall clock. "We don't want to run out of time."

"I'll be brief. All went well, and she arranged for me to have copies of her marriage certificate and her sons' birth certificates."

"Why the other son? He's got nothing to do with any of this."

Michael felt himself redden. "I didn't want to alarm her, so I said I was compiling a family tree. Her name's O'Brian with an 'a'."

"I see. So you tricked her."

Michael felt a change of subject was called for. "And

I must tell you what happened on the flight back. We got upgraded, to First Class!"

"Really?" Melanie frowned at her father.

"Yes. Don't you believe me?"

"Of course I do. It's that you just said 'we'. Girlfriend, boyfriend, secret significant other?"

"Don't be so silly. Just someone I met on the way out. Don't look like that, Melanie. She's a grandmother. She was visiting her son and daughter-in-law in Baltimore."

"So are you seeing her again?"

"Oh really, Melly, all these questions... I want to hear more about the trial preparations."

"Not much more to tell. I think David doesn't want to worry 'my pretty little head' about it all. He's that type. Of a certain age."

Like me, Michael thought. He realised he would have to get chapter and verse from the man himself. All would become clear, he thought, when I deliver the documents on Monday.

Chapter 22

"Well done," said David, "these are just what we need. I'm glad they're signed and stamped, as the other side won't be able to quibble about them."

It was Monday, 5th October. They were sitting in David's London Office. Steady rain pattered on the window trying to get in. Michael watched him quickly scanning the certificates, glad that he had contributed in some small way to Melanie's defence. It had been nearly four weeks since he had sat down in that room and handed across her file. He recalled David's predictions: that his daughter might be questioned under caution; that she could be arrested and charged; and that she might have to go to court. They'd all come true.

"So, what's next?"

"Well, we are now waiting for the trial date to be confirmed. The CPS was hoping it would all be over by now, but that would have only happened with a guilty plea. Poor Melanie, what an ordeal."

"Which reminds me," said Michael, "I saw her on Saturday, and she didn't seem too bad. She's helping out in the medical centre – mothers and babies unit – and doesn't seem too stressed about it. Thanks for fixing up the appointment, by the way."

"A pleasure. Remember, if she seemed cheerful it was probably because she was happy to see you and didn't want to worry you. Don't be fooled. Prison is not fun. I can assure you of that."

Thanks, thought Michael, that's really cheered me up.

"Let's get back to the time-table," said David, rubbing his hands. "We managed to get the Defence Statement away on time, following the receipt of the indictment. Then we went into bat at the PTPH – that's the Plea and Trial Preparation Hearing. I trust you got Caroline's summary. It all went well, I'm pleased to say, and we have been warned for trial during the last two weeks in November."

"Why does it take so long?" said Michael, anxious that the whole thing should be over as soon as possible.

"Well, for one thing, each side must contact all their witnesses to make sure they can attend the trial. November's a good month as few people are on holiday. Fortunately, we don't think it will be a marathon, so agreeing a date will be that much easier – and squeezing in a short trial is easier than a long-drawn-out one."

"But I thought these things could drag on for months, especially one for murder."

"Yes, they can indeed. But this case, although very serious, is not complicated. At the hearing, we all agreed that it came down to just the two issues. The first is whether Melanie *really* had the intention to carry out the crime – bearing in mind it must have taken some planning. The second is whether anyone else had the means, motive and opportunity to murder the man."

"Surely a person cannot be convicted if there's no evidence to link them to the scene of the crime?"

"You'd be surprised. They don't need a crime scene. They don't even need a body. Let me refer you to Regina v Shirley and Lynette Banfield, a mother and daughter who were given life sentences in 2012 for the murder of the husband and father, Don Banfield. There was no body, no suggested mechanism of death, no identified day when the murder was said to have occurred, no time and no place and no suggestion of what happened to the body."

"Bloody hell. You're kidding! And they got life?"

"I know, it's frightening, but google it if you don't believe me. It was a miscarriage of justice. Thank God it was put right in the end, but a jury did convict them.

You see, circumstantial evidence is enough for a guilty verdict if it can be interpreted in only one way. And that's what the jury was told. Happily, in Melanie's case, the circumstantial evidence *can* be interpreted in another way, namely that Rand did the deed. That's why it's so important we must prove to the jury – if we have to – that this fellow Rand was real and had the motive, the means and the opportunity. Remember, we don't have to prove he *committed* the crime.

"We can prove he's real by showing them his birth certificate. We can show he had the motive – of helping this poor soul you see standing in the dock – by showing the jury his emails. As for means and opportunity, he could well be the trained assassin he claims to be, living in London waiting for his next assignment, and he could well have purchased the fish hooks and wire from any one of hundreds of tackle shops in the South-East. We don't have to prove these things. All we have to do is show they are possibilities."

"Thanks, David. I appreciate that reassurance. So at what stage in the proceedings will you produce those certificates?"

"Not sure. Bearing in mind Melanie's wishes, about keeping Rand out of it, I think we'll keep them in reserve and only use them if we need to." David looked at his watch. "Now, I have a surprise for you!"

"Nice one, I hope?"

"I think you'll be impressed. We'd better get our skates on."

The two of them stepped out onto a wet London pavement below a gloomy dark-grey sky. The cabbie opened the rear door automatically allowing his fares to climb inside quickly, and as they closed it, he pulled out into the slow-moving traffic. Ten minutes later they were outside Fabio's, an Italian restaurant renowned for its *risotto ai funghi* and extensive wine list.

Mark Issijay was waiting in reception, a handsome man, tall and slim, wearing a well-fitting suit and a silk tie. He smiled at David and then turned to Michael. "You must be Dr Green. I'm Mark. It's a pleasure to meet you, sir."

"And to meet you, Mark," said Michael extending his hand. A young man, he thought, at least compared with himself and David. A good head of hair, growing grey at the temples. He put him at forty-five.

David briefly put an avuncular arm around Mark's shoulders. "This is the young man I've chosen to represent Melanie," he said, "the best of the best!"

Mark looked appropriately modest.

"Glad to hear it," said Michael. "I think my daughter has already worked that out."

Fabio himself came to greet the trio and show them to their table, returning moments later with three wine lists and three menus, leather-bound and heavy.

During the meal, Michael had to ask Mark the question, how does a barrister defend someone he knows is guilty. Both Mark and David smiled and looked at each other. Mark began by saying it was a question he'd been asked many times.

The two lawyers together explained that the English system of justice was an adversarial one, in that each side had a particular job to do. The prosecution had to try and prove to the jury – not the judge – that the accused had committed the crime by presenting evidence, while the job of the Defence was to challenge it and demonstrate to the jury that the evidence did not show guilt beyond reasonable doubt. What each counsel thought about the guilt of the accused didn't enter the equation.

"And it works!" said Mark, leaning back on his chair.

"Just three things I would add," said David, "having worked with and observed many silks over the years, is that the confrontation between the counsels you see in court is rarely personal. They appreciate they each have a job to do. It's rather like two professional tennis players. They play their shots in the hope that their opponent will lose the point, but at the end of the game, they shake hands and look forward to the next match.

"The second point is that the confrontation isn't quite the battle it seems. There are rules. For example, you're not allowed to introduce an argument without giving your opponent due notice. Going back to tennis, you don't serve if your opponent's not ready. Having said that, I would add that drop shots, volleys and slices are all part of the game."

"I should add," said Mark, "that we barristers are just the front men. Most of the heavy lifting is done by our solicitors." He smiled at David.

David smiled back and lowered his eyes. After a glug at his glass, he continued. "My last point – and I think Mark will agree – is that a barrister will not accept a case if the accused has told him of his guilt. It would be dishonest to do so. The overriding principle is that both sides should work towards the common aim of achieving justice."

After the expensive Barolo – just the two bottles between the three of them – followed by the compulsory home-made on-the-house Limoncello, Michael was pleased he had come by train.

He had enjoyed meeting Mark and found it fascinating to hear how barristers operate. He was pleased he asked how a barrister defends someone they know is guilty – not that it was relevant in Melanie's case; no way. But he wished he asked the other question: how does a barrister prosecute someone they know is innocent?

It was interesting to hear and could understand why

Melanie had been happy to have him on her team. He looked forward to telling her he'd met him, but it would have to wait until his next visit. It had been arranged for the following afternoon, after his lunch in Tunbridge Wells with his new friend he'd met on the plane.

When he'd phoned Celia the previous day, it had been her idea that they met down there, as she was at an art class all morning. He could easily make it to Bronzefield on time by whipping around the M25. He was hoping Melanie would approve, but until it happened, he wouldn't decide whether or not to let on.

Despite the good news about Mark, he appreciated that the meeting with Melly would be a sad one, as in the evening he would be flying back to La Manga. Daniela had emailed him pleading with him to return, as two of his colleagues had taken holidays and one was off sick. Michael's immediate thought was that the fellow should see a doctor, but he knew he should do the decent thing and report back for duty. He'd already been away for a month, and apart from enjoying nice lunches with David, he realised there was little left for him to do in the furtherance of his daughter's innocence.

Another thought occurred to him. If his pub lunch with Celia the next day did not go well, his return to Spain that evening might not be a bad thing. It would allow either of them to slide away gently – should they wish to – without causing hurt to the other. If it did go well, him flying away might cool things down a touch and allow both parties to reflect on what might come next.

He rose early the next morning, giving himself plenty of time to pack all his things and check out of his guest suite. But his plans were nearly thwarted because he'd mislaid Melanie's file. He searched everywhere for it, his main case and his cabin bag, his bedside drawer where he'd left his Brit passport and the drawer of the small desk underneath the window.

He was surprised it wasn't in his briefcase, then he remembered he'd emptied everything out before flying to America. He cursed himself for his stupidity when he recalled he'd emptied it into the drawer in the wardrobe. He smiled as he opened the wardrobe door and pulled out the drawer. Inside was a two-week-old newspaper, an airport paperback he'd given up on, a New Statesman, a free Holiday Inn pen, a half-empty packet of tissues, a half-full tube of mints, an unopened box of English shortbread for Daniela, a Lancet he'd been meaning to read – and nothing else.

Chapter 23

When Michael returned to Spain, one of the first things he did was to make the on-line payment to Sam. All twenty-four dollars fifty of it. He emailed him a short note thanking him for his help and saying he was making good progress with the O'Brian family tree. If he were ever in Pierre again, he would come and look him up.

Next he sent Celia a postcard, as promised, from sunny La Manga. It evoked an immediate response, much to his delight, with a notelet saying she was pleased he got back safely and how much she enjoyed the lunch. It wasn't the sort of communication you get from someone who never wants to see you again.

And so the correspondence began. No more than a letter or two each week and the occasional postcard. It was only natural they progressed onto more informal text messages, as it was so easy to send pictures you'd taken yourself – or even a clip of something you'd seen happening, perhaps a beautiful sunset, or waves crashing on a beach.

Celia wasn't anybody particularly special; just a friend whom he might drop in on – should he ever be passing within a few hundred miles of Tunbridge Wells. But knowing that someone, somewhere, might be thinking of him gave him a little buzz of excitement. It made him realise how sorry he was that Melanie was alone in the world. It did cross his mind that the handsome, intelligent Mark Issijay might float her boat, but he appreciated that a good-looking and successful man like Mark would have been snapped up by now. Anyway, he was probably too old for her by a good fifteen years. He would be a dribbly old man when she was still gadding about reforming the world.

As for David, he kept in contact by phone when there were questions to be asked or news to pass on. But it became clear to Michael that David and Mark had the thing sewn up; it was just a matter of waiting for the trial to commence. Michael asked if Mark was still managing to see something of his... er... family. David replied that he didn't have one.

Life at Bronzefield continued to suit Melanie, as amply demonstrated by her lengthy emails. Having heeded David's words about her putting on a brave face, he always read her letters carefully to see if he could detect a chink in her armour. There wasn't. Of course, David was right to say prison is no fun. But Michael realised that if you're on remand and innocent, there was no burden of guilt to bear, no shame to sap your confidence, no disgrace, no sleep-depriving concerns that your friends would desert you or your loved-ones would stop visiting, leaving you alone in the world. And in her case no worry that you might be unemployed when they eventually kicked you out, back into the big wide horrible western world, rife with crime and drugs.

He was fascinated by her stories. Some were wonderful, about human strength and kindness; others had a humorous side. Several were tragic, but what Michael found uplifting was that in every sad tale, Melanie found something which was positive and good. She made friends among the staff and the 'residents', as they were called. And sometimes, her position as an 'in-betweeny' – a 'resident' yet on remand and working as a medic – enabled her to oil away the friction which would occasionally occur when one side or another would rub each other up the wrong way.

She told him about the conferences she had with David and Mark. He thought it was a grand word for the getting together of just the three of them, but when he mentioned this in one of his emails, she replied that it was a legal term. Michael himself was trying to bone up on the law in his spare time, but he became concerned that his daughter was not only catching up in this respect, but overtaking him. He'd have to try harder.

Another subject which stole a significant portion of his spare time during the long wait was Afghanistan. If he were to go there with Melly after the trial, he should get his head around the salient points of the Nation's history, culture and politics in case she asked him questions.

Come off it, he had to tell himself, she's miles ahead of you already. She'd lived there for three and a bit years, not in a big, modern international city which could be almost anywhere on the planet, but in a primitive mountain village high up in the foothills of the enchanting Hindu Kush. It was an area of the planet untouched by modern civilisation and unsullied by tourism, where little had changed for hundreds of years, where communities lived hard lives, but under their own code, sovereign to themselves.

He read up about the Pashtunwali, the code of life, as Melanie had termed it, still followed by many Pashtuns, especially in the more remote parts of the country. As a doctor, he could not contemplate the amputation of a person's hand as a punishment, but he had to admit the threat of it was probably enough for it to be an effective deterrent. He felt rather smug that neither his home country nor the one he now lived in relied on such barbaric threats to control crime. But then a thought struck him. Oh yes, they do. Especially Spain.

Having married a Roman Catholic, he had gone along with the teachings of Dawn's religion but had stopped short of becoming one. However, he was well aware of the fear, drummed into Catholics from an early age, of suffering eternal punishment in the fires of hell, should you transgress and not receive absolution. Neat, he thought, because the responsibility for judging guilt and awarding such a dreadful punishment lay not with the government or the officers of the Catholic Church but with a higher authority.

Clever, he thought, because the punishment is not administered until you die, so unlike amputation, nobody suffers physically. So if they do turn out to be innocent, there's no harm done. On the other hand, as his legal friend would say, there's no-one walking around handless to deter others who might be tempted to steal.

Michael reckoned the main weakness in the concept was that post-mortem punishment is only a deterrent if you believe in an afterlife. And getting people to do that takes some doing. But if you are a believer, there's always the danger you'll die in torment, terrified that somehow or other you had upset your god at some time during your life and would thus suffer eternal damnation. He'd watched a few of those: not a nice way to go.

But Melly was not going to be punished, because she hadn't committed any crime, and once her trial was over, she would walk free. Unless there was a miscarriage of justice, and he had read up on a number of those. Fortunately – or unfortunately – many of those tragic tales were in the public domain. Michael had taken David's advice and googled the Banfield case. That took him down the rabbit hole to the unfortunate Colin Stag, Barry George and others, all of whom had been wrongly convicted of murder, not several hundred years ago in the early days of British justice, but in the last twenty-five.

To his relief, the long-awaited confirmation of the trial date came on Wednesday, 11th November 2019, when David phoned up to tell him to get over there, as the trial would start on Monday at the Central Criminal Court in London at 10.30 am sharp. Michael had to look it up. He knew it by its nickname, the very mention of which could strike terror into the hearts of even the most righteous: The Old Bailey.

Daniela was delighted to make all the arrangements, and was thrilled at Michael's promise that she could take the whole of the Christmas period off, as he would be back well before then and would be on standby should any customers come their way. He said he wouldn't need a car in London, providing she could find him an Airbnb near St. Paul's. He would use taxis and tubes in the city – and the train down to Tunbridge Wells – should he decide to go there.

The following day he received an A4 sized air-mail envelope addressed to him by hand and bearing the stamps of the United States. Inside was a handwritten note from Sam, hoping he was well and that the O'Brian family tree was bearing fruit. Get it? he said. He hoped the enclosed would help with the good work, but he realised it would be sad news for Michael and other members of the family.

Michael studied Rand's death certificate, a single sheet of closely packed boxes containing all manner of detail. He felt sorry for Martha, and he hoped he hadn't raised her expectations by telling her about Melanie. If he did ever go back to Pierre – which he admitted was unlikely – he would drop in and see her.

At first, he was grateful to Sam for sending it on but then remembered what David had said: the *last* thing he wanted was Rand's death certificate. He was in a tricky position. Did he take the certificate and give it to David? Did he leave it in Spain and not ever mention it? Or tell David about it and destroy it?

He understood the argument, that the Defence needed to prove Rand was real and could have carried out the murder, and while he didn't want to conceal anything from his friend and legal advisor to Melanie, he didn't want to put David or Mark in the difficult position of concealing evidence or lying about it in court. In the end, he decided to leave the certificate behind.

He assumed the trial would take the two weeks which David had estimated, from the 12th to 28th November, but he asked Daniela to leave the return arrangements open in case the hearing took longer – or he decided to pop in and see the odd friend or two.

In all his communications with Celia, from when they first spoke to each over above the wastes of Greenland to their recent email exchange, he'd never mentioned his daughter's predicament. It was not that he was a coward – more like he didn't trust himself to explain it without making his daughter out to be some psychopath who'd killed a respected member of the establishment.

He decided to grasp the nettle there and then by writing an email to her. He'd make it look as if he'd dashed it off, between patients, so it appeared less like a signed confession, and he'd spare her the alarming details. However, it was many hours before he had a version he was happy with:

Hi Celia – many thanks for the pictures of your two grandchildren. They look wonderful kids, and you must be very proud of them. I'm glad you liked the one of Melly. That was taken a few years ago now, when she was on leave, but she's the same old Mel, full of life.

I must say it was a surprise for us when she joined the Royal Army Medical Corps. Although I'm a medic myself, nobody in my family, or in Dawn's, has ever had anything to do with the Army; at least not since the Second World War. But it was no surprise to us when she got posted to Afghanistan. Everyone in the forces seemed to be doing their fair share out there. She loved it, the country, the people and the job which gave her professional and personal fulfilment.

But in the fog of war strange things can happen, and indeed a strange thing happened to our girl: she went out in a helicopter to bring in a casualty and got left behind. She took shelter in a remote community and treated their sick and injured, until one day a special forces team raided the village and Melanie was mistaken for a deserter. The British officer leading the raid took her prisoner, interrogated her and mistreated her – rather brutally I'm afraid – but a couple of years later she was back in England suffering from PTSD but physically in good shape.

She decided to report him, having seen him on the news as a new MP, but then he died in suspicious circumstances in London and – naturally – Melanie was suspected. Not that she'd ever do anything like that, but the police had to go through the motions. As you can imagine, she wants to clear her name, and the opportunity for her to do this formally in court has come up next week. Quite an ordeal, but as her dad

I want to be there to give her any support should she need it.

Which means I'll be coming over and staying in London for a while. It will be nice to be in England again and meet up with some old friends. My days might be a bit busy but I could find myself at a loose end in the evenings. There is a musical I'd love to see, and a new play which has had good reviews. It might not be the sort of thing that would interest you, but if you did fancy an evening out, I'd be very happy if you cared to join me.

Very best wishes,
Michael

His mouse-pointer hovered over 'Send' as he wondered if he should check it for a final time. All was in order – except he noticed that after his name, at the bottom of the letter, was a garble of words, sentence fragments, punctuation marks and part-paragraphs which he rejected in his attempt to strike the right note. Having deleted those, his forefinger made the commitment. Publish and be damned, he thought.

The response was enthusiastic. Celia's casual mention of Bretton-Willis took him aback. She'd read about his death, but the general opinion from 'disgusted of Tunbridge Wells' – the collective view from dinner party prattle, from friends of friends who knew him at school or at Sandhurst or had served alongside him in his regiment – was that he was a wrong'un. She wished Michael and his daughter good luck and said she looked forward 'very much' to meeting him in London if the opportunity arose and he could spare the time.

Chapter 24

The Airbnb was perfect, located five minutes walk from the court. It had a double bedroom and a study with a put-you-up. He arrived on the Sunday morning, allowing him the afternoon to do a dummy walk to the Old Bailey and locate the Capable Travel Company. The last thing he wanted to do was get lost and be late on the first morning.

How English, he thought. If you go to the public gallery of the Old Bailey, you can't take in any electronic device, including a mobile phone. But there are no facilities for leaving one in the building, so you have to find a shop or a café in the vicinity willing to look after your phone for you. The Capable Travel Company was one such establishment recommended to him. It charged £1 for the privilege.

The day had finally come. Michael watched from the public gallery as a policewoman led Melanie up the steps and into the dock. She looked fresh, smartly dressed and well-groomed – and he wondered if anyone at Bronzefield had given her a helping hand. He saw her eyes searching the gallery until she found him. She smiled and gave him a little wave. His knees knocked together as he furtively returned it, not quite sure what the rules allowed.

After introductions by the judge, the swearing-in of the jury and the reading of the indictment, Melanie was asked how she pleaded. Not guilty, she said with confidence and sincerity, clearly and loud enough so all could hear. There was no sign of the tiredness and stress Michael was feeling following his restless night of worrying.

Counsel for the Prosecution was a plain woman of an indeterminate age who went by the unfortunate name of Miss Moody. She began her opening statement by describing to the jury how the newly elected Member of Parliament for Richmond and Putney, a man of great talent with a bright future in politics ahead of him etc. etc., had been found dead in his apartment on the morning of Monday, 7th September, having been brutally and cruelly murdered. She explained about the files which the ushers were distributing to the jury but asked them not to open them until asked to do so. She said she would be showing them that the crime had been planned in meticulous detail, well in advance, and had been carried out with the intention, not only of killing the poor man but also of making him suffer in the most horrific way.

She would show them that the defendant had, without any shadow of doubt, a strong motive which drove her to murdering him in that vicious manner, and had indeed spoken of her sadistic intentions to kill him to several people, some of whom she would be calling as witnesses. Furthermore, she would be providing written evidence – written by the defendant herself – of how she was driven by rage to take the law into her own hands and commit this most terrible crime.

Her witnesses will testify as to the defendant's medical knowledge and ability which were needed, and some will be giving evidence proving beyond any doubt that the accused had access to the medical and other paraphernalia required to complete this terrible deed.

She said Counsel for the Defence might try to say some of the evidence was 'merely circumstantial', but during the course of the trial, they the jury would see that all the evidence – all of it, when put together like a jig-saw puzzle – pointed fairly and squarely to the woman sitting in the dock before them.

Miss Moody told the jury that they might be tempted to conclude such a vicious act of torture and execution could only have been committed by someone who was criminally insane. But she would be calling an expert witness who will testify that the defendant was perfectly responsible for her actions and, although she had experienced trauma in the past, she was mentally fit enough to be tried and convicted. Don't be persuaded by her appearance, she urged the jury, you are looking at a monster.

When Miss Moody said this, she scowled at Melanie. In contrast, Mark looked at Melanie with a twinkle in his eye and sympathetic smile on his lips. He then looked at the jury and allowed the smile to develop, slowly shaking his head from side to side. His body language was clear: look at the defendant, you don't really believe this beautiful young lady is a monster, do you?

For Michael, the prosecution opening was a ramble. The woman had not presented any facts that were new to him. For much of the time, he watched the jury, realising that they were hearing it all for the first time.

He also watched Mark, noting that his performance in mime had already begun. Whenever Counsel for the Prosecution said something damning about Melanie – like how she was driven by rage to commit this vicious crime – he would raise his eyebrows as far as they would go and half close his eyelids and allow the beginnings of a smile to form on his lips. He would look at Melanie, then look at the jury, as if to say 'you don't want to believe all this nonsense'.

Miss Moody wittered on about the injuries, explaining that both sides accepted the postmortem report and had agreed not to call the forensic pathologist as a witness. She drew the attention of the jury to Exhibit 1, an A3-sized binder full of photographs and mock-ups of the deceased and his injures. Michael could see them from his position in the gallery and was relieved that in the snapshots of the body, most of it had been pixelated out. However, from the blow-ups of the fish-hooks, he could make out which parts of the body they had been pushed through. Miss Moody referred to them as 'murder weapons' and encouraged the jury to study in detail each photo. Finally, Michael heard the words he wanted to hear.

"My Lord, I would like to close my opening statement-"

Michael wasn't the only person in the courtroom to breath a sigh of relief. But the woman hadn't quite finished.

"- by referring to evidence the jury will hear provided by cyber-forensics. It has been agreed by both sides that there is no need for them to be presented in person. With your permission, I will ask my junior counsel to read out the relevant passages."

The judge grumbled his acceptance.

"My Lord, members of the jury. The statement referred to is Exhibit 2. It is in two parts. The first part is the defendant's contributions to and replies from a Facebook group she joined, a closed group offering bereavement support. The second part contains personal emails she wrote to another member of the group; forensics were not able to trace his replies, but we understand it's a man named Randolph O'Brian. I will read out the relevant extracts."

The woman started with what Melanie had shared with the Facebook group:-

'To be honest, I'm really angry.'

'I can't seem to handle the anger.'

'I have an almost unbearable desire to kill him.'

Michael wanted to leap to his feet and cry "FOUL!". The extracts were totally out of context. He glared down at David who was lolling in his chair behind Mark, seemingly unconcerned. David must have sensed it. He looked up at Michael, mouthed 'it's OK', and smiled.

The foul was compounded when the girl moved on to Melanie's emails:-

'Thank you for your email advising me to kill my partner's murderer. I think this is an excellent idea.'

'Any suggestions of how to 'execute' the deed would be very gratefully received.'

'I want to watch him die slowly, in pain, terrified.'

Michael groaned. He could see the jury were shocked, but neither David or Mark seemed worried. The girl continued:-

'I could kill the shit-fucker if you helped me plan it.'

'I want you to cheer me up with lots of ways in which I could kill Mr Nasty.'

'Thanks for the tutorial on assassination. It's got my mind buzzing with possibilities. How about fish-hooks?'

'I was so angry. I hoped he would lose the by-election, but he won. That made me fucking furious!'

Holed below the waterline, thought Michael. He watched the startled frowns of the jury. He expected Mark to be hanging his head down in defeat, realising that turning them around after that lot would be impossible. But the man was smiling to himself as he went through the papers on his desk, pencilling in the odd note.

Mark was still smiling when he stood up to give his opening address. Michael noticed from the jury's faces that they'd recovered from the shock of hearing about all the viciousness and cruelty, and some of them were smiling back at Mark. He then welcomed them and thanked them for their attendance, flicking his eyes from one to another, so each one felt they had been personally welcomed by this nice man.

It was clear to Michael that Mark's display of happy confidence had an effect on the jury. He imagined what was going through their minds: 'this guy obviously thinks he can get her off. Perhaps she's innocent after all'.

Mark echoed the Prosecution's revulsion of the crime, agreeing it was indeed an especially cruel way to finish a life. He didn't look at Melanie at all while saying this, as if she had nothing whatsoever to do with it. Only later did he turn to his client to say that she did have a strong motive for killing the man and that he would be explaining this to the jury in the course of the trial.

Yes, thought Michael. He's good. He has captured their attention already. They'll be itching to find out what on earth the victim had done to this lovely girl which allegedly drove her to kill him.

Mark then told the jury in no uncertain terms that wishing someone were dead was not the same as killing them. The nodding heads indicated their agreement. He said that his witnesses would show that this young woman before them was, in fact, incapable of hurting anyone, let alone killing someone in cold blood. She was a doctor who had dedicated her career to saving the lives of our servicemen and servicewomen fighting the Taliban in Afghanistan and making our streets safer. Of course, he said, she had the medical knowledge it would have taken to have killed the man, but knowing how to kill someone – and at this point he chuckled – doesn't make one a murderer.

Michael looked at the jurors. Some were smiling; others were nodding, agreeing that knowing how to kill someone and doing it were definitely not the same thing.

Michael wasn't the only one watching them. Mark was reading each one, sizing them up, making eye contact with them in turn, nodding slightly as he did so, telling them they were on the right lines. He then agreed that the defendant might have had access to the kind of medical equipment used by the murderer because she was working in a medical centre. His face said: what could be more obvious? Of course she did. But how many others, he added, might also have had access to that equipment?

As for the 'hardware' – the murder weapons – required to carry out the killing, he continued, any one of us could have gone in one of a hundred or more shops within twenty miles of here and purchased them over the counter. Here's a packet I bought yesterday, he announced, holding up a hand-sized polythene bag of large fish-hooks. Am I a murderer? The jury smiled. They liked his style.

And finally, he agreed that although she had suffered serving her country in Afghanistan, she was indeed mentally fit, not only to stand trial but also to give evidence herself to show she was entirely innocent of the charge.

He wound up by telling the jury that throughout the trial they would learn that all the evidence was circumstantial, and while the Prosecution make the absurd claim that it all points to his client, the jury would also learn that it could equally well point to others. He reminded them that they could only convict his client if they were sure she was guilty. If they were not sure, because they had the perspicacity to understand that another person or persons could have committed the crime, they would have no option but to find her not guilty.

Michael wondered if all the members of the jury had understood the word 'perspicacity' and whether they thought it was a good thing or a bad thing to have.

Mark turned to the judge and declared there was no case to answer, on the grounds that the Prosecution had nothing whatsoever to link his client to the crime: no DNA, no fingerprints, no positive ID, in fact nothing. And he respectfully asked for the case to be dismissed. The judge said no. Mark smiled, looked at the jury and shrugged his shoulders. His expression said 'I tried, but it looks as if we are going to have to go ahead with this nonsense'. Some of them smiled back, in sympathy.

After a welcome break for lunch, the Prosecution called its first witness. It was the cleaning lady who had discovered the body. Miss Moody extracted the story from her witness with pedantry beyond belief, goading the poor woman to describe every gruesome fact. The barrister kept looking at the jury, relishing their shock as each detail was revealed. Michael noticed Mark was tut-tutting with his head lowered, but every now and then casting an eye towards the members of the jury to see how each one was taking it. Everyone in court seemed to sigh with relief when Miss Moody finally said 'your witness' and sat down.

It was Mark's turn. He began by saying how sorry he was that Mrs Mahinga had had to suffer such an ordeal, and he thanked her for coming to court and describing with such courage what she'd seen. He didn't actually say 'on behalf of the jury', but his head swivelled from jury to witness and back again thereby confirming that impression. Michael noticed that some of them were nodding.

Mark caught the eye of one of the ushers and indicated that the witness might like to sit down. With a nod of approval from the judge, a chair was hastily provided, and Mark began. As it was a cross-examination, he was not prohibited from asking leading questions, but his first could not have been more benign.

"Mrs Mahinga, it must have been such a shock for you when you first saw him, but can you tell the court how you felt when it dawned on you later that your employer had died?"

"Well, he's not the only person I work for. He paid well, so I'll miss the money, but I-"

"You'll miss the money. I understand. Times are tight, aren't they?"

Mrs Mahinga smiled. Michael guessed she rarely got any sympathy from anybody.

Mark continued. "Did you miss *him* at all? Did you feel sorry that he had suffered in that horrible way?"

"No. I didn't miss him. I wasn't close to him. In fact, I didn't see much of him-"

"Why was that?"

At that point, the judge interrupted to ask Mark whether his line of questioning was necessary and if so, to where was it leading.

"My Lord, with respect, if we are to understand my client's alleged motive for killing the deceased, I think we need to understand more about him. And I believe Mrs Mahinga to be a thoroughly reliable witness who, having been in his employ, can perhaps shed some important light on his character."

"Mr Issijay, you may proceed."

"Thank you, my Lord. Mrs Mahinga, why did you not see much of him?"

"Because I used to do his place when he was out. I preferred it. I didn't feel comfortable when he was around. He looked down on me, like, as if I was his slave. I found him a bit creepy. He'd smile at me in a certain way, more like a leer, it was. I might have imagined it, but I felt threatened."

"In what way, Mrs Mahinga?"

"In a sort of sexual way. He had them magazines, bondage I think they call it, and I used to find things. Under the bed. You know. And sometimes the place had a smell – perfume it was. I think he used to entertain. In the evenings. It's not my place to say any more."

"Quite so. But did you feel sorry for him, dying in that manner? Suffering pain and knowing he was going to die?"

"No, your worship, I didn't. I thought 'well, Mr Hoity-Toity' – he was posh, like– 'it looks as if you've got your comeuppance!'"

"Mrs Mahinga, do you have any idea who might have given him his comeuppance?"

"None. One of them girls, probably. Or boys. I dunno."

Mark turned to the jury and raised his eyebrows as if to say neither do we know. A girl? A boy? Could have been anyone.

"No more questions, my Lord, but I think there is a short point of law that needs determining, and I suspect the jury would welcome the opportunity for a cup of tea."

Michael wasn't sure if Mark had given the jury a wink when he smiled back at them. To everyone's relief, the judge decided to adjourn the court until the following morning, as it had been a long first day.

Chapter 25

Michael was up bright and early on the Tuesday, ready for the second instalment of R v. Green. Having watched Mark Issijay give his opening speech and cross-examine the first witness, he did think David had chosen him well.

It wasn't just what Mark said that impressed him, but the way he very subtly handled the judge, the witnesses and most important of all the jury, his audience. Using a combination of carefully chosen words, facial expressions and body language, he had very quickly got them on his side and had become almost one of them, part of their team, if not their leader.

He felt Miss Moody was heavy going. While a murder trial was not a venue for cracking jokes, he believed there was a place for humour in the grimmest of situations, not to entertain and make people laugh but to relieve tension. Miss Moody had yet to demonstrate she had any. Michael felt she had over-egged the pudding in forcing the poor Mrs Mahinga to describe in detail what she had seen. He hoped he wouldn't have to listen to it all again when Moody called her other witnesses.

Michael was disappointed. First up was the constable who'd been called to the scene by Mrs Mahinga. Using his notebook and with suitable prompting, he described the building, a newly converted Victorian mansion. He took the court through the front door, into the communal hall, up in the shared lift and to the fourth floor where the victim's apartment was situated. There he found the cleaner waiting outside; she was too shocked to speak to him. He entered the flat and was drawn by the stench into the bathroom where he found—

It was too much for Michael. He crept out of the public gallery, remembering to bow to the judge on the way. He guessed it would take Miss Moody at least half an hour to winkle it all out of the poor fellow, and decided he would see what was going on in the other courts.

On the stairs down, he bumped into Bob, Melly's psychiatrist, who asked Michael how she was.

"She did okay yesterday, giving her plea, and quite honestly, I think she's handling everything very well. David reckons it will be Friday before she goes on the stand, and I guess that might be more difficult for her."

"I've been told I'll be called this afternoon, so I thought I'd take a peep now and see how things are going."

"But I didn't think witnesses were allowed in the court," said Michael, "until they've given their evidence."

"You're right – unless you're an expert witness. And apparently, I am. For the Prosecution, but it's only to declare Melanie fit to plead. The defence will cross-examine me, so I might have the chance to put in a good word for her."

"You sound as if you've done this before."

"A few times. In this case, it's not too arduous, as I've been treating her since she came to Beechwood. I expect they asked me for that reason, as I can comment on her state of mind at the time of the crime."

"So, no mountain to climb, eh?"

"No. Should be a doddle. I'll have to wait until the weekend for some real climbing. Just some guiding at Harrison's Rocks at the weekend. It's always fun with the kids."

"Yours, Bob?" Michael had never thought of him as a family man.

"No. From the climbing club. We don't have any, but we do plan to marry and start a family soon."

"They'll have you climbing up the wall! Been there

done that – but just the once... Melanie said you've written a book. What's it about?"

"Gross exaggeration, I'm afraid. All I did was to update a book about climbing written in the thirties. Called *The Night Climbers of Cambridge*, that's the univ-"

"Good Lord," said Michael, "I was there. Jesus College, 1973 to '75."

"Melanie did mention that. You were an oarsman, I believe. I was at Cat's, and the only physical activity I managed to fit in was climbing."

"I remember the book!" said Michael. "Climbing college buildings in the days when undergrads had to be in by midnight. Amazing pictures! Quite frightening. Some of those climbs looked really dangerous."

"Difficult would be the word I would use. I became fascinated by the psychology of doing something dangerous despite the primitive instinct of fear. The challenge is to overcome it, but also to lower the risk as much as possible. In Cambridge, we would plan the climbs meticulously – having done a couple of recces by daylight, of course, then taking it steady the first time. The guys you see in those photographs, it wasn't their first time doing those climbs."

"Have you done any of them?"

"Oh, yes. The lot. When I was up there. And some

new ones on buildings which weren't there when the original book was written. Great fun."

"Bloody hell. You need to see a psychiatrist."

Both men laughed at the silly joke, then Michael asked Bob if he'd ever tackled the peaks of the Hindu Kush. Bob said he'd never been there, but it was on his bucket list.

Michael looked at his watch and decided it was time to go back. Their conversation on the stairs had saved him from a rerun of the horror film, but little did he know it was only the trailer for the main event.

As the two men took their seats in the public gallery, the forensic investigator – Mr Mills – took to the stand, a man in his early forties. With Miss Moody inciting him with her questions, he started to describe the corpse and the dreadful things which had been done to it. To both Michael's and Bob's relief, Mark jumped to his feet and addressed the judge.

"My Lord, I think by now the jury is well aware of what happened to the victim and are perhaps ready to move on and hear how the crime was committed." As he was saying the words, he glanced back at his audience a couple of times, giving the impression he was their spokesman, looking after their interests, fighting their corner.

The judge glared at Mark, but when he saw the jury

nodding, some of them quite vigorously, he suggested to Miss Moody that she may wish to move things on.

There followed a detailed explanation of how the killer must have had a key to the apartment or was let in by the victim. They stabbed him with an auto-injector rendering him incapacitated before administering a spinal anaesthetic causing paralysis. The killer stripped him, put him into the bath and filled it up. The fish-hooks were applied and their wires secured to the shower fitting above. The water was drained away by puncturing the sheet of cling film which had been placed over the plughole, thus lowering the body and tightening the wires. One of the hooks had ruptured the penile artery causing fatal blood loss.

Mark's first question to the forensic investigator was how much did the victim weigh.

Mr Mills looked at the ceiling for a moment, as if he was working things out. "My opinion is that he weighed between eighty and a hundred kilograms – twelve to fourteen stone – about five foot ten inches tall, slim-"

"Thank you, Mr Mills." Mark glanced at the jury. His look said, 'you know what's coming next?' They all sat up, eager to hear the next question and the answer to it.

"Mr Mills. You have given us a very good

description of how the victim came to meet his end, but I would be grateful if you could share with us your theory of how the killer managed to get the body into the bathtub."

"Well, sir." The man scratched his head; he was off script. "The killer must have done the injection in the spine when the victim was on the floor, lying on his front. Then he dragged him over to the bath and heaved him into it."

"Heaved him into it?" Mark raised his eyebrows in utter disbelief. He looked at the jury with his jaw slack in shock. Then he turned to look at his client standing in the dock, and twelve heads followed his gaze.

"Mr Mills. How strong do you think the killer must have been to have 'heaved' the victim into that bath?"

"Quite strong, sir. He must have-"

"He, Mr Mills? He?"

"Yes, sir. He would've had to have been strong to lift someone of that size."

A scrape of a chair on the hardwood floor next to the desk of the CPS solicitor distracted him. Mr Mills shot a glance at Miss Moody. She glowered back and flashed her eyes at the slender young woman in the dock.

Mr Mills looked at her too. He got the message. "He, or a... strong she, sir." His cheeks were turning red. He realised he'd blown it.

"He?' said Mark, raising his voice. "Or a strong

she?" he added, even more loudly, looking at the jury and managing in a second or two to achieve brief eye contact with every member.

They looked back at him, waiting for his next question. Michael and Bob leaned forward to get a better view.

Mark's next move was a master-stroke. He said nothing. He started to look around the courtroom, in an exaggerated way as if he were trying to locate the 'he' or the 'strong she'. When he looked under his table, nearly everyone present burst into nervous laughter, enjoying the release of tension. The exceptions were Miss Moody and the CPS solicitor.

Mark stood there, waiting patiently for the court to regain their composure. His timing was perfect. Only when complete silence had returned did he announce he had no more questions. He turned to the jury and almost imperceptibly bowed his head as if to acknowledge their silent applause.

Michael didn't think he had scored a massively important point, but it was clear that his audience – the jury – loved him. When he spoke, they listened.

Next on the stand was the constable who had taken Melanie's complaint at the station. Michael smiled when he thought this particular policeman wasn't getting any younger.

Miss Moody extracted from him every little detail,

not only about the crime and the events leading up to it, but also about the policeman's personal history and his long record in the force, obviously to establish his credibility.

Michael noticed the jury were beginning to get restless, and he caught the judge yawning behind a hand carefully raised to conceal it from the mere mortals in front of him. The courtroom only woke up when the constable repeated the expletives which the accused was alleged to have said.

He was reading from his notebook. "And she said to me 'well, mister ploddy-bloody-woddy, if you're not going to do anything about that fucking arse-hole, I'm going kill the c, blank, blank, t with my bare hands'."

Miss Moody feigned shock by dropping her jaw and taking a little gasp. She took a sip of water then bravely carried on. "Tell me, constable, how did the accused appear to you when she exploded with that torrent of abuse and that blatant threat."

"Terrible, ma'am. Out of control. In a blind rage. At that juncture," he was still reading from his notebook, "she raised both hands and made out like she was a lion, with claws. Snarling, she was. Then she hexited the building."

"Thank you, constable," said Miss Moody, smirking at Mark. "Your witness." She sat down.

It was a warm-up act for the jury. It stirred them into consciousness. The star himself, their hero, was about to take centre stage. It was the moment they'd been waiting for.

"Constable Lawson," Mark began. "Firstly, my client has asked me to apologise to you for the disrespect she showed you on that day. She is truly sorry."

The constable stood up straight and puffed out his chest. He looked a little surprised as if apologies to him were few and far between.

"That's all right, sir." He turned to Melanie. "Ma'am," he said, with a quick nod of his head in acknowledgement of her apology. He turned back to face Mark. "I know she didn't mean it. I've met her type—"

He was stopped in his tracks by a loud cough from Miss Moody. Michael saw the expression on Mark's face change. He detected the beginnings of a smile, a slight twitching of the lips. Michael looked at the jury. One of them, a man in his twenties, had his head down, resting his chin on his hand. When he looked up for a moment, Michael realised he was trying not to laugh.

The question and answer exchange between cross-examiner and witness began. For Michael, it was like listening to a good joke you've heard many times being retold by a professional. You know the punch line, but you relish the lead up and laugh even more when it's finally delivered. Or was it like the nursery rhyme, *There's a Hole in my Bucket*? You know how it's going to end, but it still makes you smile. He wondered if it was amusing *because* you know how it ends. Michael was ready to be amused:-

"Constable, when did you first hear about the death of the victim?"

"That morning, sir, just before dinner time. I'd come in for the afternoon shift—"

"And how did you feel when you heard about this poor man?"

"Shocked, sir. Truly shocked. But I knew it was her that did it. Must have been. After those threats of hers."

"And what did you do then, when you heard the man had died?"

"I reported it, sir. Straight away. To my boss. I told him I knew the hidentity of the murderer—"

"How did you know at that stage that the victim had been murdered?"

"I put two and two together, sir!" He straightened himself up again. "She told me she was going to do it when she left the station."

Mark nodded, in order to say – without actually saying it – that the constable had done well to have deduced who'd done it and reported it immediately up the chain of command. His smile completed the effect, and the constable stood to attention, looking straight ahead with a satisfied grin on his face.

"Constable, would you say that an important part of police work is the prevention of crime?"

"Most certainly, sir. If we can prevent it, stop it happening in the first place, everybody gains, don't they?"

Mark's enthusiastic nodding encouraged the constable to continue.

"I mean, if you think a crime is about to be committed, you can arrest the person and take him into custody."

"But it must be difficult to foresee a crime. I would imagine one would need years of experience to make that judgement. Is that right?"

"Yes, sir. I would agree with that, sir."

"And do you believe your long years in the force, which you told us about earlier, have given you that skill of sizing someone up, of looking into their minds and working out what their intentions might be?"

"Most definitely, sir. I can remember the time—"

"And, if you did have the persp— the intuition, the feeling that someone had the intention to commit a crime, would you arrest them? Or would you just let them go, in the hope that they might, perhaps, change their mind and not commit the crime they had in mind?"

It was time for Michael to put his hand over his mouth. He looked at Bob and noticed he was doing the same, and his shoulders were shaking. Cruel, he thought, but if it prevents a miscarriage of justice, it's worth it.

"Arrest them, sir. Definitely. You see, if you arrest someone in those circumstances, it prevents the crime. You nick 'em, take them down to the station and give them a good talking to, let them cool down and if – and only if – you think it's safe to do so, you can give them a clip round the ear – not really, but you know what I mean. And then you let 'em go."

"Did you arrest the accused after she 'exploded' at you in the police station that day?"

The constable looked across at Melanie. He smiled. "No, sir," he said, rolling his eyes to heaven as if it were a ridiculous question. Michael and Bob had both stopped laughing and looked at each other. It was unkind. The poor man still didn't see the punch coming. Get on with it, man, Michael wanted to shout at Mark. He looked down at Miss Moody; he could almost see the steam. The CPS solicitor behind her was quietly growling.

"Did you *think* about arresting her?"

"No, sir. Not at all. I felt sorry for her. She was in a state. You know what women can be like—"

"Did you report her outburst to a senior officer?"

"Certainly not. I wasn't going to bother him. It was well within my authority to handle the situation, to use my discretion. She came from that home, Beechwood something, up the road from us. They're all a bit funny there. No trouble they are, though. Never had any bother from them. I thought she was just having a turn. She wouldn't hurt a fly. Not the type. I offered to take her home, but she didn't want me to. It was then she shouted at me and left. All mouth, she was. I didn't mind. I've been called a lot worse. And been spat at. But you get used to it. Maintain a professional approach at all times is what I do. Part of the job, I always say..."

Mark was kind enough to let him carry on. To Michael's surprise and relief the Counsel for the Defence, the barrister who was defending his daughter, had the magnanimity to pull the punch at the last moment.

Mark turned to the witness box and took two steps towards it. He lowered his voice, but in that courtroom, at that moment, there was utter silence. Everyone heard what Mark said to the witness.

"Constable Lawson. Even for a person of your experience, it can be a difficult ordeal standing up in a courtroom like this in front of lots of people. And having someone like me in a wig and gown asking you lots of questions. But you have answered them all with dignity and honesty and given a great deal of credibility to your profession. You can be rightly proud of the fact that your integrity has today added a few drops of oil to the wheels of true justice. Thank you."

Nobody laughed.

Mark turned to the judge. "No further questions, my Lord." In return, he received a nod and a smile.

It was 1.15 pm. For Michael, the time had raced by. The judge called an adjournment for lunch, meeting again at 2.15 pm.

Chapter 26

Michael and Bob left Court 1 of the Old Bailey and made the short walk to the All-Bar-One in Ludgate Hill. They settled for a pint and a sandwich, and Michael insisted it was on him. He wanted to hear more about the Hindu Kush.

"Sure, what do you want to know? As I said, I've yet to go there, but I've read up a few reports on climbing expeditions."

"I'd like to hear about that. Has it become like Everest?"

"Overcrowded? Hell no. It has some of the least explored mountains in the Himalayas. Because of the war, very few American expeditions have gone there recently. It has the highest concentration of 7000-metre peaks in the world. Some have never been climbed."

"So you are going to tackle those?"

Bob smiled. "The most I can hope for is to join

an expedition, but one day I will. What about you? Where are you and Melanie intending to go?"

"Good question. She wants to go back to that village where she stayed. A sort of pilgrimage, I suppose. Visit the grave of her son if she can find it. And to see her 'family', as she calls it, the villagers who took her in and looked after her."

"Where is it?"

"A bit of a mystery. Its name is something like Khuh Tabar. I've tried googling it, but no luck there. Melanie's no help either, even though she lived there for three years."

It was Bob's turn to look at his watch. "I'd better report in. Mustn't be late! And thanks for the lunch. See you soon."

"A pleasure. Are you here tomorrow?"

"Sadly not. Something called work. Let me know how it goes."

"Will do. Give me your number and I'll text you."

Proceedings that afternoon in Court 1 began slowly. The first high point was when Mark cross-examined the middle-aged lady who'd been manning the constituency office when Melanie had called in. Michael had noticed Miss Moody slipping in the odd leading question or two, which had enabled her to elicit from the woman the opinion that Melanie was angry and emotionally unstable. He was surprised

Mark hadn't objected, but then he guessed it was of no great importance compared to the extracts read out the day before.

On cross-examination, Mark was able to establish that Bretton-Willis was not very popular with her or her colleagues and was a 'bit of a martinet'. Michael reckoned that even though some of the jury might not have come across the term, they got the message: he was a shit.

Next on the stand was Bob. Having established his identity and qualifications, how long he had been practising and since when had he been treating the defendant, Miss Moody asked him to explain what PTSD was, how it was caused, what its symptoms were and how it was treated. Michael thought he spoke up well and with authority, and from the expressions on the faces of the jury, he reckoned Bob had come across as a professional and reliable witness.

This proved to be important when Miss Moody asked about Melanie. Despite her valiant attempts, she wasn't able to persuade Bob to say that a person suffering from PTSD was more likely to murder someone. As for Melanie Green, he said, she had never shown any signs whatsoever of being a danger to the public. Had that been the case, she would have been confined to the secure ward at Beechwood Hall, at least at night and during the weekends.

Bob declared her fit to plead to the charge of murder, despite PTSD being a registered condition. The judge intervened to explain to the jury that some mental conditions might allow the defendant to be found not guilty of murder but of the lesser charge of manslaughter. Miss Moody beamed at the CPS solicitor. Her skilful questioning had blocked off that particular escape route.

Before taking a bow and passing her expert witness over to the Defence, Miss Moody slipped in the reminder to the jury that the Defendant had confessed in writing to her intention to kill the deceased in the emails she had sent to Mr O'Brian.

The judge looked at Mark as if asking him if he objected to Counsel for the Prosecution prodding the jury in that way. Mark smiled and shrugged his shoulders.

"Your witness," declared Miss Moody, smiling at Mark.

The jury shifted in their seats, making themselves comfortable for what was to come.

Mark slowly stood up. He looked down at his notes on the lectern in front of him. With one hand, he flicked through the sheets; with the other, he squeezed his cheeks. Michael guessed that had he not been wearing a wig, he would have scratched his head. He took a deep breath.

"Dr Weston, thank you for coming here today. My

learned friend has just reminded us of the rather disturbing comments the defendant made in her emails to Mr O'Brian, the ones saying she was going to kill the deceased. Let me give you a couple of examples."

Hang on, thought Michael, what on earth are you doing? Surely the last thing you want to do is remind the jury of those.

But he need not have worried. Mark chose the ones with the most swear-words in them, making a pretence of being shocked when he read out the expletives but smiling as he did so. Clearly, he didn't believe she meant it. But hey! We have an expert here, let's ask him. All in body language.

Turning to Bob, Mark said, "What do you make of them?"

Bob smiled. "Well, they are no more than revenge fantasies. Dark thoughts, about what you'd like to do to someone who has harmed you. It's quite natural, and we actually encourage it. For most patients, it's cathartic, providing psychological relief through the open expression of strong emotions. They often smile at the thought of vengeance or even laugh out loud. Of course, at the right moment, we tell them revenge is not the answer: we don't want them actually doing it. But that wasn't a problem for Melanie. She liked the thought of doing something terrible to the man, but that was all. In fact, she often felt remorse that she'd even had those thoughts.

"As for Mr O'Brian, I think it did her a world of good, having that kind of relationship with someone she'd never met who'd listen to her. I've never seen her emails, but she told me about them, and about Rand, as she called him. I have no doubt that for every one of those quotes from her emails, she assured Rand there was no way she'd do anything stupid. She's not a stupid person."

"Dr Weston, I don't quite understand what you mean. We have a copy of her emails here. With his Lordship's permission, perhaps you'd be good enough to scan through them and give us some examples. Those quotes the Prosecution read out are sidelined in red." Mark handed him a copy of Exhibit 2.

The court waited while Bob opened the file.

"Here we are. On the first page. 'I can't bear it – but I couldn't kill him. I couldn't kill anyone. I only joined the army as a doctor because I wanted to help soldiers survive the horrors of war; to save those young lives – boys, really.'

"Ah. This one makes the point well: 'However, despite my army training, I don't think I'm capable of carrying out such an operation for two reasons. Mentally, I could not bring myself to do such a thing. And practically, I can't think of a way to do it and get away with it. But any suggestions of how to 'execute' the deed would be very gratefully received so that I can imagine them in my dreams: the nastier the means, the better.'

"Just dreams, I'm afraid... Sorry."

Michael couldn't believe it. Bob had shot the Prosecution's case down in flames and was apologising.

Mark waited. Everyone was silent. He looked around the courtroom, up at the public gallery, across at his jury eyeballing each one. He frowned at the Prosecution. Only then did he speak.

"No more questions, my Lord."

The trial continued with Miss Moody calling her next witness, the investigating officer, DS Simmons.

The woman had plainly spent time in court before. She was offering up her evidence in a clear and confident voice when prompted to do so. Michael listened as she read out a rambling statement describing her interview with Melanie under caution.

When Miss Moody had achieved what she was after, she handed DS Simmons over to Mark. He reminded her of the DNA incident by playing the recording up to the moment when she asked Melanie to come clean. By turning up the sound fully, the court could just make out above the mush the words stage-whispered by the constable who brought in the folder.

"DS Simmons, what was in the folder?"

"A DNA report."

"Of whose DNA?"

"I can't remember – people involved in the case, the cleaner, the policeman who was first on the scene."

"Did it state that the defendant's DNA had been found at the scene?"

"Er, no."

"Then why did you give the defendant the impression that hers had been found at the scene? As we have just heard – and I believe it was when you closed the folder – you said to the defendant 'don't you think it's time to tell us the truth?' Did you intentionally mislead her to think that her DNA had been in that folder?"

"Sir," she said, straightening herself up. "I believed the suspect had committed the crime. I felt sorry for her. I'd been told about the complaint she had filed, about being allegedly raped by the deceased. I didn't know if it was true or not, but I wanted to help her. I pointed out that with her medical record, the charge could be reduced to manslaughter – if she pleaded guilty. I explained that it would allow the judge to pass a lesser sentence."

"And did you think your 'trick' would persuade her to confess?"

DS Simmons reddened. "It was not a trick. Sir. More of a life-line. If she'd killed him, it would make a great deal of sense for her to confess to manslaughter. The judge could then take into account her unfortunate experiences, the character of the man she killed, her motives for doing so... "

Mark waited for her to fizzle out. Then said, "She didn't take you up on your kind offer, did she?"

"No, sir."

"Were you surprised?"

"Yes, sir. I thought she would at least want to talk it over with her brief. He could have advised her."

"Do you think she's stupid?"

"No, sir. Not at all."

"Yet you said that it would have made a great deal of sense for her to come clean – assuming she'd killed him."

"Correct, sir."

"Let's assume for a moment she hadn't killed him. What do you think this intelligent woman would have done?"

"Not up to me to say, sir. I think she would have maintained her innocence."

"And what did she do, in fact?"

"She shouted at me."

"What did she say?"

"I... I'm not exactly sure-"

"No matter. Let's hear the recording."

Mark pressed the button. Despite the overloading, the voice was obviously Melanie's. 'I've already told you FOUR FUCKING TIMES that I DIDN'T, BLOODY-WELL, DO IT!'

"DS Simmons. You are an intelligent, experienced police officer. What did you think at the time when she reacted that way?"

The policewoman buckled. If not physically, she certainly did mentally. She replied in a very quiet voice, but the whole court was waiting on her words.

"I thought she must be innocent."

"I'm sorry. I don't think the court heard that. Would you mind repeating your answer, please?"

The woman coughed. "I said I thought she must be innocent."

"Thank you." Mark turned to the judge. "No more questions, my Lord."

Michael was disappointed Mark hadn't turned the knife. If he'd been cross-examining the woman, he would've asked why she didn't close the case or find the real suspect. Then he remembered David telling him that the police would be under pressure from the CPS. And the CPS would be under pressure from on high.

It was a few minutes after five when the judge halted the proceedings – having waited for Mark to finish the cross-examination. He announced they would recommence at 10.30 the following morning.

Chapter 27

That evening, Michael had arranged to meet David in a little Turkish restaurant off the Strand. David had recommended it, but it was on Michael as he was very much looking forward to grilling David on things so far. His friend was already at the table he'd reserved, and in front of him was an ice bucket with a bottle of champagne.

"Hey, this looks good. Are we celebrating already?"

"We are celebrating the end of the beginning, my dear friend, having got off to a cracking start. In rowing terms, we are just approaching Ditton Corner and closing on the opposition."

The name was familiar to Michael. He could picture the bend in the river, about halfway along the Bumps course. If you survive the Gut, the narrow stretch of the river leading into Ditton Corner, you've done well. But in Bumps races on the Cam, anything can happen. He remembered the strategy: go like hell off the start, then keep going like hell until you bump the boat in front or reach the finish line.

"That's great. But the case for the prosecution seems to be collapsing. You don't think you could ask for it to be stopped?"

"No case to answer? We could make a submission at the end of the Prosecution case, but it has its risks."

"Surely not. From what I've learnt, it's the judge who decides. He can acquit the accused there and then. Or, if he turns down the submission, the case simply carries on. He cannot declare the accused guilty, so there's nothing to lose."

David smiled. "I see your law studies are coming on well, but there are risks. If a submission is made and rejected by the judge, and the jury got wind of it, it might prejudice their verdict against the accused. Of course, it's up to the client, but my advice would be to see it through to the end."

He leaned forward, and Michael did the same. David lowered his voice. "It's looking good for Melanie, but we have some special circumstances here. Remember, it normally takes a lot longer for the two sides to get their acts together. My team have done well, but these days the CPS and the police are understaffed, and I'm concerned they've been rushed. There may be more evidence on the way, yet to rear its ugly head.

"The last thing we want is for Melanie to be

acquitted now, only to find that some new and compelling evidence turns up a week later and the whole process starts again. Also, I think a unanimous not-guilty verdict from twelve good men and true somehow carries more weight than an acquittal agreed by a judge, possibly on a technical point of law. Legally, they mean the same thing, but out on the streets there is a nuance – especially if the police produce a press release saying they are 'not looking for another suspect'.

"Mark's done well. He's effectively turned a couple of prosecution witnesses, and he's got the jury eating out of his hand. While you can never be sure of these things, on the evidence produced by the prosecution so far, I believe the probability of a not-guilty verdict from them is high."

"Over 50%?"

"Oh, yes. I'd put it at 80%."

"That's wonderful!"

"No, it's not wonderful. It means there's still a one-in-five chance that your daughter could spend the best years of her life in prison. I want to get that probability up to 99.9%."

"How are you going to do that?"

"By submitting as evidence Rand's emails. We must make him a suspect. We don't have to prove his guilt, but we do need to show the jury he *could* have done it.

That's why that birth certificate was so important. It proves he's real and alive."

Michael nodded, perhaps more than he should have done, remembering the latest certificate from Sam. "What about Melanie? Would she be happy for us to do that?"

"I think so. I know the Prosecution has drawn a complete blank on Rand, so I think the chances of the police tracking him down and arresting him are – frankly – nil."

"So, how do you propose to introduce that evidence? If the police can't find his emails—"

"You, Michael. I want you to present them in court as a witness. You can state under oath their provenance. Melanie sent them to you in that file of hers, you printed it off, and now you produce it in court."

Michael's heart skipped a beat. He would be under oath to tell the truth, and the *whole* truth – which would include him receiving a copy of Rand's death certificate, just the thing David would not want revealed when he's trying to show the court the man could have committed the crime. Could a father breach his oath to save his daughter? Yes, he thought, and get charged for perjury and contempt. He was saved by the light-bulb in his head.

"A snag. I don't have Melanie's file."

"Ah. So who does?"

"That's the thing. I don't know. I think I threw it away. You see, I put it in a drawer along with an old newspaper and a couple of magazines, and I binned the lot when I left Beechwood Hall."

David was stroking his chin and frowning. He looked up at Michael and smiled. "No matter. I'll get hold of the copy in our safe, the one with your notes in the margins. Even better."

"Thanks. You're a brick... And Mark, of course. You chose well there. I just hope his fees are not too high."

"Fees? You may find he'll be wanting to pay you."

"Why would he want to do that?"

"I think you'll find that when reporting restrictions are lifted there will be a lot of public interest in this case. It could propel him forever onwards and upwards and get him his QC."

When the mezze arrived, David was the one to change the subject. "Talking of Ditton Corner, do you remember the time... must have been the Mays... when we were chasing Lady Margaret – a canvas between us – and they bumped Peterhouse? We had to go for the over-bump. God, it was hard work! Then you, or was it what's-his-name..."

Michael remembered the incident well, but not the name of the unfortunate individual who caught a crab and got catapulted out of the shell, over the rigger behind him and caught his strip on the top of the gate, splitting his blade in the process. Michael enjoyed having a break from legal-speak – all that jargon.

Michael got to the travel agent in good time the following morning and joined the short queue of people wanting to deposit their phones and electronic watches. He couldn't help overhearing a man asking one of the girls behind the desks about Afghanistan. He turned around and looked at him, a smartly dressed middle-aged man carrying a black briefcase. In his other hand was a Trilby, and he was wearing steel-rimmed glasses. Clean-shaved, shiny shoes, and a bald patch on the top of his which Michael was able to look down on, being a good half a head taller.

Not a climber, he thought, perhaps a businessman. He wondered if this was the place to fix up his trip with Melanie. To his astonishment, he heard the man mention what sounded like Khuh Tabar, Melanie's village. A minute or two later, he heard the man repeat it.

The queue had moved on, and it was his turn to hand in his phone. Having done that, he was just in time to see the man walk out of the shop and stop; something in the window had caught his eye.

Michael went up to him. "Excuse me, I wonder if you could help me. I heard you mention a village in Afghanistan, just now, to the girl behind the desk."

The man smiled and raised his eyebrows. "That's right. Khuh Tabar. Do you know it?"

Michael could not believe his luck. "Only by name, but I'm hoping to go there. But I'm not sure where it is. Silly, isn't it?"

"What a coincidence! I know it well. Why don't we pop into that café opposite and chat about it over a coffee?"

"That's awfully kind. Are you sure you don't mind? It'll be on me – I insist."

As they took their seats at a table in the corner, the man introduced himself. "I'm Jim, by the way." His eyes darted around the room, not in a nervous way, but as if he were casing the joint out of habit.

"And I'm Michael." He called the waitress over, and she took their orders. "So tell me, Jim, how do you know that village?"

"Ah!" he said, "it's a long story, but I will tell you."

Michael looked at his watch. "I'm sorry, I don't have much time as I need to -"

"In that case, Dr Green, I'll get straight to the point." The avuncular smile had gone.

Michael frowned at the man. "Who the hell are you?"

"It doesn't matter who I am. Just somebody who could help you. If you could help us."

"Me, help you? I've never been to Afghanistan."

The man's smile returned as he stirred his

cappuccino. "I will give you the lat and long of that village to the nearest 200 metres if you sign something for me. And if you do sign it, I can explain to you what this little charade is all about."

"How do I know you will keep your word?"

The man took a sealed envelope out of his inside pocket. "In here is the location of your village. It could be authentic, or just numbers off a bus. If the latter, all you have done is to sign something. If it's true, you will be able to take your daughter there."

"What do you expect me to sign, a big fat cheque?"

"Certainly not." The man smiled as he lifted his black briefcase onto the table and removed an A4 envelope. "In here is the document. It's in two parts. The first is a non-disclosure agreement; the second is a statement saying that you have read and understood the agreement. An Italian concept, I'm afraid, but when the stakes are this high, we prefer the belt and braces."

Michael was stunned. He wondered if he was signing his life away – perhaps it was a scam to get his signature. Or some sick trick which was being filmed for reality TV. He checked his watch again."

"Dr Green, I understand why you are in a hurry. Have a quick scan of the document now, then come back here at, say, 5.30 pm. You can then read it at your leisure, and I can explain anything you are not sure about. Then you can sign it. If you want to." He removed the document from the envelope and handed it to Michael.

The two words in red at the top of the first page – TOP SECRET – above the Royal Coat of Arms, were enough to convince Michael it was not a scam. The man directed him to the last page which had the two signature blocks. Next to the first one, sealed into the page, was Michael's passport photo. He handed the document back to the man, and they agreed to meet back at the café at 5.30 pm. As the two men emerged from the cafe, a black taxi drew up next to them. Jim climbed in and it departed.

In comparison to the meeting with 'Jim', the trial that day was not that exciting for Michael. Miss Moody presented her last three witnesses , the first was John, the 'estates manager' from Beechwood Hall. She tried to persuade him that two of his pike hooks could well be missing. While he did not deny that the hooks taken from the corpse – Exhibit 3 – could have come from his fishing tackle box, he explained to Mark on cross-examination that they came in packets of forty, and that the packet had printed on it 'contents 40 (approx.)'. Like this one? Mark asked, holding up the packet he'd recently bought. When asked why he didn't keep them locked up, John said he'd never regarded them as offensive weapons – unless you were a pike.

The next witness was from the firm which manufactured the auto-injectors. He admitted that the trials batch of twenty-five supplied to Beechwood Hall did have the same ratio of sufentanil and naloxone as that which the PM report had estimated from blood analysis. On cross-examination, he also admitted that the pens weren't sealed – because they were trial ones – and anyone who could manage a pair of electrician's pointed pliers would be able to unscrew the top and alter the dose. He explained that that was the purpose of the trial, to measure reaction times for different ratios of the two drugs.

Miss Moody's final witness took the stand after lunch. She was a QARANC nurse who had been in the Army in Iraq but currently worked part-time at Beechwood Hall. She'd given a statement to the police, but her job that afternoon had been to imply that Melanie was the only person in the Medical Centre who had access to novocaine, the local anaesthetic found in the spine of the corpse. Mark asked what it was used for, and the nurse explained that 'guests' who had lost limbs sometimes experience great pain, and the only way of relieving it quickly was through an injection directly into the epidural cavity.

Mark asked if it was ever given in an emergency.

The nurse said, "Sometimes pain can be so acute it becomes an emergency. That's why Melanie was given the one and only key to the drugs cupboard so they could quickly be obtained, out of hours if necessary, as she lived in."

"But what about when she was away," asked Mark, "perhaps at another hospital or staying with friends?"

"The key would then be given to someone else, sir. Someone responsible, or locked in the guardroom safe."

"So why," asked Mark, "did you say in your statement that the defendant Dr Melanie Green was the only person who had access to those drugs?"

"Because it was true, sir. Melanie was the only person who had access to the cupboard during the weekend when it happened, 5th/6th September."

"Just during that weekend?" Mark repeated. "And during the week before?"

"Well, it was a working week. She would not have had the keys then."

Mark thanked her with a smile. Then he smiled at the jury. Michael noticed that four or five of them smiled back and, almost imperceptibly, nodded as if to say 'yes, we got it'.

"No more questions, my Lord."

As Mark sat down, Miss Moody rose to say that is the case for the Prosecution. As it was approaching four o'clock, the judge decided – bearing in mind the late finish the previous evening – to adjourn until the

morning when the court would hear the case for the
Defence.

Chapter 28

Michael was early for his meeting with Jim, so he decided to explore an idea which had come into his mind while watching Melanie in the dock that afternoon. She needed a holiday when all this was over. Somewhere special, just for a week or so. He'd committed himself to working over Christmas but wondered if a New Year's winter holiday in the Alps would suit, given that there would undoubtedly be other people of her age around.

He had never indulged in winter sports, but Daniela was a keen skier, and as Melanie was of the same generation he wondered if his sporty daughter would also get the bug. Who better to ask about winter holidays than the nice young lady in the travel agent's?

"Yes, sir, I understand what you are after, but I must warn you New Year is a busy time and hotel rates can be quite expensive. What I would recommend is a catered chalet which you share with other people.

At this late stage, you might have difficulty finding a place, although we do get cancellations."

"So who does the cooking?"

"A catered chalet means all the cooking and housekeeping is done by trained professionals – or passionate amateurs who are out in the Alps for the season. I've been on a few holidays in catered chalets, and they generally work well. People normally get on, as enjoying the mountains in the winter seems to unite them. A lot of life-long friendships start on skiing holidays."

"Sounds good to me," said Michael. "Would it be possible to come up with something? It would be for my daughter and me, just the two of us. She is single and 29."

"I get the picture, sir. So, two single rooms. Will you be leaving your phone in here next week?"

Michael nodded.

"Let me see if I can come up with something for Monday. In the meantime, I'll give you some brochures to browse."

Michael took them across to the café to read while he waited for Jim. On the dot of 5.30 pm, the man appeared, complete with battered black government-issue briefcase. Just any old civil servant, thought Michael. He wasn't sure whether he should jump to his feet, smile and shake hands – or scowl from his chair. He remained seated and smiled.

"Dr Green, may I suggest we go for a little walk? It will allow me to explain a few things."

A suggestion, or an order? Michael gathered up the brochures and put them back in the carrier bag. "Suits me."

"Dr Green. You may want to add this."

Michael took the wodge of A4 sheets. The first line on the front page told him what it was:

From: Rand@djb9x2103i9.com
Subject:
To: Melanie55@gmail.com
15/08/19
>
Just do it.
Rand

The pair walked out of the café and strolled northwards up The Old Bailey, the street which gave the Central Criminal Court its name.

"You see, we understand the situation, and we want to help. As for the trial, we must let justice run its course, and we hope – as you must – that your daughter gets off. As for the alleged war crimes, I believe you were right to report them, and I believe in normal circumstances they should be investigated for all the reasons you gave to General Smedley. But as I will explain later – if you sign the non-disclosure agreement – the circumstances are not normal."

"Tell me about the document. What exactly are you expecting me to sign?"

"It binds you not to disclose anything about any alleged war crimes, or about this meeting or anything I might tell you."

"And what if I decided not to keep my mouth shut? Would you take me to court?"

"Dr Green, I don't think it would ever come to that. You see, we have other ways of shutting you up."

Michael had to smile at the phrase 'vee haff vays'.

Jim continued. "You see, by signing the document you are promising HM of your commitment to silence and acknowledging that any breach of it would amount to treason."

"So I would end up in court, but on a charge of treason?"

"No, Dr Green. The document would merely be submitted as evidence to a sub-committee of the Privy Council. They would then issue the authority for certain Departments of State to take whatever action was required to safeguard the best interests of the Nation. I think you know what I mean."

"Bloody hell! So, in effect, I would be signing my own death warrant?"

Jim smiled. "No, Dr Green, In fact, by agreeing our terms and signing the document, you will guarantee your freedom and, hopefully, a long and happy retirement."

"So are you saying that if I don't sign it, my life is in danger?"

"If I were in your shoes, I'd sign it. You and your daughter will find your village, and if you keep your side of the agreement, you have nothing to fear. Just one more thing, if I may. You would also be agreeing to your daughter's silence on the war crimes."

"How on earth can I do that? She's her own person."

"You will just have to persuade her. By the time you get back to your lodgings, you will have received an email. It might help if you show it to your daughter."

Michael thought through his options. He only had the two, and it didn't take long for him to realise it was a no-brainer. Signing the document in the light of a street lamp emphasised to him the bizarreness of the situation. He handed the single copy back to Jim who in return gave him the sealed envelope containing the co-ordinates of Melanie's village. He added it to his bag.

"So what are the special circumstances? The crimes happened. Why not investigate them?"

"Let's walk on... Major Bretton-Willis and his team were taking part in a joint operation with other Coalition forces. Three simultaneous raids were mounted on three villages, the mission being to seize a terrorist leader who had hitherto evaded capture. As you will find out, the village you call Khuh Tabar is in an area where the international borders are, shall we say, vague. A terrorist who knows the area and the mountains can happily skip across them. One of the villages was across the border in Russia, the other in China. Only just, but the operation breached international law. Had it been discovered, we would have had two highly sensitive diplomatic incidents on our hands, and on our allies' hands."

"God. I can believe that. Was the operation a success?"

"Sadly not. Major Bretton-Willis escaped with his life, bringing out a woman whom he suspected was someone known as the White Queen, an Englishwoman believed to be the mistress of the terrorist leader. She turned out to be your daughter. The other teams – what was left of them – came away with nothing. Subsequent intelligence indicated a fourth possible location. An airstrike on it was carried out in which the terrorist leader was killed. Along with thirty-nine locals – collateral damage, I'm afraid."

"But why shoot civilians? And unarmed women?"

"A favourite tactic of the Taliban is, or hopefully was, to use women and children as suicide bombers. If a woman wearing long flowing robes runs towards you screaming 'Allāhu Akbar!', you have two choices. You can hope she is not wearing an explosive vest, or you can shoot her dead."

"Why did that major rape my daughter?"

"Allegedly, Dr Green. My answer is, I don't know. But it takes a certain sort of man to lead a raid like that – a ruthless one. The kind and compassionate don't last long. To survive and succeed, you need to be able to focus on the mission to the exclusion of all else. Driven, perhaps by basic instincts to kill, or be killed."

He paused and they walked slowly on.

"Not a nice man… There is no excuse for it… I have no idea who killed Bretton-Willis in that horrible way, but I'm not shedding any tears."

"What happened to her afterwards? Once that bastard had… After he'd finished with her?"

"Standard procedure, I'm afraid. After in-theatre interrogation, terrorists – or suspected terrorists – are sent back up the line for deep interrogation with a view to prosecution, or giving evidence against others. Suitable candidates might receive psychological correction in the hope of turning them against their former comrades—"

"You mean brainwashing?"

Jim sighed. Michael watched him in the light from the lamp post. It glinted on his glasses. The man smiled and his eyebrows went up.

"That's a dramatic term, Dr Green, don't you think? Treatment might be a more sensible term for it, to rid them of their psychopathic tendencies and political extremism. Successful subjects are then returned to the battlefield, or exceptional cases may be assigned elsewhere. It's not something my department gets involved with, so I have no idea what happened to your daughter."

At that precise moment, a black cab drew up next to the two men.

"Dr Green, a lift to your accommodation, perhaps?"

"No thanks, it's only just round the corner."

Jim climbed in the back, and the cab drove away.

He was right about the email. Michael read it, lying on his bed.

Dear Dr Green,

Further to your recent meeting with General Smedley, I am writing to thank you for informing us about certain incidents which are alleged to have occurred during operations overseas involving British Army personnel. As a result of your timely submission, the Special Investigation Branch of the Royal Military Police have been tasked with conducting a full enquiry into all aspects of the accusations and report directly to the Secretary of State for Defence.

You will appreciate that such an exercise will take time and we would ask for your patience in this regard. I am sure you will also realise that, meanwhile, such matters must remain sub judice, and any publication of any of the details of the allegations could prejudice the outcome of the investigation and be subject to charges of contempt of court. Your co-operation in this respect is kindly requested.

Cases of this nature rarely happen, but if it is established beyond doubt that a civilian community has in some way suffered from an unjustified military action, reparations will be considered, providing all parties involved agree that any such settlement remains confidential.

We will endeavour to keep you informed of progress.

I am, sir, your obedient servant—

The signature was illegible, but below it was the appointment of the writer, Chief of the General Staff. Michael liked the idea of having an obedient servant, but the stick the general wielded and the carrot he offered made him the master.

Chapter 29

It was Thursday. The judge began the proceedings by explaining to the jury that judges used to give them guidance right at the end of a trial, but nowadays it was deemed to be more useful to provide it as and when they thought it appropriate.

He said they would shortly hear from the defendant who had been on operational duty in Afghanistan. The details of these military operations were classified and could not be disclosed in open court. The prosecution and the defence have agreed they are not relevant to the case, but should either counsel feel the need to raise these issues, or a member of the jury sought clarification on any of these matters, the court would have to be cleared and sit in camera.

He reminded them about their obligations and stressed for the umpteenth time the strict requirement not to discuss the trial with anyone nor remove any papers from the court. Then, having checked that everyone was in place, the judge nodded at Mark.

"My Lord, I would like to call as my first witness: the defendant, Dr Melanie Green."

It was a tense moment for all present in Court One of The Old Bailey when the girl was led out of the back of the dock, through the well of the court into the witness box. Michael watched her from the public gallery. He felt sick. Having confirmed her identity and profession, his daughter read out the oath in a clear voice, then smiled at Mark, indicating her readiness.

He began. "Dr Green. Could you please tell us the nature of your work?"

"I am a captain in the Royal Army Medical Corps. At the moment I'm a patient at Beechwood Hall, a convalescence facility for military personnel. I was sent there six months ago, suffering from post-traumatic stress disorder."

Mark turned to the judge. "My Lord, if it pleases the court, I will ask the witness to tell us in her own words about the traumas which led to the disorder. This will not be easy for her, but she has specifically asked if she may do this."

The judge agreed, and Melanie began her story, from taking off in the helicopter on her casevac mission to arriving at Beechwood Hall nearly four years later. Michael was as moved as anyone. He thought he knew it off by heart, but each time he heard the harrowing tale an extra little bit of important detail had been added.

When she finished, Mark made a pretence of going through his papers, obviously, thought Michael, to give the jury a few moments to reflect on what they had just heard. Then he stood up straight and addressed the judge.

"My Lord, may I perhaps say on behalf of all of us here in this room how grateful we are to the witness for sharing with us the horrors she was so unfortunate enough to have experienced in the service of this nation." The jury nodded enthusiastically. Mark looked at the courtroom clock. "With respect, may I suggest we adjourn for twenty minutes before continuing with questions?"

The judge agreed, but before giving the order he addressed the jury.

"Ladies and gentlemen, you have heard a distressing tale. Of a young woman who has experienced a succession of traumata, some of which were part of her job as a doctor in a war zone, which she could have expected.

"Some were not. She has bravely told us that she was the victim of rape, a most serious crime in any jurisdiction. However, I must remind you that this is not a rape trial; the alleged rapist is not here to defend himself and whether or not he was guilty of the offence is not a matter for this court. While you may rightly assume that a rape victim deserves the full support of the law, you must not let sympathy persuade you of the defendant's innocence of the offence for which she is charged."

The break was well appreciated, not least by the witness herself who was able to handle the questions which followed without her voice cracking or having to resort to a paper tissue. Mark asked her how she found out about Mr Nasty and how she felt when she did so. He made a point of using Melanie's nick-name for her abuser whenever possible. It was less of a mouthful than Major Bretton-Willis, but Michael suspected Mark used it as a mild form of character assassination.

Mark asked her why she'd joined the bereavement support group and why she had accepted an invitation from a Mr Randolph O'Brian to engage in private correspondence. He reminded the court that the defendant's emails to the man were contained in Exhibit 2, but explained it contained no record of his responses.

Michael leaned forward in his seat, anxious not to miss any of the drama which he thought was going to follow.

"What did you do with his replies?"

"I kept them, but when I heard Mr Nasty had died, I thought I'd better delete them."

"Why was that?"

"I didn't want Rand – Mr O'Brian – to become involved. He told me he was a trained assassin and would help me kill Mr Nasty, but I thought it was more likely that he was a lonely crank looking for friendship on the internet."

"Would anyone else have seen his emails?"

"Yes. I sent a copy of them to my father in Spain. He then gave a copy to my solicitor, Sir David Goodman. I told him not to use them. They were personal-"

Miss Moody leapt to her feet. "My Lord, I wish to raise a point of law."

The judge agreed and gave the order for the jury to withdraw. As lunchtime was fast approaching he said the court would adjourn straight after the point of law had been dealt with, reassembling at 2.00 pm. Michael could hardly bear to wait for the fireworks.

The public gallery was allowed to remain and watch the point of law being discussed between the two counsels and the judge. Miss Moody claimed that the replies from Mr O'Brian could be vital evidence which the defence had failed to disclose. Mark admitted that the evidence had not been referred to in the Defence Statement, as there was no intention to use it. He reminded his Lordship that, unlike the Prosecution, the Defence did not have to disclose evidence which would harm their case.

Mark had baited the trap, and Miss Moody fell straight into it. She insisted the Defence produce the emails from Rand, on the basis that they could shed further light on the defendant's state of mind, which was a vitally important issue of the case. Grudgingly, the Defence agreed.

After lunch, Exhibit 4 was distributed to the jury. Mark explained what it was: a file containing a copy of Melanie's emails to Rand with all his replies. He told them his learned friend, the Counsel for the Prosecution, had requested it be produced as further evidence and the Judge had agreed. He would be questioning the defendant on certain aspects of this new evidence which he would read out.

He began by reading out Rand's first email: 'Just do it.'

He looked at Melanie. "What did you think he meant?"

"I didn't know," she replied, "so I wrote back asking for him to explain."

Mark read the reply: "'Kill him. I assume he is still alive and that justice has not taken its course. If you can be sure of your facts, that he murdered your partner, I suggest you avenge him. The anger will then go.'"

He looked up again at his witness. "How did you feel when you read that?"

"I thought it was a good idea. It made sense..."

Melanie, oh Melanie! Michael wanted to shout at her, shake her and tell her she was doing herself no favours. He couldn't understand why Mark was following this line of questioning. It went on and on, but eventually, Michael recognised there was a pattern. Mark was asking Melanie the kind of questions the Prosecution would be asking, but each time he was giving his client the opportunity to refute each and every suggestion that she had ever seriously intended to kill the victim. Mark was spiking the enemy's guns.

Furthermore, Michael realised that as the afternoon wore on, Mark was building up a picture – by reading out carefully chosen extracts from the emails – showing that the murderer was far more likely to be Rand than Melanie. Michael remembered David's assurances: all they have to do is cast doubt.

Michael noticed the worried look on Mark's face when he finally announced he had no more questions. He hoped it was a pretence, aimed at emboldening his adversary. Certainly, it seemed to have that effect; Miss Moody was smiling when she stood up to question the witness.

It soon became clear to Michael what her plan was. She, too, read out extracts from Rand's emails, making fun of his claims to be a 'trained assassin', raising her eyebrows at the suggestion and smiling at the jury as if it were some fantasy a five-year-old had come up with. Was this 'trained assassin' *really* trained in 'close-quarter combat'? And he lived in *Greater London*, did he? Surely she wasn't taken in by him, was she?

This went on for about half an hour. The raised eyebrows gradually became a frown, the kindly voice of the parent doubting the five-year-old became a growl as she mocked the very existence of 'Mr Randolph O'Brian'. Finally, she accused Melanie of making the whole story up, of fabricating this fictitious character, of inventing his very existence, forging his replies in order that she – the real murderer – might escape justice. A cunning deceit, carefully prepared over weeks, designed to fool magistrates, judges, lawyers and indeed the whole judicial system.

Michael noted that when she said the word 'lawyers' she extended her right hand, palm turned up, towards David and Mark, as if to say 'here, look at them, they've been fooled'. She then turned towards the jury, smiled and shrugged her shoulders as if to say, 'but you haven't been taken in, have you?'.

Michael had to admit it was an impressive performance. But not the best in the house. That accolade had to go to his daughter. During Miss Moody's venomous rant, Melanie had remained silent and passive. Not a frown nor a smile. Not a silent plea to the jury. Not a wringing of hands, not a slump of the shoulders, not a quiver of lip, not a lone tear rolling slowly down a cheek begging sympathy. No Kleenex clutched in a trembling hand. Nothing.

Miss Moody ended her diatribe by almost screaming at the accused, "End your lies NOW! Tell the court the TRUTH! Remember, you are UNDER OATH! You made it ALL UP! DIDN'T YOU?"

It was the cue for Melanie to say her lines. Or line. Or to be precise, just one word, delivered with the drama of someone replying to the question, 'has it stopped raining?'

"No," said Melanie.

Michael could hardly wait for the coup de grâce, but wait he had to, for the jury to be wheeled out of the court and for the wigged lawyers to discuss the next irregularity.

"My Lord," said Mark, "with your permission I would like to present to the court a further exhibit."

"My Lord," it was Miss Moody's turn, "I must object. It is quite irregular for the defence to behave in this manner, of drip-feeding new evidence during a trial of this nature, whenever it suits them."

"My Lord," it was Mark, "you will recall my learned friend was quite happy for us to introduce new evidence earlier today – the emails from Mr O'Brian – when it suited the Prosecution. In fact, she insisted.

May I respectfully request that the Defence is offered the same privilege?"

"Mr Issijay. What is this new evidence?"

"Just two sheets of paper, my Lord, a birth certificate for Mr Randoph O'Brian and his parents' marriage certificate."

"And why did you not present these before?"

"My Lord, you will recall that my client explained earlier that she thought Mr O'Brian could have been a lonely crank simply trying to find a friend on the internet. For this reason, she was adamant he was not to be drawn into this trial in any way."

"Has she now changed her mind?"

"No, my Lord. My client was not consulted on the matter. It was the Prosecution who insisted his emails were submitted to the court. We only wish to present these certificates now because the Prosecution are trying to make out the man doesn't exist."

"Mr Issijay, please prepare the copies of the certificates for distribution to the jury. I direct you to present them as a new exhibit, explaining what the certificates are and why it is relevant to the case. Miss Moody, you will have an opportunity to continue your cross-examination of the defendant after Mr Issijay has done this."

Exhibit 5 was the wrecking ball to the Prosecution' accusation that Melanie had lied under oath. Mark proved it was impossible for her to know anything about Rand except the information he'd provided in his email. And the certificates showed, without doubt, the information was correct, specifically his name and those of his parents. Rand was not a figment of her imagination. He was a real person – and now a suspect.

Miss Moody declined the judge's offer to continue her cross-examination. The defence called no further witnesses, and Mark declared that was the case for the Defence. The court was adjourned to reconvene the following morning.

When Michael returned to collect his mobile from Capable Travel, the girl asked him if he had read the brochures and come to a decision. Yes, he wanted to go; no, he hadn't the faintest idea where; he needed her guidance.

"Well, sir. We do have two singles in a chalet in Zermatt. Normally it's very expensive, but the company are anxious to fill it and are offering it at half price. We only heard about it this morning."

"I'll take it before anyone else does. American Express?"

He was pleased he'd taken the plunge. He knew it was a bit of a gamble, but if Melly were found guilty, the last thing on his mind would be £2328 going down the Swanee. He decided to keep it a surprise for the time being and give it to her as her Christmas present. It would be one seasonal problem solved.

The next thing he looked forward to was seeing her. He'd been warned it was unlikely the trial would be over in one week, so he arranged a meeting on Saturday afternoon during visiting hours. And Sunday was the day he would go down to Tunbridge Wells. Celia said she'd pick him up at the station and do a traditional Sunday lunch for him, at her little place in the country a few miles outside of town.

But he had Friday to get through, the summing up by the Prosecution followed by that for the Defence.

Chapter 30

It was the end of a busy week in Court 1. By the time Michael arrived, the public gallery was filling up fast. He guessed some were law students anxious to learn from the summings-up. Others looked like tourists come to be enlightened and entertained by the English justice system. A couple looked as if they could be military.

After the preliminaries, the judge called on Miss Moody to sum up the case for the Prosecution. As Michael expected, it was largely a rerun of her opening statement but adding suitable verbiage saying that the defendant's intention to kill the deceased had now been proved beyond doubt, and it was now absolutely clear she had the knowledge needed to plan such an attack and the means at her disposal to carry it out.

She drivelled on that some of the evidence 'might be circumstantial' and that other persons 'might have been capable' of the crime, but Dr Melanie Green was the only person who had the means, the motive and the opportunity. Obviously, the accused couldn't claim she acted in self-defence, and she herself had rejected with utter arrogance any of the many partial defences which might have justified a lesser sentence, no doubt in the mistaken belief that she could 'fool us all with her lies'.

She acknowledged the defendant had been unfortunate enough to have suffered deep trauma while serving her country. She admitted that rape victims did harbour wishes to see their attackers suffer. But Dr Melanie Green had taken the law into her own hands, and, egged on by an internet troll seemingly well versed in assassination techniques, she actually murdered, in a most vicious way, a retired British Army officer who had also served his country and was about to continue to do so as a Member of Parliament.

Finally, she harangued the jury with her assurances that there could only be one verdict beyond reasonable doubt; that this, this 'person' in the dock before them was guilty.

The jury seemed unsettled. Some were scratching their heads; others were whispering to their neighbours while a couple of them were wading through the documents in front of them as if the answer lay within.

Michael worried he might have been premature in

booking the winter holiday. The only factor which calmed the butterflies was David's reassurance that if by some chance the jury did convict her, he and Mark would launch straight into an appeal which would stand a very good chance of overturning an unsafe verdict.

He was itching to hear Mark's speech, but his Lordship adjourned the court for an early lunch break. It would reconvene at 2.00 pm.

Michael walked northwards following the route he and Jim had taken two nights previously. There was no way he could stomach lunch. He was reminded of the letter he was to show Melanie and was pleased the opportunity to do so would be the coming weekend. He wondered how she would take it. Perhaps he should wait until the trial was over.

The general expectation was that the Summing Up for the Defence would conclude that afternoon, with Monday and possibly Tuesday being taken up by the Judges Summing Up and Guidance. But then there were the deliberations of the jury. He'd been warned it could take days.

It was just after 2.00 pm. A hush descended over the packed public gallery. The usher boomed out the order, all stand, and with a shuffling of feet and chairs, all present rose to their feet as the judge walked in.

After everyone had settled down, he announced, "We will now hear the Summing Up for the Defence."

Mark rose, "Thank you, my Lord." He waited until there was utter silence. "My Lord... Ladies and gentlemen of the jury... My learned friends." He paused again and looked around the courtroom and up into the public gallery.

"This week, we have heard how a Member of Parliament had been brutally murdered. It was no ordinary killing, as the attack had been designed not only to kill the man but also to make him suffer. It was not carried out in the heat of the moment. There was no evidence of a struggle. It had been meticulously planned over possibly weeks. It wasn't a last-minute thought, a seizing of an opportunity. The killer must have had a reason for wanting the man to die. They must have wished for his death. They must have intended to cause it. They must have carried out a number of actions in order to bring it about.

"A few weeks before the murder, we heard how a woman had submitted a complaint to her local police station against the victim, claiming he had killed her partner and child and raped her while in Afghanistan two years previously. On leaving the station, she said that if the police didn't do anything, she would kill him.

"It was only natural that the investigating officer would want to interview her. Further investigations made the team realise she had not only the motive, but also the means and opportunity to kill the MP, and it was only natural that the investigating officer, with guidance from the CPS, would charge her.

"Ladies and gentlemen of the jury, that woman is before you now. Your verdict will decide whether she walks free, or is imprisoned for life. You can only find her guilty if you are satisfied that you are sure, *sure*, she committed the murder. How can you be sure? How can any one of us be sure? There was no forensic evidence that she killed him. There was nothing that linked her to the scene of the crime. We agree that she had the knowledge and access to the means of execution. We agree that she *could* have carried out the crime; perhaps she is, after all, the 'strong she' who would have been needed to heave the man into that bathtub."

Mark smiled when he said the words and looked across at Melanie. The pause gave the jury time to look again at the young woman in the dock, then to exchange knowing glances with eyebrows raised in disbelief. Some gently shook their heads.

"But we disagree strongly with the prosecution that she actually did it. Why? There are two reasons.

"Firstly, we do not believe this young woman had any serious intention to carry out the crime. She might have said things, in the heat of the moment. At times she might have thought herself capable. But we do not believe she had the sustained intention necessary to plan the crime in such detail and then carry it out.

"Let's look at that word, intention. It is an essential ingredient for murder. If there's not an intention to kill or seriously hurt someone, there is no murder. Is intention the same as motive? No. A motive is a reason, a justification for carrying out an act. My house is on the other side of the road. I have a reason for crossing that road, but I have no intention to cross it because the lights on the pedestrian crossing are red.

"Is intention the same as a desire, a want or a wish or a hope? I might desire a new car, but that does not mean I'm planning to steal one. I might want to go on holiday, but – sadly – that does not mean I'm packing my suitcase. I might wish I were a rich man, I might wish to fly to the moon, but that does not make me a millionaire or an astronaut.

"It is perfectly true that my client had a motive, a reason for wanting to kill Mr Bretton-Willis. It is perfectly true she wanted him to suffer. It's true she wished him dead and hoped he'd die a grizzly death. But that does not make her a murderer. Your job is to decide, based on the evidence you have heard, whether or not she killed him.

"Secondly, I put it to you, members of the jury, that the evidence you have heard this week has not eliminated the possibility that someone other than Dr

Melanie Green killed Mr Bretton-Willis. We've heard his cleaner didn't like him. We've heard that the staff at his constituency office thought he was a martinet. Perhaps he had enemies. Perhaps he had other victims. We've heard how the mysterious Mr O'Brian offered to help her, how he thought she was in danger from him. Perhaps a member of her partner's family obeyed the code of his tribal ancestors and took revenge.

"To reach a guilty verdict you must be satisfied that you are SURE of two things. You must be SURE she intended to kill him. And you must be SURE that there is no possibility whatsoever that another person could have carried out the crime.

"It's not enough to think she did it. It's not enough to think she probably did it. You have to be sure she did it. It's not enough to think it unlikely that anyone else would have killed the man. It's not enough to think it's an extreme possibility that someone else was responsible. You must be sure that only, only Dr Melanie Green could have killed him.

"There is no shame in not being sure. It's not because you cannot make up your mind. It's not because you have missed or misunderstood a vital piece of evidence. Let me tell you; there is no 'vital piece of evidence' which points to this woman's guilt. Remember, the officer who took her complaint reckoned she 'would not hurt a fly'. Remember, too, that even the investigating officer was unsure of her guilt. You will recall that the officer said, under oath, that she thought the defendant 'must be innocent'.

"If you are not sure – like the investigating officer – of either Dr Green's intention to kill, or that no-one but her could have committed the crime, the only verdict you can return under the law is not guilty."

Mark looked around the courtroom, at the judge, at his learned friend and each member of the jury. Only when he was satisfied that they had taken in and understood his points did he sit down. There was no applause. No acknowledgement that he had delivered a brilliant summing up. Only an all-pervading fear that the jury might make a terrible mistake.

The judge adjourned the court, announcing that it would reconvene on Monday morning. Michael guessed his lordship would need the weekend to work on his summing up.

Chapter 31

Unlike the judge, the last thing that Michael wanted to think about over the weekend was the trial. Fortunately, he did have some distractions. He dedicated Saturday morning to finding out all about Zermatt; where it was, what goes on there and why it was so popular.

After lunch, he set his mind to working on the 'Jim issue', of how he would present to his daughter the letter he'd received from the Chief of the General Staff. He hoped it would do its job, which was to persuade the young lady to forget all about the war crimes.

He was not optimistic. The best he reckoned he could do was to convince her it might not be wise to do any investigations himself when they went to Khuh Tabar next spring.

The meeting with Melanie went well. He was

pleased she didn't dwell too much on the trial. She did refer to it, as if it was a soap on TV, and said she was looking forward to the next episode. She seemed more interested in finding out what was happening in another soap, if he'd seen anything more of 'the grandma'.

When he clammed up, she let him off the hook and told him what had been going on at the prison. As usual, some funny stories, and some sad ones. He was pleased she seemed to be enjoying her voluntary work and the sense of achievement it was giving her.

He did not tell her about meeting Jim, nor about the agreement he had signed. But he did get around to showing her the letter.

"What do you make of it?" he asked.

"Good! At last. Reparations, eh? They need a new water supply – and a mobile phone mast. The genny was on its last legs – probably given up the ghost by now. The footbridge isn't safe either..."

Michael let her continue. She was back in Khuh Tabar.

"Dad!"

"Yes, darling?"

"Don't say anything about the war crimes. I know you've worked hard on them, writing to the MoD and having those meetings, but I think we ought to leave it to the SIB. Do you mind?"

Sunday morning was bright and clear. Michael decided to walk to Charing Cross station, some twenty minutes away. The overnight rain had left the streets wet, but a faint mist formed above them as the sun began to dry them out. He bought flowers for Celia from a florist on the station forecourt and a bottle of champagne from an off-licence in Villiers Street. He dismissed the butterflies as a rogue response to a primitive instinct.

Any apprehension on his part was rapidly dispelled by the enthusiastic welcome, and something inside him said he was doing the right thing. The two of them just seemed to click. She laughed at his jokes, and he loved her stories.

He'd been itching to tell someone about the surprise winter holiday he had arranged for Melanie, and he was thrilled that Celia thought it a splendid idea. She'd been skiing many times, but all that ended three years ago. Zermatt, she said, was super, a must before you die. He was relieved he hadn't been sold a pup.

He brought her up to speed about the trial, playing down his concerns and playing up what a bore it all was for his daughter. He proudly told Celia that she was working in the medical centre at Bronzefield but was looking forward to returning to Afghanistan. He would be going with her and spend a few days there before returning to Spain.

Monday finally came. The judge walked in and sat down. Michael thought he looked bright and breezy, ready for the final act in which he would be playing the principal role. In contrast, Michael felt awful after a near-sleepless night, and he wondered if he would manage to stay awake for the summing up.

His Lordship began with some general guidance to the jury, repeating many of his remarks in his opening address concerning burden of proof and the role of the jury. He flattered them by saying they were the true judges in this trial, basing their conclusions on the facts of the case. He, on the other hand, was there merely to judge the law and make sure it was followed correctly.

He continued in general terms explaining some of the 'trips and traps' on English law relevant to the case, and Michael wondered if the jury were taking it all in. Then he noticed the great relief on their faces when the judge said he would be giving them a written brief, so there was no need to take notes.

He then turned his attention to the case in hand, saying that in some ways it was a straightforward one. There was only one defendant and only one charge, that of murder. The defendant had pleaded not guilty to that charge and also to the lesser charge of manslaughter. And finally there was agreement on how the crime was committed: it was not an accident, it was not in self-defence, and it was intended not only to kill but to cause suffering.

However, it was a complex case in that there was no evidence to link the accused directly to the crime or even the crime scene. She clearly had a motive for the murder, access to the means by which it was carried out and the opportunity to do so. He conceded that motive and intention were not the same thing, and the jury had to be sure the accused did have the intention to kill the victim. This, he said, was the first issue on which the jury had to decide.

He reminded them that although the evidence was principally circumstantial, in law, it can be sufficient to warrant a guilty verdict if it can only be interpreted one way. He said that the second issue on which the jury had to decide was whether this evidence could be interpreted in another way. The Prosecution maintains it could not. The Defence maintains it could. It was up to the jury.

So far, so good, thought Michael. The judge then warned the jury they must judge the evidence and not the manner in which it was delivered. He said it was unusual for new evidence to be introduced during a trial, but he was satisfied that it was not only admissible but necessary. He then warned the jury that they were not judging the performance of the advocates; it was not a talent show, although they could be forgiven for thinking that at times it was.

The remark produced a nervous laugh, enough to wake up the elderly man in the back row of the jury and sent the proverbial titter around the public gallery.

His next warning concerned the victim and whether or not he had committed the crimes alleged by the accused: they were not a matter for this court, and the jury must ignore them. He warned the jury that while it was natural 'for us all' to feel a great deal of sympathy for the defendant, this too must be put aside when judging the facts of the case.

To Michael's dismay, the judge then proceeded to go through every piece of evidence, explaining its relevance or not to the case. While it was boring if you'd heard it all before, Michael conceded that it was a useful summary for the jury, especially if it appeared on the written brief the judge was going to give them.

The final frustration for Michael was having to listen to the judge summing up his summing up with a repeat of the guidance he'd given the jury to begin with. He was reminded of the adage: tell them what you're going to tell them; tell them; then tell them what you've told them.

The judge ended the torture by telling the jury only a unanimous verdict was acceptable unless and until they receive a further direction from him. He said they would need to select one of their number to act as the foreperson who will deliver the verdict in court and possibly chair any of their discussions during their deliberations. Any exhibits they wish to see would be made available to them, but there would be no more evidence.

The court clock showed that it was five to one. His Lordship had timed it perfectly.

Chapter 32

Michael reckoned the bars and cafés in the immediate location were doing good business over lunch, as most people in the public gallery were going to hang around for the verdict. They all hoped it would be delivered that afternoon, but he thought the law students at least would appreciate that these things can take time.

One customer they would not be getting was Michael; lunch for him was simply not going to work. Instead, he took a walk, making sure he was back well before two to be sure of getting a place in the front row. He was determined Melanie would see him.

He was third in the queue, standing on the stairs trying to stop his knees knocking. Melanie's whole life was flashing past his eyes. He remembered the scares he and Dawn had fretted over, how he had dragged the toddler out of the fish-pond at Dawn's parents' house, amazingly none the worse for the experience. He remembered rescuing her from a friend's sixteenth birthday party when some joker had spiked her Fanta. He'd always been there for her, but now all he could do was watch. He just wished he could do something to help.

The doors at the top of the stairs remained locked and the queue steadily extended until it stretched out into Wick's Passage and the street beyond. Michael asked the usher checking people in what was the delay. Waiting for the jury to return, was the reply.

Gulp.

There was a hum of excitement. The usher had his radio to his ear. He fished a bunch of keys out of his pocket and unlocked the door. For Michael, it seemed to take ages for the usher to search the couple in front, explaining that the his-and-hers electronic watches on their wrists were not allowed.

Michael dreaded missing the verdict, of not being there for Melly when it was announced. Fortunately, he managed to get a seat in the middle of the front row, well in time. The gallery continued to fill up, and in the well of the court, ushers refilled water jugs and emptied waste-paper baskets. There was some hushed talk between them, but Michael couldn't hear what was said.

People on the rows behind him were whispering to each other. He heard a woman laugh, a quip in French and a laboured explanation in Hoch Deutsch which he couldn't quite follow. Surely it can't take this long, he thought, to get the jury back in their box. Perhaps they've changed their minds. Or one of them has got stuck in the loo. Something must have gone wrong. She wouldn't have confessed, would she? Had she finally broken under the strain? Maybe she snapped and tried to escape: punched the policewoman guarding her and made a run for it. Don't be daft, he told himself. She's not that stupid, not normally.

Then in trooped the legal teams, David and the CPS solicitor and the two barristers. A few hours later – or so it seemed – Melanie was led into the dock. She looked up into the public gallery and caught her father's eye, breaking into a broad grin when he smiled back.

He'd always looked forward to the day when he would be leading her down the aisle, to give her away in holy matrimony to some handsome up-and-coming professional who'd had the cheek to fall in love with his beautiful girl. Now he feared he might be losing her in a different way, to a life in prison. Perhaps the nightmare was about to become a reality.

Finally came the order for the court to rise and in walked the judge. A few words and nods were passed between the judge and the two advocates, and the jury bailiff led his charges back into the courtroom. Everyone took their seats, and when the quiet hubbub had eventually died down, the judge called upon the two counsels to stand.

"Members of the jury, have you reached a verdict?"

The jury foreman stood up. "Yes, my Lord." He coughed nervously. "We have."

For Michael, time stood still. And he waited. Come on, he wanted to shout out loud. All eyes were on the foreman. Michael was convinced he was milking it for all it was worth, revelling in his moment in the sun.

The man looked around the courtroom. Another cough. A nod from the judge. Then finally, he spoke. "Not guilty."

Michael let out the breath he had been holding. He looked at his daughter, a picture of innocence. She smiled and looked up at him as if to say, 'there, I told you it would be okay.'

He heard the murmurs around him and saw the smiles.

The judge turned to Melanie and said she was free to go. He turned to the jury and thanked them for their service and said that they, too, were free to go. He nodded to the legal teams in front of him and stood up. Nobody heard the bailiff saying all rise. The judge walked out.

Michael saw the two advocates shake hands. He noticed Miss Moody was smiling. It reminded him of a curtain call at a Christmas pantomime when the wicked witch removes her mask to reveal a pretty girl in her twenties. Was it just an act? Was she simply doing a job?

David was smiling, too – and sharing a joke with Mark. The only person who did not look pleased with the outcome was the CPS solicitor. Michael wondered if he was in for a roasting.

The court began to clear, and Michael made his way downstairs and out into the crisp November air. Having repossessed his phone from Capable Travel, he texted Bob with the good news. Then he walked to a café in Ludgate Hill where he had arranged to meet David, Mark and Melanie. David had warned him that although a not-guilty verdict would immediately free Melanie, she would have to return to the cells to sign out and pick up her things; Mark would meet Michael at the café and David would join them later with Melanie.

Two cups of Earl Grey later, David arrived. He was alone – and as white as a sheet.

"Michael, I'm so sorry..."

"What is it, man?" said Michael, "where's Melly?"

Mark banged the table with his fist, "Damn it! Shitshitshit!! I thought we'd got away with it."

David slumped down in a chair. Michael was shocked at his appearance. It seemed that life was draining away from his friend; he looked ten years older. Mark poured him a cup of tea.

After a couple of sips, David spoke. "They've arrested her. I'm so sorry, Michael. It's all my fault."

"Bloody hell!" said Michael, "Why? The judge said she was free to go."

David took a deep breath and looked his friend in the eye. "They've charged her with conspiracy to murder. She goes to the magistrates' tomorrow morning."

Mark turned to Michael. "It's what we feared. It was a risk. Putting Melanie's emails and Rand's together has given them all the evidence they need. God knows why they didn't bring that second charge during the trial. That's what they should have done."

"A two-edged sword," mumbled David. "Melanie's file. I should have seen it coming. She says to Rand 'how about fish-hooks?' and he replies 'I'll see what I can do', and bugger me, that shite of a bastard gets himself killed by a couple of bloody fish-hooks! You couldn't make it up! It's the proverbial open and shut case. I'm so sorry..."

Michael couldn't bear to see his friend so deflated. He'd given the case his all, spending a huge amount of time and effort on it, and keeping Michael fully informed throughout.

"David. Look. You raised the risk during our first meeting in London. You did see it coming. It was a risk, and we took it. But sadly it didn't pay off. Look on the bright side. Thanks to you and Mark, Melanie has been found not guilty of murder. Nothing can take that away from you. You won. And I know you'll sort out this second charge. Head up, old man. Eyes in the boat!"

It was Michael's turn to be the strong one. David was taking it personally because he was the one who decided to introduce the email exchange, and Mark was upset because he felt he should have sewn up the downside.

"Come on, guys," said Michael. "It can't be that bad! Surely, only talking about bumping someone off isn't that serious. What's the maximum sentence?"

David stirred. "Life."

"Blimey!" said Michael. Be strong, he told himself.

David continued. "At least I was there when she was arrested and cautioned. I told her not to say anything... Sorry, Michael, to have sent you all that way to South Dakota to get proof Rand was real, and now he's biting us in the bum."

"Hey guys," it was Michael again, trying to jolly everyone along including himself. "Let's go next door and have a pie and a pint. I haven't eaten since breakfast."

They were on their third round, perched on stools at the corner on the bar. David was beginning to lighten up. "Michael, don't get me wrong. You did a good job in South wherever it was. Splendid work.

Those certificates were important. Vital. They showed Rand was real and that she wasn't making it all up. And your daughter's emails showed he was a suspect. Without those, the result could have gone the other way."

"I understand," said Michael, draining his third glass. "So how are we going to get her off this second charge?"

"Easy," replied David. "Prove Rand's not real and that she made it all up."

"Very funny," said Michael, but not laughing at David's attempt at humour. "I'm being serious. How do we proceed?"

"I'm being serious, too," said David.

"What? But if we did that, they'd re-arrest her and find her guilty on the first charge."

"Actually not," said Mark. "You can't be tried twice on the same charge unless new evidence comes to light."

"But if we prove he doesn't exist, isn't that new evidence?"

"Possibly, but the new evidence also has to be compelling. The law was changed in 2007 to allow retrials, principally so that DNA evidence could be used to convict in cold cases. And if there is a retrial, none of the evidence heard in the first trial is allowable. So the 'compelling new evidence' has to be enough on its own to secure a conviction. Something like a confession might qualify."

"Guys," it was Michael, smiling, almost giggling. "Talking of confessions, I have one to make."

"What's that? You've drunk too much?" said David.

"No, no. Do you remember telling me that the last thing you wanted was a death certificate for Rand?"

"Absolutely. That would have scotched it. Rand had to be alive to have carried out the murder. Or at least to have been a suspect. Anyway, what's your confession?"

"I have it! In my possession!"

"Have what?"

"His death certificate! The private eye from South Dakota sent the copy over, stamped and signed like the other certificates."

David and Mark exchanged worried glances. David spoke first. "Bloody hell! You kept that pretty quiet, didn't you?"

"Sorry, David. I thought it best—"

"Sorry? Don't be sorry. You, my friend, have saved the day! I'll produce it tomorrow morning and claim there is no case to answer."

"A snag, David. It's at home in Spain. But I could go over tomorrow and be back by the end of the week."

"Could work. What date of death did it give?"

"2014, I think. Ages ago. Went missing in action, in Afghanistan. One of the two thousand or so

Americans who died there. I think they have to wait five years or something. Depends on the state."

"Perfect, so she could not have conspired with him!" David was beaming. "Let's have another round. It's on me!"

"David," said Mark, "I hate to spoil the party, but that's not going to work."

"Why on earth not? She could not have conspired with him, because he was dead when the email exchange took place."

"A conspiracy charge doesn't have to identify the person or persons with whom the accused conspires. It could have been someone pretending to be Rand. All the prosecution has to do is to give evidence that the defendant planned the crime with another person. It doesn't matter who the person is or whether the crime was actually carried out."

"Shit," said David, "well, in that case, we need to show that there was no other person. Bright ideas anyone?"

Michael's phone pinged. It was a text from Bob.

Delighted to hear the good news, you must be very relieved. Congrats to your team.
Bob.

He groaned at the prospect of being a bearer of bad news, but he texted Bob back a quick summary with a promise to keep him in the picture.

"Who was that?" David asked. "Your new girlfriend?"

Michael didn't react to his friend's teasing. His mind was elsewhere. "I think I have."

"Have what? A new girlfriend? Not another one?"

"A bright idea. David, you asked if anyone had a bright idea. I think I've got one, but I need to make some inquiries."

The two legal eagles exchanged smiles; as if a doctor could come up with a solution to a legal problem.

"One for the road?" said David. Without waiting for an answer, he ordered three malts. Doubles.

Chapter 33

Michael woke up late the next morning, feeling a bit under the weather. He hoped he'd feel better by the time he was due to meet Celia. He managed to get two tickets for *The Lion King*. She'd assured him she hadn't seen it and that she loved musicals.

He felt awful he'd missed the hearing at the magistrates' court, but David's call from the court cheered him up. Melanie had pleaded not guilty and was remanded for trial in the Crown Court. The good news was she'd been granted bail, the only condition being that she should remain in the country. The bizarre news was that she'd asked to go back to Bronzefield as she was on the night shift that evening. She'd told David to 'send my love to Dad' and to say she hoped to see him before he returned to Spain.

After a black coffee and a dry piece of toast, Doctor Michael Green's condition improved slightly, and he was able to bend down without overbalancing. His next task was to phone Bob. Unfortunately, the phone said he was unable to take his call right now, but please leave a message with your name and phone number, and he will get back to you.

Blow that, thought Michael. Nobody listens to voice mails any more. His text was simple:

Can I meet you for lunch tomorrow, at the Dog and Duck at 1.00pm, on me?
Michael Green

Half an hour later, the reply came back confirming the meeting. Michael was pleased with his morning's work and went back to bed, setting the alarm on his phone for 4.00 pm.

Celia's train was due in at 17.10. He was there in good time, and the headache had gone – but with it went the numbness which had protected him from the emotional sledgehammer which had walloped him the previous evening. He knew Celia would ask about the court case, and he had no idea how he would break the news. But it wasn't Celia he was concerned about. He knew he'd have to put on a brave face if her first-ever evening with him – apart from the aircraft – was not to be ruined by him losing control.

For Michael, the aperitif before the show was somewhere between being the hair of the dog and a slug of Dutch courage, enabling him to relate to Celia the slight legal technicality which had detained his daughter temporarily. She seemed genuinely concerned, but Michael hoped the wave of his hand and the smile on his face convinced her there was no reason to worry.

After the performance, he suggested a quick nightcap at his Airbnb. He wasn't sure why he burdened Celia with all his worries. She'd asked about the skiing holiday he'd planned for Melanie, and it suddenly had dawned on him that she wouldn't be able to come. Celia had asked him what the matter was, and it all bubbled to the surface: Melanie had now been charged for conspiracy to murder which had a maximum sentence of life. She'd been remanded for trial in the Crown Court at a date yet to be decided. She was on bail but would not be able to leave the country, meaning that his carefully laid plans for her spending Christmas with him in Spain, followed by the winter holiday, would all have to be cancelled.

Was it the sympathetic ear which his outpouring had found? The hand that reached out and touched his arm, or her soothing words? Or that mysterious perfume? Not at my age, he thought. Perhaps just a meeting of soul-mates, not driven by some primaeval urge to procreate, but by a desire to share the good and the bad which life doles out, seemingly at random. He lent her his best shirt as a nightdress and gave her, as a souvenir, the toothbrush he saved from their first-class flight across the Atlantic.

The following morning they parted company with a kiss and a hug, and she agreed to join him in Spain for Christmas and go with him to Zermatt.

Bob was waiting at the bar when Michael arrived at the Dog and Duck. They went straight into the restaurant and chose a corner table where there was little risk of being overheard. Michael briefed Bob on the full story and asked the psychiatrist the simple question: can Melanie be Rand?

Bob looked puzzled. "I'm not sure what you mean."

"Well, you remember you told me some weeks ago that PTSD victims sometimes can't tell what is fact or fantasy, that their brains can split into two and they are not sure what are dreams and what's real-"

"Hang on, Michael. Yes, in extreme cases, it can cause dissociative identity disorder, DID. Split personality is what it used to be called. Although in some cases, a patient can have more than two identities, each one completely independent of the others."

Michael's mind was racing. "So would these different identities be aware of each other?" He was thinking of Melly's ghost.

"Sometimes they can be. Often one identity is dominant and aware of the others, whereas in other cases they can simply appear to the world at large as

two different people. Like Jekyll and Hyde. Or, if you
like, a single person with a severe mood-swing."

That's Melanie. Exactly. He let Bob continue.

"Multiple personality disorder is perhaps a better
name. But coming back to Melanie, what exactly are
you driving at?"

"Simply, that if Melanie had DID, the exchange of
emails between her and Rand could have been
between her two identities. She conspired with Rand,
but he was her 'alter-ego'. We know the real Rand died
years ago. Her Rand wasn't a person, just an identity
of hers. She would not be guilty of conspiracy. You
can't conspire with yourself. And she couldn't be
found guilty of murder because she'd already been
found innocent-"

"Steady, Michael. Great idea, but there's no way
we could make that one stick. DID is a very complex
disorder, and some professionals don't even
acknowledge its existence."

"We don't have to make it stick. All we have to do
is suggest to a jury that it's a possibility. They cannot
find her guilty of conspiring with another person if
there is a chance she'd conspired with herself."

"You're well ahead of me on the legal side, but I
do remember a very strange story about an American,
Billy Milligan, charged with multiple rape. He was
diagnosed with the disorder and was able to plead
insanity, evading conviction and claiming one of his

other identities had done it. And last year there was that case in Australia of a woman giving evidence against her abusive father, and she had over two thousand identities.

"There are some genuine legal difficulties with DID, for example concerning the civil and political rights of alters, particularly which alter-ego can legally represent the person, sign a contract or vote. And sufferers other than Billy Milligan have been known to deny culpability of a crime on the grounds it was committed by a different identity-state. But I don't think it's going to help Melanie much to say she's a sufferer. They'll just say she's insane. True, Billy Milligan escaped a rape conviction, but he spent many years in and out of mental hospitals. We don't want that to happen to Melanie."

Back to Square One, thought Michael. We might as well have lunch, and I can let Bob get away. Over the meal, they had an interesting chat about their medical careers so far. Michael told Bob how he'd started as a GP, then went into anaesthetics before returning to general practice in his semi-retirement in Spain. In contrast, Bob's foreign travel was limited to South Africa, where he did his elective.

Wonderful experience, he said, as the students are sent out into the townships to provide every sort of medical care you could imagine, free to anyone who needed it. He personally had delivered several babies, carried out amputations, set numerous bones, sucked a few snake bites and even faked the last rites for an ardent believer, an elderly woman involved in a road accident who was terrified she was going to die before the priest arrived. And did she? asked Michael. She died, Bob said, in his arms, peacefully.

The flash of inspiration came to Michael on the tube travelling back to Central London. First, he phoned David to bounce it off him; then he phoned Bob.

Bob picked up the phone. "Michael! I'm just about to see a patient. Is it a quick one?"

"Very quick, Bob. About Billy Milligan. One of his identities did actually commit the crime for which he was charged. The rape took place; there was a real victim. But if Melanie had been writing to herself in a state of dissociative identity disorder, there would've been no crime at all. At least not of conspiracy! You can't be found guilty of a crime that never happened! And, now she's so much better, they can't section her!"

There was a moment of silence at the other end of the phone. Michael waited.

"Give me 'til Monday. I'll write the assessment. Text me the address of Mel's solicitors."

Michael dedicated his last full day to seeing

Melanie. They met in the staff quarters where she had been allocated a bed-sit. He received his usual warm welcome with a hug and two kisses, but he sensed there was something troubling her. It was peculiar. She'd almost laughed off the charge of murder, yet here she was on the less serious charge of conspiracy and not taking it too well.

Or perhaps it was the shift-work. Or was it cumulative fatigue, the effects of not sleeping properly, of the stress and worry? Or had she caught some bug? He reckoned that in an institution of that size, there must always be a high risk of contagion, either through touch or airborne transmission. Stop it, he said to himself. She's not a patient.

He did wonder if in the weeks before the trial, she had been putting on a brave face just for him, and now the mask was beginning to slip. Perhaps it was his turn to be brave. So, when she asked about 'the grandma', he told her everything; almost. She said it was lovely he had a friend-who-was-female at long last and that he deserved to be happy.

He told her about the Christmas present he'd planned for her, but she replied that she couldn't have gone anyway, as she'd signed up to work full time at the prison for three months. Father and daughter agreed they would go to Afghanistan together in early March, with him returning to Spain after a week or so.

He was dreading her going back to that country,

as he knew she'd remain there; it was her home. She assured him he and 'the grandma' could come and stay whenever they wanted to – if they didn't mind living in yurts. And she would certainly come back to visit him in Spain.

"That's lovely to hear you say that, but I suppose, being a father, I'm hoping that one day you'll—"

"Dad! Same old song? So who are you trying to pair me up with now?"

Michael felt himself going red. "Well, to be honest, I did wonder about Mark. He seems a nice young man – youngish, anyway – and you seemed to get on well with him. And I believe he doesn't have a family-"

"Dad! For Heaven's sake! You're right. He is great, and he's a very good barrister. We get on well, and I feel I can relax with him, be myself."

"But Darling, that's a wonderful basis for a relationship-"

"Shut up a moment." She was smiling at her old-fashioned father. "I'm comfortable with him because he's already taken. You're right; he doesn't have a wife and kids. He has a husband. I've met him. They've been together for years and married for the last three." She laughed. "You can't get rid of me that easily!"

She looked at her watch. "Dad, I'd better go."

"Oh. I was hoping we might have lunch together!"

She groaned at his suggestion. "No, thank you," she

mumbled, "that's the last thing I could do with. Next time perhaps."

As they said goodbye, he realised she was well into adulthood and that he'd have to get used to it. She was no longer his little girl, but a mature woman taking life on the chin, coping with the setbacks and enjoying the good moments. He still wondered if she had given birth to a son, out there in Afghanistan, in Khuh Tabar.

Chapter 34

He returned home to find southern Spain enjoying a mild spell, warm in the day and cool at night. He hoped it would remain for Celia's visit. It was going to be a state visit, not quite with a red carpet, but he would make every effort to give her a good time. Daniela was a bit miffed when he told her, but he'd managed to assure her that nobody or nothing could ever replace her as his very highly valued personal assistant.

Planning the visit had taken his mind off the trial, but when the email arrived from David with Bob's statement about Melanie, he had to read it.

There were pages of it. Dr Robert Weston began by stating his credentials – his training and qualifications and details of his last three posts. Michael was certainly impressed. Bob then described the role of Beechwood Hall in the treatment of military personnel with mental issues, ending with his own job description.

One of the main issues he dealt with was post-traumatic stress disorder (PTSD), a condition triggered by a terrifying event — either experiencing it or witnessing it. The likely symptoms included flashbacks, nightmares and severe anxiety, as well as uncontrollable thoughts about the triggering event. He explained that these could get worse, last for months or even years, and interfere with normal day-to-day functioning.

Next, Bob described in broad terms the treatment for PTSD, followed by a succession of cases he had handled. His report had several footnotes referring to papers written by eminent psychiatrists. Some were by Dr Robert Weston, either as sole author or co-authored with other highly qualified members of his profession.

In the following section, Bob zeroed in on a related mental health issue: dissociative identity disorder. Michael read it carefully.

Dissociative identity disorder (DID), previously known as multiple personality disorder, is a mental condition characterised by two or more distinct and relatively enduring personality states. This is accompanied by memory gaps beyond what would be explained by ordinary forgetfulness. In about 90% of cases, there is a history of abuse in childhood, while other cases are linked to experiences of war.

Treatment generally involves supportive care and counselling. If not treated the disorder can persist. It affects about 1.5% of the population and is diagnosed about six times more often in females than males.

DID is controversial within both psychiatry and the legal system. In court cases, it has been used as a rarely successful form of the insanity defence. In questions regarding the civil and political rights of alters, other issues have arisen, particularly which alter-ego can legally represent the person.

Bob then went on to describe Melanie's condition when she first arrived at Beechwood Hall, referring to the gap in her memory of where she had been and what she had done during the previous fifteen months. She also had flashbacks to her service in Afghanistan where she had apparently been sexually abused. Other symptoms of hers included sleep-walking and abrupt and unexplained changes of mood. He was pleased to report that following the death of her alleged abuser, these symptoms had disappeared.

While emphasising that one could never be sure about these matters, Bob stated that in his opinion Melanie had been suffering DID, brought on by a combination of severe combat trauma followed by psychological conditioning in an unknown medical institution.

The wall sockets! Michael remembered the sockets with the upright slits. An 'unknown medical institution'. It was beginning to make sense. He continued reading.

Bob proposed that this conditioning, building on her PTSD, could have created her alter-identity, that of Rand, an American serviceman trained in assassination techniques. He understood that a Randolph O'Brian, a US Special Forces soldier, had died in combat in Afghanistan in 2014. His identity could have been deliberately planted in Melanie during her missing fifteen months.

Bob them referred the reader to Project MKUltra, a CIA mind control programme which began in 1953 and lasted until 1973. It was one of a small number of similar research projects run in the US and other countries, in which subjects for experimentation were specifically chosen if they had suffered trauma, as this was believed to make them more malleable mentally.

Michael stopped reading. You've got to be joking. He was grateful to Bob for trying but felt he had strayed too far into the realms of fantasy for any court of law. MKUltra? Who dreamed up that one? He had to google it.

Bloody hell! The Wikipedia article was a long one with ten external links and fourteen recommendations for further reading. Then he started looking up the 110 references. After five he gave up; he'd seen enough to realise this was not simply fodder for conspiracy theorists.

He returned to Bob's statement and read the conclusion. It didn't claim she'd been a guinea-pig in a mind control programme. All it said was there could be a possibility that Dr Melanie Green had been suffering from dissociative identity disorder during the period 7th August to 6th September when she exchanged emails with a man calling himself Randolph O'Brian. He could have been a false identity-state existing only in her own mind but without her knowledge. It is significant that after the death of her alleged abuser, Rand never replied to her emails and his mail box was closed down. She had been healed.

Good, thought Michael. That should do the trick – if there is indeed something called dissociative identity disorder. He thought he'd better check it out, too. The article was just as long with 109 references. Michael glanced down them. One caught his eye. It was a research paper entitled *Personality differences on the Rorschach of dissociative identity disorder, borderline personality disorder and psychotic inpatients*. One of the co-authors was listed as Dr Robert Weston.

He immediately wrote back to David, thanking him

for sending over Bob's excellent report. The reply came straight back:

glad you like it more success in the attached

The attached was another report, this time from their IT department.

Dave – Some of Rand's emails and Melanie's emails were typed on the same computer. No question. Hope that helps. Let me know if you want to give me a pay rise.

Darren

P.S. Should have said same keyboard. A key-bounce analysis proved it to fingerprint standard. Luckily it was an oldie, the sort which didn't scrub out repeats. The WP program back-spaces them (like when you type a full stop, then a space then a lower case character, it back-spaces it and pops in a capital). You can't see the BSs unless you look at the raw code. Then it's obvious. The L, R and F on the shared keyboard were dodgy.

Michael was glad things were beginning to look up, case-wise. No question. But he found it hard to get his head around the fact that his Melanie had typed all those emails. He consoled himself with the other 'fact' that she hadn't truly lied in court, as it was her alter-identity which had composed Rand's missives. Yeah, yeah. But if it buys her freedom...

A phone call from David a week before Christmas confirmed two things: that he'd received the indictment, and that he'd got his mojo back.

"Michael, my dear chap! We're on a roll here. We're going to hit them with the Defence Statement before Christmas, then press for an early Plea and Trial Preparation Hearing after the break if they haven't buckled by then. What with Bob's assessment and Darren's report it's looking good – and both men are prepared to take the stand."

"Great news. Who's Darren by the way? Sounds a bit of a weirdo."

"Darren? He's my grandson, actually. Cheeky little sod. I said he mustn't call me grandpa in the office, so I'm Dave. He knows I don't like it, but that's the young for you – no respect."

Michael thought that if he had a grandson, he wouldn't mind if he became Mike to him, once he became an adult.

"Is there anything I can do?" he asked.

"Actually, yes. If you could scan that death certificate and email it over, with a note to say where it came from, I think that will be sufficient for our statement, and probably for the hearing. If we do end up in court, we will need the certified copy you were sent by that chum of yours in South Dakota."

"Sure. I'll do that today. How's Melanie? She seemed a bit down when I saw her last."

"Okay. We – that's Mark and I – popped down to Bronzefield a couple of days ago for a conference. It went well although she seemed upset when we gleefully suggested she'd written Rand's emails. Of course, she denied it, but then we explained about the DID thing. She didn't like that, either. We said it was only a remote possibility, but we had to show it as a defence. That also went down like a lead balloon. She said it meant there was a remote possibility that she was the murderer. It got complicated when we tried to explain that it would not have been her but an alter-ego. Honestly, Michael, I wish Bob had been there. He could have explained it much better than we did."

"That's a thought," said Michael. "Couldn't you get hold of Bob and ask him to go and see her?"

"Good thinking. I'll try. And there was something else. I just got that feeling that she was sad when we told her that Rand didn't exist. Do you remember, when we first read those emails, we both thought she'd grown fond of him? I think he was real to her."

"How odd. To grieve for an identity which only existed inside you."

"Michael, are you all right? You don't actually believe all that tosh, do you?"

Michael laughed, relieved to hear that his friend had got his feet firmly on the ground.

"Remember, all we have to do is to convince a jury of the *possibility* that she only conspired with herself.

Actually, that's not quite the case. I don't want to raise your hopes in any way, but I'm keeping my fingers crossed that all we have to do is to convince the CPS that they don't stand a chance in hell of securing a conviction and should cancel the case. Then we can all go home."

Michael was reassured by his friend's words, but he'd learned from bitter experience that things can go horribly wrong. But it got him thinking about Melanie and what she would be doing once it was all over. She'd be going home, too. To Khuh Tabar.

Celia proved to be a most appreciative state visitor, loving everything they did together, and very happy to amuse herself when Michael had to work. Christmas itself seemed to pass in a flash, and before they knew it, the time had come for Celia to return to England. The parting was more sweet than sorrowful, as they would be meeting a week later in Zermatt. They shared their amusement and amazement that two late-middle-aged second-time-arounders had somehow – in a relatively short time – managed to cobble it together.

Zermatt was magical in many ways, and neither wanted the holiday to end. On the morning of their departure, he got a text message from David. He had to read it twice before being able to decypher it:

at ptph mel pleaded not guilty mark made a no case to

answer submission which was upheld all good this end
hope snow is too

"So, Michael, are you going to tell me the good news?
An avalanche has blocked the line and we're going to
have to stay here for another week? Or have you won
the lottery?"

"Sort of. Won the lottery, I mean. Not me, though.
Melanie. She's off the hook. They closed the
conspiracy case. She's free. It's over!"

"That's wonderful news. What a relief!"

They had a celebratory hug. Then Celia frowned.
"Are you hoping to do some skiing there?"

"What do you mean, 'there'?"

"Afghanistan. I assume you will be going with her
and leaving me all alone in Tunbridge Wells?"

Michael frowned.

"Just teasing. I want you to go, then come back and
tell me all about it. Perhaps we could both go next
year."

Chapter 35

Melanie had spared her father from becoming involved in the arrangements for the trip. He'd simply given her the coordinates provided by Jim. She'd done everything, from organising an exclusive 4×4 with driver and sat-nav, to persuading various consulates and embassies to cough up the necessary documents.

She insisted on paying the airfares, as she was the one dragging her father, kicking and screaming, out to Afghanistan. Not that he was protesting too much. He did want to see her village and meet those she referred to as her extended family, but for him, a couple of weeks without Celia would be enough.

He was much relieved that Melanie had put the awful business of her trial well behind her. Mentally, she was relaxed and happy. Physically, she looked a picture of health, certainly compared with how she was when he had met her before Christmas at Bronzefield. At Heathrow, he said how lovely it was to see that twinkle in her eye and the ready smile, but he stopped himself remarking on the fact she had perhaps put on a bit of weight. He knew she'd tell him in her own good time – if his hunch was right.

The journey from Kabul was an experience he would never forget; three days along a mix of motorway-standard tarmac roads and hard-to-follow dirt tracks, staying overnight in guest houses which in some cases were no more than shacks. The countryside was stunning, and the people they met on the way were all delightful and welcoming, even if some of them did require a small 'gift' before letting them pass their unofficial checkpoints.

The arrival in Khuh Tabar was a tense moment for Michael, as he had no idea whether they would remember his daughter. If they did, they might even hold her responsible for the raid. But he need not have worried. As she stepped out of the vehicle in the middle of the village, a woman stopped and stared.

"Mellah?" she said, looking her up and down. "Mellah?"

Melanie smiled and nodded. The woman ran away, shouting, "Mellah! Mellah!"

Doors opened and villagers peered out. When they realised who it was, they came running. The word soon spread and a crowd of about twenty, mainly women, gathered around the vehicle, laughing and shouting, touching Melanie and pointing at her clothes.

Some children stopped their game and came to see what was going on. Michael noticed that none of them wore shoes. Some were in rags while a couple had trousers made from old army uniforms. One of them carried a stick which he pointed at Michael, pretending it was a rifle. Michael was happy to see that the little lad was smiling. He smiled back and noticed the glinting discs around the boy's neck. Just like a real soldier, he thought. When Michael walked towards him, he ran off laughing.

Melanie was deep in conversation with the ladies of the village. Michael couldn't understand a word. He gathered they were asking her lots of questions, all at the same time, and she was doing her best to answer them using her hands and facial expressions when she couldn't remember the right words.

At times, hands were covering shocked mouths or clapping in excited approval. Giggles turned to laughter, then to commiserations. Frowns to smiles and back again. She'd removed her sunglasses when she got out of the car but was shielding her eyes with her hand. She was looking for someone, perhaps a missing friend, someone she expected who hadn't joined the throng.

The gathering continued to grow, and Michael thought it best to hold back and let them get on with it. He walked over to where the boys were playing and got down on one knee. Smiling, he beckoned the boy with the toy rifle to join him. The child approached him and transferred the rifle to his left hand so he could greet this foreigner properly. Michael followed suit, raising his right hand to his heart and adding the standard reply, peace be with you.

The boy stepped forward and offered Michael his rifle. He took it and made the appropriate signs of admiration and approval. He pointed it at a tree and pretended to fire it. The boy laughed.

When Michael returned it with a nod and a smile, he noticed that behind the black eyelashes the boy had blue eyes. Michael strained to see what was on the dog-tags hanging around the boy's neck. They were glinting in the sun. He caught sight of a name. It was so familiar to him that he could read the pattern of letters upside down and at ten paces. Steady, he said to himself, he could have found the discs. His eyes were watering as he handed the rifle back.

He wanted to go over to Melanie and tell her, but he feared the boy might run away and join his friends. He called to her. After three attempts, she heard him. The throng parted to allow her to go over to him. She smiled at Michael, but when she saw the boy with the stick, her jaw dropped.

She slowly walked towards him. She stopped and crouched down, smiled and held out her arms. Her eyes welled up. A tear rolled down her cheek. The boy took a step towards her. He was frowning. The crowd was watching, waiting to see what would happen. Nobody said anything. They were smiling and listening, waiting. The boy looked at Michael then back at Melanie. He was the first to break the silence. He spoke quietly. "Mama?"

The impromptu celebration lasted well into the night. Food and drink appeared as if from nowhere. There was incessant chatter, all in Pashto which Michael couldn't understand, despite his efforts to memorise his phrase book.

Eventually, father and daughter were able to retire, he into the one and only guest bedroom of the 'hotel', and Melanie to her hut which had been her home until the raid over two years previously. With a sigh, she effortlessly scooped up the sleeping Jangi and carried him off to bed.

The following morning, Melanie explained it all to him, what had actually happened when the village was attacked. Sadly Shahpur had died instantly, but the English soldier who had Jangi in his arms turned around just before the shot was fired, putting his body between the major and the baby. He died, but the baby somehow crawled away from underneath his body, covered in blood but unharmed.

The major fired a second shot, this time at the other

soldier who had been with him. It was at point-blank range; he hadn't stood a chance. The villagers couldn't understand why the officer had done it. He then struck their 'Dakhtur' with the butt of his pistol and dragged her away. The other soldiers joined the major and withdrew to the three helicopters. About two hours later, they took off.

They left behind the two dead soldiers; they were buried the day following, along with the other dead. In addition to Shahpur, seventeen villagers had been deliberately executed. A further four had died later of their wounds. Of the twenty-two civilian casualties, eighteen were women. Four were found where the helicopters had landed; some of them had had their clothes ripped off; all had been raped.

Later that day Melanie, Michael and his grandson walked up to the graveyard, some two miles from the village. Piles of stones marked the shallow graves, many of which had been marauded over the years by bears and other scavengers. Melanie hugged Jangi at the grave of her late husband; she sobbed. Michael noticed the two wooden crosses.

It was a sad trek back, with hardly a word said between the three of them, Jangi sitting on Grandpa's shoulders and Melanie leading the way. The warm reception back at the village changed the mood, and Michael realised that for the inhabitants many moons had passed since the massacre. The village had recovered, and the tribe had got on with their lives, herding goats and sheep, hunting game and growing what crops and vegetables they could on the rocky soil.

Chapter 36

On his second-to-last day, Melanie took Michael on an expedition up to the snowline. It was Jangi's day at school, so there were just the two of them. Melanie had prepared a packed lunch, and with some help from friends, she had kitted out her father with suitable boots and attire.

He found it hard going, his lungs straining to get enough of the rarefied high-mountain air, his heart thumping hard to pump the blood around as they climbed and scrambled their way up. Easy for someone like Bob, he thought, young and fit and born to climb.

He didn't have enough air or energy to talk on the way up, but when they reached their picnic spot – an old favourite of hers and Shahpur's – he was able to get some of his breath back. "Wow!" was all he managed as he drank in the stunning view.

To his relief, Melanie did the talking. "See that peak

over there? The really high one beyond the ridge? That's Tirich Mir, the highest mountain in the Hindu Kush."

"How high?" Michael managed to ask between gasps.

"Getting on for 8,000 metres – 25,000 feet, if you prefer. The name means 'King of Darkness.' It's actually in Pakistan."

"So how close are we to the border here. His majesty looks quite close to me."

"No, Dad. It's at least thirty miles away. But the air is so pure, you don't get much haze here... And look over there, over that saddle. See it? With the cloud on top? That's our mountain, Naw Shakh, the highest in Afghanistan. Actually, it's on the border with Pakistan but the summit is just on our side."

"Wow. It's so beautiful..."

The two of them enjoyed the breathtaking views and the silence. After a while, Melanie took the picnic out of her backpack. It was not a western-style picnic with nicely prepared sandwiches with the crusts cut off. And there was no bottle of rosé to wash it down. It was a loaf of bread, baked that morning in the communal bread oven, a hunk of goats cheese and a skin of something which actually tasted wholesome and delicious."

"What's this then, it tastes good!"

"Don't sound so surprised, Dad. Would I give you

something that wasn't nice? If you must know it's fermented camel's milk."

Michael spat it out and wiped his lips on his hand. His daughter laughed.

Dad?"

"Yes, Darling."

"There's something I need to tell you."

"What's that, Melly? Is it something nice? Will I be pleased – or half pleased?"

"No, you won't be pleased at all. I did something bad-"

"I think I know, and I want to talk to you about it. What is bad in some places is not bad in others. You remember telling me about the Pashtunwali code? I've read up all about it, and I understand. Anyone who commits a crime can expect retribution from the victim or his family to match the harm done. Mr Nasty's crime was committed out here, on Pashtun territory where revenge is part of the justice system. He took life, and he deserved to die. The fact that the punishment was meted out in England is beside the point. You did what was right for you and your village-"

"Dad—"

"No, Melly, let me finish. Please. Hear me out." Despite having rehearsed the speech many times in his head, he stumbled over the words. "It was not bad.

It was good. You did your duty. You honoured the code, and I am proud of you. I want you to know that. It must have taken a great deal of thought, and effort, at a time when you were not well. But you succeeded, and by the grace of God and the efforts of David and Mark, here you are, at your home, as free as a bird, with Jangi, a great kid, and maybe one day..."

He fizzled out.

Melanie waited a couple of seconds, then she spoke. "Dad?"

"Yes?"

"I didn't do it."

"I know, darling. It wasn't actually you. It was Rand. But we know he doesn't exist, except... except as an identity, who was, who came to be inside you..." He looked at his daughter, beseeching her to try and accept the only explanation which would fit both his theory and her adamant denial.

Melanie rolled her eyes and took a deep breath. "Dad. Rand does exist, and I guess he carried out the execution on behalf of the village and me. Do you honestly think I could have done it? Could I have heaved that shit-head into that bath?"

"Well, under hypnosis perhaps. Bob told me you were a good subject, and that people can do incredible things under hypnosis. As Mum used to say, you're a strapping girl."

"Okay. So I was under hypnosis doing incredible

things – like finding out where the slime-ball lived and opening his front door? Or was I hypnotised to climb up the side of the building and squeeze through a kitchen window? I'll tell you something, Dad. I wish I'd done it. I wish I'd had the courage to do it. It was my duty. I should have done it. But I don't have the strength – even under hypnosis – to have done that, nor the brains to have worked out how to do it. Rand had what it took, and he did for me."

Michael was concerned. She was fantasising, in a make-believe world of her own. He remembered Bob saying that it can take years to cure PTSD and that sometimes it never goes away.

"Darling, I met Rand's mother. As I told you, in South Dakota last October. Rand died many years ago, in Afghanistan." He waited for Melanie to take in the sad fact.

She spoke slowly, softly, more to herself than to her father. "I was there."

"I know you were, darling. I understand what it must be like in a war-zone."

"No, you don't. You're nowhere near understanding."

He noticed her breathing was getting faster. She was agitated, her cheeks were flushed, and she was frowning. What have I done? he thought, his head in his hands. Neither spoke for a few seconds.

"I was there when he died." She smiled at Michael. The frown had gone.

She continued. "It was so sad. Remember the letter I found on the casualty Foxy and I went to pick up? The American soldier? He was in a bad way. He wanted to give me the letter. I took it and opened it. It wasn't sealed. It started 'Dear Mom and Dad'... One of those 'if-you-read-this' letters. I told him he was going to be fine and I put the letter pack in his pocket. We loaded him up, the heli took off, and you know what happened.

"I know what you're going to ask, did I remember the address on the envelope and the names? No. I didn't. Couldn't. But they must have registered somehow. Bob told me what they were. Apparently, I was babbling on about the incident during one of his hypnosis sessions."

Michael nodded, not daring to utter another word. She was back to her normal, lovable self. The flash of anger had melted away.

"You see, Dad, there were actually two Rands, the lad who died when the heli went down – the son of the woman you met in South Dakota – and my Rand. My Rand used the identity of that young soldier to hide his own. My Rand was the one I met in that bereavement support group, and I guess he killed Mr Nasty.

"He was nice. We got on, and he wanted to help.

I didn't believe him at first, but he was good for me. I don't think I 'conspired' with him at all. We just chatted. It was good therapy, thinking about killing that turd of a man. Of course, I was delighted when I heard the arse-hole had actually been killed – once I'd got over the shock."

When Michael had regained his courage to speak, he had a burning question for his daughter. "Did you ever find out who your Rand was?"

"No. At first, I thought he was some lonely nutter looking for company, and I didn't give it much thought. Then I wondered if he really was a CIA assassin or something. But when he stopped replying to my emails and then closed down his email address, I assumed something had happened to him. It was a bit like Foxy going. You have to get over it and get on with life. I grieved for my Rand, but I wasn't interested in who he was. For all I knew, he could have been a she, or an it. Perhaps he was just a treatment."

Michael could hardly bear it. "But surely you must have wondered who the real person was who was hiding behind the identity? The man – or woman – who had murdered Mr Nasty?"

"No. For one thing, he or she obviously didn't want me to know. Otherwise, he or she wouldn't have kept their identity hidden. The other is that I just wasn't fussed."

"But darling! He – or she – played such an

important part in your life, and in your recovery, that you must want to know more about them."

"Dad, I guess your mobile plays quite an important part in your life. But are you concerned how it works? Do you care? You drive a car, watch television, sit at your computer, but do you ever wonder how those devices do all the clever things they do? Did Mum ever try and work out how the wine and bread got changed into the body and blood of Christ? Of course not."

Michael wasn't sure whether to nod in agreement or shake some sense into her.

She smiled, as a mother might smile at a bewildered child. "It's part of the human condition to want to know everything, to answer the big questions – and the little ones. This natural curiosity has been the driving force behind humankind's greatest achievements. But it can also be destructive. 'Why did God let this happen if He loved the world?'. A consequence of traumata can be guilt if you start asking the wrong questions. You witness a terrible thing – like a road-side bomb tossing the vehicle in front of you high up in the air. You see the rag dolls tumble to the ground, bounce, roll and just lie still. You do your best. Afterwards, you torture yourself with the question, why them and not me?

"At Beechwood, one element of our treatment programme was learning how to switch off that question. A sort of mind control but over your own mind. If you like, a discipline. Bob says it's regaining control of the memory channels which are opened every time you ask that question. Eventually, you free yourself from the torment. I don't ask myself why I wasn't in that helicopter with Foxy. At least, not any more. I don't ask myself who my Rand really is or was, and I never will.

"Dad, you're shivering. Time to go back. Don't worry, you'll warm up on the way down, as you absorb all that potential energy you accumulated when we walked up. And we can talk."

They moved down the rough track, carefully stepping over the boulders and avoiding the little stones which might slide – and the pockets of snow which had somehow survived the harsh rays of a spring sun unfiltered by pollution or cloud.

Michael plucked up the courage to ask his next question. "When we first stopped for lunch, you said you had done something really bad. What was it?"

"Oh, yes. That. I'm really sorry. You going to be so disappointed."

Michael was dying to know if he was right. He'd seen enough early pregnancies to recognise the signs. His problem was knowing how to handle it when the expectant woman just happened to be his own unmarried daughter. In one way it was unfortunate, but in another, it was great news. He decided to come straight out with it.

"Boy or girl?"

Melanie threw back her head and laughed. "Girl, actually. I did the scan myself during a night shift at Bronzy. ETA August-ish."

My God, thought Michael, I'm going to be a grandpa all over again. The couple stopped, and he gave his daughter a big hug.

"That's excellent news. I'm so pleased for you. And these days there's nothing to be ashamed of. A little sister for Jangi, that's wonderful. What's bad about it?"

"Nothing, as far as we're concerned. We're thrilled, actually. But I know you'll be upset. It was a breach of medical ethics, I'm afraid. A serious one, by us both. My fault, actually. We had to stay schtum, otherwise... Hey, look! It's Jangi. Can you see him, down there? He's coming up to meet us. How sweet!"

He didn't miss that little word 'we'. Not someone here, he thought, the dates don't work. Obviously a patient of hers. Dear oh dear. At Beechwood hall? At Bronzefield? Not a prisoner, I hope. Perhaps a member of staff she was treating. She'll tell me – when she's ready.

Back at the village that evening, Melanie

announced she had another surprise for Michael. He braced himself.

"Tomorrow, a helicopter is coming to pick you up and whiz you down to Kabul. You'll have one night there and then fly directly to Heathrow on Saturday."

"Wow, Melly. That must have been expensive. Is it just for me?"

"Yes, Dad. But you're a VIP and deserve appropriate treatment. Actually, it's costing nothing. I arranged it with the Embassy. They're flying out some water supply stuff, solar panels and medical supplies for the village, all paid for by DfID from their overseas aid budget. They said they had to spend it before the end of the financial year, otherwise they'd lose it – and have the budget cut by that amount next year. It could all go by road, but some of the goodies might get 'lost' on the way.

"And, it's bringing out my assistant. Or my boss, if you're that old fashioned. You see, there's a project to install a mini-medical centre in every village like ours – so many injuries and illnesses get worse because of the time it takes to reach a hospital. And we are the pilot! Why they chose Khuh Tabar, I have no idea." She opened her eyes as wide as they would go, turned up her palms and slowly shook her head.

Michael got the message. He wasn't going to wreck her scheme by investigating any war crimes. He wondered who her boss would be. No doubt someone who would be overseeing the reparations. Jim, perhaps? Unlikely. He's more of a desk wallah.

It was a sad parting, but Michael was looking forward to seeing Celia, and he knew he would be back soon to see his daughter and grandchildren, hopefully with their step-grandma-to-be. The last thing he wanted to do was to spoil the last moments with Melly by prying, but he had to ask, just the one question, which in his mind was the most important one.

"Darling, do you love him?"

She answered, straight away. "Yes, Dad. I do. And he loves me. We're in love. And he would do anything for me."

"Anything?"

"Yes, Dad. Anything."

The heavy-lift helicopter landed outside the village in a swirl of dust. Michael waited while the pilot powered down and watched as the side door slid open, and steps were unfolded. The crew began to unload the aircraft. A man in a Tilley hat was helping. Michael guessed he was Melanie's new boss? A civil servant, no doubt. Michael wondered if he had a battered black briefcase. He looked for the steel-rimmed spectacles but the man wore sunglasses.

He looked familiar. It was something about his

walk, his build. When the unloading was complete the man disappeared into the body of the aircraft.

The pilot gave Michael the signal to proceed. He turned and waved to his daughter and grandson. As he walked towards the helicopter, he saw the man in the Tilley hat come down the steps carrying his hand luggage. He walked towards Michael. It wasn't Jim.

When he smiled, Michael realised who it was.

He smiled back. "Hi, Bob! What a surprise! Come to do some climbing?"

***

After completing the crossword on the back, David flicked back through the sports pages of The Times. The football photos looked odd with backgrounds of empty seats. Like most of his colleagues, he was working from home, coming into the London office only if mask-to-mask meetings were absolutely necessary.

He didn't stop to read the weather page, nor the adverts which preceded it. But, as usual, he scanned the legal notices on the last page of the Register. Then the deaths on the left, relieved that none of the names were familiar.

Above them was a birth announcement. Just the one; it made him realise that the young these days prefer social media to announce such happy events.

He wondered if it was a first child, or an unplanned late arrival to older parents, a sister or brother for a clutch of teenagers. Four names caught his attention.

> WESTON On 14th August 2020 to
> Mel (née Green) and Bob, a daughter,
> Annabel Dawn, sister to Jangi.

The End

Author's Notes

This novel is a work of fiction, and none of the characters is real. Any resemblance to anyone living or dead is entirely coincidental. The village named Khuh Taber is also from my imagination; I understand from a 19th Century Pashto-English dictionary it means 'Good Place'. I imagined it to be somewhere in the north-east of Afghanistan, perhaps in the Wakhan Corridor which does have a border with China at its eastern end.

However, the criminal cases quoted are real, and their details can be readily found on the internet. Likewise, Jessica Lynch is a real person, a US soldier who served in Iraq. The story goes that following a hard-fought battle she was taken prisoner, badly treated by the enemy then 'rescued' by a daring operation. Her own account was very different.

No record exists of any massacre in any Afghan village by the British Army. However, US and Coalition forces did conduct counter-terror operations in the country. A report in The Times of

London on 16th September 2019 told of the death of Bin Laden's son, Hamza, in such a raid. Sources said he was last based in a mountainous eastern province bordering Pakistan but changed his location often.

'Massacre' is an emotive word implying deliberate killing. The term 'collateral damage', when applied to human casualties, is less so because it suggests they were accidental and unavoidable. In asymmetrical warfare, where the 'innocent unarmed civilian' could be a woman or even a child wearing a suicide vest, those two terms might sometimes overlap.

Thank you for reading this book. I do hope you enjoyed it. If so, I would be most grateful if you could leave a review of it on Amazon.

Douglas Renwick
10th September 2020